Don't miss . . .

ADJUSTED TO DEATH: A visit to a chiropractor—who has a corpse on the examining table—teaches Kate that a pain in the neck may be pure murder. . . .

THE LAST RESORT: Kate muscles her way into a ritzy health club to investigate a murder—and finds that detective work may be hazardous to her life!

MURDER MOST MELLOW: Kate teams up with a psychic to solve a murder—and the message channeled through is crystal clear: Butt out or die.

FAT-FREE AND FATAL: Kate takes a vegetarian cooking class where a student is found murdered . . . and she must find the killer before she's dead meat herself!

TEA-TOTALLY DEAD: Kate attends a dysfunctional family reunion—and someone turns the homecoming into a homicide. . . .

MORE MYSTERIES FROM THE
BERKLEY PUBLISHING GROUP . . .

JENNY McKAY MYSTERIES: This TV reporter finds out where, when, why . . . *and* whodunit. "A more streetwise version of television's Murphy Brown."

—*Booklist*

by Dick Belsky
BROADCAST CLUES
THE MOURNING SHOW
LIVE FROM NEW YORK

CAT CALIBAN MYSTERIES: She was married for thirty-eight years. Raised three kids. Compared to that, tracking down killers is easy . . .

by D. B. Borton
ONE FOR THE MONEY
THREE IS A CROWD
TWO POINTS FOR MURDER
FOUR ELEMENTS OF MURDER

KATE JASPER MYSTERIES: Even in sunny California, there are cold-blooded killers . . . "This series is a treasure!" —Carolyn G. Hart

by Jaqueline Girdner
ADJUSTED TO DEATH
THE LAST RESORT
TEA-TOTALLY DEAD
MURDER MOST MELLOW
FAT-FREE AND FATAL
A STIFF CRITIQUE

FREDDIE O'NEAL, P.I., MYSTERIES: You can bet that this appealing Reno private investigator will get her man . . . "A winner." —Linda Grant

by Catherine Dain
LAY IT ON THE LINE
WALK A CROOKED MILE
BET AGAINST THE HOUSE
SING A SONG OF DEATH
LAMENT FOR A DEAD COWBOY

CALEY BURKE, P.I., MYSTERIES: This California private investigator has a brand-new license, a gun in her purse, and a knack for solving even the trickiest cases!

by Bridget McKenna
MURDER BEACH
CAUGHT DEAD
DEAD AHEAD

CHINA BAYLES MYSTERIES: She left the big city to run an herb shop in Pecan Springs, Texas. But murder can happen anywhere . . . "A wonderful character!" —*Mostly Murder*

by Susan Wittig Albert
THYME OF DEATH
WITCHES' BANE

LIZ WAREHAM MYSTERIES: In the world of public relations, crime can be a real career-killer . . . "Readers will enjoy feisty Liz!" —*Publishers Weekly*

by Carol Brennan
HEADHUNT
FULL COMMISSION

A STIFF CRITIQUE

JAQUELINE GIRDNER

BERKLEY PRIME CRIME, NEW YORK

A STIFF CRITIQUE

A Berkley Prime Crime Book/published by arrangement with the author

PRINTING HISTORY
Berkley Prime Crime edition/May 1995

ISBN: 0-425-14719-3

Berkley Prime Crime Books are published by The Berkley Publishing Group, 200 Madison Avenue, New York, NY 10016.
The name BERKLEY PRIME CRIME and the BERKLEY PRIME CRIME design are trademarks belonging to Berkley Publishing Corporation.

PRINTED IN THE UNITED STATES OF AMERICA

10 9 8 7 6 5 4 3 2 1

To my agent, Deborah Schneider,
for her wise advice, encouragement and support.

And to my doctor, Anna Vertkin,
for solving the real-life mystery.

Thank you both so much.

- Prologue -

IT CAME BACK, as if in a dream.

Hands on the wheel of the Volkswagen van. Heart pumping. Mind racing. The sound of the engine roaring, the wind screaming through a crack in the side window.

And then he is there, in front of the van, his arms waving. His eyes widen with the realization that the van isn't going to stop.

One last desperate yank at the wheel, to the left. But the man dives in the same direction. At the same instant.

And then the thud. A noise that was sound and feeling. Forever repeated.

Tears obscuring the windshield. Foot on the gas.

One more bump as the Volkswagen rolls over the dead body. The dead man. Dead. He had to be dead.

And then a whisper. "What have I done?"

– One –

" ' "I SHALL NOT stay behind. I will dress as a man if I must, but I shall go with you," Aurelia declared, her opal eyes sparkling with fresh determination.' " Nan Millard paused in her reading to slap yet another white sheet of paper face down onto the stack on the glass-topped table in front of her. The stack had to be a quarter of an inch high. She went on. " ' "No, you must not!" Dalton cried. He reached out for her silken white hand . . .' "

Nan had been reading for at least half an hour on that Saturday afternoon in July. I resisted the urge to look at my watch. That would be rude. And it was my first time at this writers' critique group. I didn't want to embarrass my friend Carrie.

I snuck a look at Carrie. She at least appeared attentive. Carrie was a short, round, African-American woman with freckles scattered like cinnamon over her caffe latte skin. She was even shorter than I was, but unlike me she had a very tall personality. She had to. She was an appellate attorney. Her dark eyes were wide with what might have been intelligent interest in Nan's reading. But when I looked at her hands, sure enough, she was wiggling her fingers, one by one. I recognized the habit from some twenty years ago when we had come fresh out of college to work together in a mental hospital. If Carrie was wiggling her fingers like that, it meant that she was either bored or worried or angry. Or all of them combined.

I tried and failed to catch her eye, then guiltily jerked my head back to Nan, promising myself to focus on what she had written and was so lovingly presenting to us.

" "It would be no life for you, my darling," he said. "It's still a frontier out there. No running water. No electricity. And nothing but men." " " Nan smiled widely, showing perfect white teeth. Maybe she was thinking of all those men. She recrossed her long, tan legs. " 'A bird called outside the window. The call seemed sad to Aurelia suddenly, infinitely sad. "Must you go?" she asked softly . . .' "

I let my eyes drift to the others sitting in Slade Skinner's living room. I had been briefly introduced around when I came in with Carrie, but I had lost most of their names as Nan read on. And on.

There was the very thin woman perched on a carved wooden chair. Was her name Vicky? I wondered why she was so thin. Maybe she was sick. AIDS? I hoped not for her sake. And the woman sitting by her dressed in swirls of purple cotton was Donna. I remembered her. She had tripped over one of the coffee tables on the way in.

Those tables, made of curling wrought iron with glass tops, looked like incorrigible leg-biters to me. The whole room seemed aggressively Western. Red-tiled floors, with Indian scatter rugs, coppery leather sofas and tall, carved wooden chairs. At least it was cool in here, mercifully cool after the July heat outside.

Slade himself held a dumbbell in his fist, which he was rhythmically pumping up and down, inflating and deflating his biceps muscle. And he was staring at that muscle with unabashed admiration. It was his living room. I guessed he could do what he wanted. It didn't seem to bother Nan. He switched the dumbbell to his other hand. Up, down. Up, down.

" ' "I wouldn't have a poor man marry you, not even myself,"
Dalton whispered. Aurelia tossed a stand of bronze-burnished
hair from her fair face.' " Nan tossed her own blond hair from
her tanned face as she spoke. She had a model's good looks, a
California model's. Good tan, good teeth, good legs. I could
see most of her legs below the cream-colored miniskirt she
was wearing. " ' "And I shall return, my darling. I promise
you . . ." ' "

It seemed to me he had already made this particular promise
to Aurelia. More than a few times. But I might have been
wrong. I continued my survey of the living room.

A woman with black, permed hair who looked like she
should be a blonde sat on one of the leather sofas, her eyes
half-closed, breathing in through her nose and out through her
mouth noisily. I hoped she wasn't having an asthma attack. A
well-built man with Asian features was on her left, staring
through tinted glasses, his body and head completely still. It
was kind of spooky to be that still, I decided with a little shiver.
The elderly woman on the black-haired woman's right side
wasn't still or spooky, though. Her eyes were bright and her
face animated as she listened to Nan. She nodded as Nan
slapped another sheet of paper facedown.

"Good golly, that's mighty interesting stuff you've got
there," she put in quickly. Her raspy voice was a welcome
contrast to Nan's smooth tones. She took off her thick glasses
and wiped them with the hem of her lavender jacket as she
spoke. "Might want to skip to the chase, though. There's a lot
of good grub in the kitchen waiting to be eaten."

"Only for you, Mave," Nan said with a flash of white teeth.
She blew the older woman a kiss and thumbed through the
chunk of paper in her hand.

Right, I remembered, the older woman's name was Mave
Quentin. And then the others popped into my head. The woman
with the black, permed hair was Joyce something-or-other. The

Asian man was Russell, Russell Wu. And the drop-dead handsome man sitting next to Carrie on the other sofa was Trevor. No, Travis. God, he was gorgeous. He looked like a gypsy with his long black hair, swarthy skin and big brown eyes. I wondered why he was scowling, not that it detracted from his looks any. Was he angry with Nan? Or maybe—

"I'll skip ahead to chapter thirteen," Nan said, interrupting my speculation. She took a deep breath, then resumed. " " "I haven't heard from him in months," Aurelia told Polly. Her eyes shone with impending tears. "Is he dead? Has he found someone else to love, someone else to caress as he once caressed me?" Polly shrugged her square shoulders. Then she bent forward, her cold blue eyes glinting. "Marry Harry," she said. Aurelia put her face into her hands. A bird called nearby. . . .' "

Maybe Polly could shoot the bird, I mused. She seemed pretty practical.

" ' "But I don't love Harry . . ." ' "

I leaned back in my chair and asked myself how the hell I had ended up at this critique group. It was all Wayne's fault, I decided. My own eyes got misty. I had put Wayne on an airplane to visit his uncle for a couple of weeks the night before, and now I was suffering all the separation anxiety of . . . well, of Aurelia and Dalton. God, it was true, I realized. Disgusting but true. No wonder I was having such a hard time listening to Nan.

I sat up straighter until I felt the carved wood of my chair pressing against my shoulders. I pushed back, hoping the pressure would keep me alert. I was here for the critique group and I ought to listen. Of course, Wayne was the real writer. He wrote wonderful short stories, gentle dissections of human nature surprising from such a shy man. A couple of his stories had even been published. And then suddenly, in the midst of designing the gag gifts I made for a living, I had felt an urge to write something myself. Something besides silly slogans for the sides of coffee cups. Something like poetry.

Not that I would have ever shown the poems to anyone. I had only told two people of their existence, Wayne and Carrie. And when Carrie had suggested I come to this critique group to hear working writers discussing their work, I had agreed. But only after instructing her to tell people I wrote short stories if she was asked. Somehow, writing short stories seemed a lot less embarrassing to me than writing poetry.

I took a deep breath, clamped my eyeballs onto Nan Millard's face and willed myself to listen.

" 'The man with the heavy brown beard looked somehow familiar,' " Nan was reading. " 'The way his golden eyes folded at the edges. My God, it was Dalton!' "

What a surprise.

" 'She opened her arms, forgetting Harry. Forgetting everyone but the man who stood before her . . .' "

My mind drifted back to the design I had been working on before Carrie had come to take me to the critique group, a necktie in the shape of a computer with a matching tie tack in the shape of a computer bug. My ex-husband had convinced me there was money to be made in computer-nerd gag gifts. A vision of computer earrings danced into my mind.

" 'But Dalton did not return Aurelia's embrace. "You're a married woman now," he hissed. His familiar eyes glittered with anger—' "

"No shit," a voice muttered.

I looked around, afraid for an instant that my own mind had spoken out loud. But Nan was looking at Travis, her eyes narrowed with anger, if not glittering. Uh-oh.

I stiffened, waiting for the explosion. But then Nan bared her white teeth in a smile.

"I'll take that as a compliment, Travis, dear," she said, her voice high with false sweetness. "I'm so, so very glad you're involved in the story sufficiently to identify with Dalton."

"Me?!" Travis protested, leaping from the sofa. "Me? I don't identify with that jerk. He's a complete idiot!"

Carrie stood now too, putting a restraining hand on one of Travis's oscillating arms. Travis muttered something under his breath. But he sat back down.

"Grow up," Slade advised a beat later, his eyes still on his biceps.

Travis jumped back to his feet, his mouth open, his arms spread wide. But Carrie spoke before he had a chance.

"You will both stop this behavior right now," she commanded. She straightened her back, seeming to grow a good three feet. "We are intelligent adults here, not squabbling children."

Slade shrugged his shoulders as he passed the dumbbell from one hand to the other. Then he started pumping again. I could see why he chose his biceps to look at. The rest of him wasn't as impressive: a tall, stringy body with a small but distinct pot belly for all his weight-lifting, and a weasely kind of face complete with close-set eyes and weak chin. His thin, graying hair was pulled back into a pony tail.

"But I—" Travis began.

Carrie glared at him. It was a good, laser kind of glare, born of years of practice with her two children. Not to mention numerous recalcitrant judges.

Travis shut his mouth and sat back down, scowling silently once more, looking even more handsome than he had before. The dark eyelashes shading his big brown eyes must have been nearly a full inch long. I wondered if Slade was jealous of the younger, better-looking man. That might explain the way he had goaded him.

"I suppose the reading portion of the afternoon is over,"

drawled Nan. She reached her arms behind her and stretched before adding, "By popular demand."

Smiles broke out on some faces. Mavis chuckled.

"Okay," Nan said, all business now. "Most of you have read the whole manuscript anyhow. How about some feedback?"

Travis opened his mouth, but Carrie beat him to the verbal punch once again.

"It's difficult for me to judge a work of this genre," she admitted, waving a hand in the air. "But perhaps a little more subtlety with the main characters would be in order. And a bit more development of the minor ones."

Nan frowned and crossed her arms. This was obviously not the kind of feedback she wanted to hear.

"But other than these minor flaws, I would say that it is a very well-written novel," Carrie added quickly. Carrie never has been slow on the uptake.

Nan nodded in agreement, her face relaxing.

"The story could use more intrigue, especially in the scenes with Dalton out West," Slade threw in. He put his dumbbell down on the coffee table. "Beef it up. And give the guy more personal power. When he finds out who falsely accused him of thievery, have him meet the accuser man-to-man. Just because he has a woman waiting for him doesn't mean you have to make him a wimp."

Nan nodded again after Slade had finished, but there was a flush beneath the surface of her tanned skin. I didn't think she really appreciated his advice.

"Oh, but I think Dalton's incredibly sweet," the woman wearing purple said. Donna. She seemed sweet herself, with her wide honey-colored eyes and masses of tangled black hair. Her voice was that of an enthusiastic child. "He has real integrity. I mean, he could, you know, like shoot it out or something, but he doesn't. He comes back to be with the woman he loves—"

Slade snorted.

"But that's real integrity," Donna insisted, her childlike voice rising an octave higher. "To survive a trauma like that and retain your personal dignity. That's incredibly appropriate, I think."

"Maybe it's appropriate," pronounced Slade. "But he's not a real man. And that's where the real power of the novel is, giving the reader characters he can admire, characters he can identify with—"

"Might just be that most of Nan's readers are she's, not he's," Mave put in. She grinned. "Maybe they appreciate a more sensitive human being."

"You're no more an expert on what a *normal* woman wants to read than I am," Slade told Mave dismissively.

I wondered what he meant. Whatever it was, it didn't seem to bother Mave much. She just tilted her curly gray head to the side and eyed him for a moment.

"Maybe," she said. "Maybe not."

Slade picked up his dumbbell and began pumping again. Up, down. Up, down.

"I only have one or two comments," Russell Wu said into the silence. He had the voice of a classical radio announcer, low, rich, and soothing. "Your use of archaic language isn't always consistent. And you repeat certain phrases too often."

"Like what?" Nan demanded with a glare. Maybe Russell's voice didn't seem so soothing to her. Or maybe she was tired of criticism. I certainly would be.

"'The bird called,'" Russell answered mildly.

Nan's nostrils flared. "The bird is symbolic—"

"That's not the problem," Travis cut in indignantly. I had almost forgotten him. "You're all talking about these stupid little points. The real problem is that you set this story in the West at a time when the Native Americans were in their last death throes, and you never even mention their oppression!

What the hell point are you making? What are you writing—"

"Oh, for God's sake," Slade interrupted. "This is a romance, not a serious novel. It's entertainment."

Travis wasn't the only one scowling at Slade now. Nan had joined him. Not that Slade had noticed.

I watched as Nan took a deep breath, uncrossed her arms and bared her teeth in another smile. Why had she challenged Russell Wu, but not Slade Skinner? Maybe it was because Slade was the expert. Carrie said the thrillers he wrote were close to best sellers.

"'Literature flourishes best when it is half a trade and half an art,'" Mave pointed out. "W.R. Inge said that. He was the Dean of Saint Paul's."

"The quotation might have some relevance if we were talking about literature," Slade fired back. "A romance novel is not literature. It's not even a real novel as far as I'm concerned."

I took a peek at Nan's face. It was a battleground of conflicting emotions, though anger seemed to be winning.

The woman with the permed, black hair, raised her hand hesitantly.

"Yes, Joyce," Nan said impatiently.

"I wanted to say that I appreciate your story for its lack of violence," Joyce told her slowly, her voice barely above a whisper. Her skin pinkened as she spoke. "That in itself is a kind of statement, with all the obsession with violence these days."

Nan just stared at Joyce, unsmiling.

"That's all," Joyce finally added. "I can't really comment on the romance angle."

"No," drawled Nan. She drew herself up straight in her chair. "I guess you can't at that."

Joyce's skin went red to the roots of her black hair. Damn.

What was that all about? I was liking the idea of spending time with working writers less and less.

"Now, Nan," Mave said, waggling a finger. "We all get a mite testy when we're critiqued, but that doesn't mean you can just ride roughshod over the rest of us—"

"Mave, will you knock off the folksy routine?" Slade demanded. "You grew up here in Marin just like I did and you had fucking well better—"

Travis leapt from his seat. "Don't you talk to Mave that way!" he shouted. "Or I'll—"

– Two –

"OR, YOU'LL WHAT?" Slade cut in. He rose from his chair, dumbbell in hand and squinted his close-set eyes. "Tell me how politically incorrect my actions are?"

Travis's mouth opened and disjointed words came sputtering out. "You—can't—Mave—"

Carrie stood then too. She placed her small, round body between the two men and spread her arms like an umpire.

"You two cut it out right now," she ordered, her voice low and firm. "Both of you."

The order wasn't up to her usual formal standard of speech, but it did the trick. Both men glared for a moment longer, then lowered their eyes simultaneously and returned to their respective seats.

Carrie sat back down, muttering to herself and shaking her head. I caught "ye gods and goddesses" and "damn fools," but none of the other words in between. It was probably just as well, because Mave was talking at the same time.

". . . is all right, Travis," she was assuring the younger man. She leaned back against the cushions of the sofa and let out a braying laugh. "An old warhorse like me has heard plenty worse, let me tell you. Good golly, seems to me—"

"Well, this has been oodles and oodles of fun," Nan

interrupted. "But I for one need a break." She stood and stretched, her fingers laced behind her head as she arched her back. It was quite a sight. Even Travis seemed to forget he was mad at Slade as he turned to stare at her.

Once Nan had everyone's attention, she dropped her arms and asked, "Can we eat now?"

So we ate. Food was potluck and spread out on a long wooden table in the kitchen. There was lots of it and it all looked good. And better yet, most of it was recognizably vegetarian. I helped myself to a pasta salad studded with broccoli and almonds, green salad, French bread, marinated asparagus and Carrie's homemade carrot muffins, which, on the way over, she had assured me were vegetarian. Then I added a scoop of my own Thai-style noodles. The other dishes might have been free of animal products too, but I was suspicious of the little brown chunks in one and the brown broth in the other, so I left them alone and carried my full plate back to the living room to join the others.

Travis was shoveling food into his face as fast as he could swallow, looking a little less gorgeous than usual as he did, but not much. In fact, everyone seemed to be packing it in. Well, not everyone. Donna had spilled something on her blouse and was busily shredding a paper napkin on it in an effort to scrub it away. Joyce was prodding bits of food with her fork but had yet to raise that fork to her mouth. And Vicky, whose emaciated body looked like it could use the food more than the rest of our bodies put together, was ignoring her own plate with its small serving of green salad to watch everyone else eat.

I opened my mouth to ask why she wasn't eating, then realized it was none of my business. Anyway, I had a better use for my mouth. I was hungry. I broke off a piece of carrot muffin. The tantalizing scent of oranges and cloves wafted up to my nose.

"Well, Kate," Mave said just as I was about to stuff the piece in my mouth. "Tell us about yourself."

My stomach clenched. I set the untasted piece of muffin back on my plate unhappily.

"Oh, I own a gag-gift company, Jest Gifts—"

"Gag gifts?" Her gray eyebrows shot up above the violet rims of her glasses. "Holy gee, do you mean goofy things like whoopee cushions and joy buzzers?"

"Not exactly," I said, wriggling uncomfortably in my wooden chair. "I design and sell specialty items for different professionals—"

"Items such as shark mugs for attorneys," Carrie put in, her dark freckled face lighting up in a smile.

"And shark earrings," I added.

"Shark earrings?" Carrie demanded. "I wasn't aware you were making earrings now. You've been holding out on me, girl. I will expect a pair of your best sharks at your earliest convenience." She lowered her voice and winked. "If not sooner."

"I'm doing earrings for all the professionals," I went on, encouraged by her enthusiasm. "Toothbrushes for dentists, shrunken heads for therapists. That kind of thing. And I'm starting a whole new line of computer-nerd gifts—"

"Do you really make a living this way?" Slade asked. The sneer in his voice matched the one on his face.

So much for encouragement. I nodded and broke off another piece of muffin, hoping my face hadn't turned too red.

"So, do you make good money?" Nan probed. She leaned forward, her blond pageboy swinging gracefully as she moved.

"Well, not really good," I admitted. "After I get through paying manufacturing costs and employee salaries, there isn't a whole lot left. But it's enough for me to live on."

"You'd better stick to selling real estate," Slade advised Nan with yet another sneer. I wasn't sure if that sneer was for me or for Nan.

"Your business must be incredibly fun," Donna piped up. She had shreds of white napkin all over her purple blouse, but at least she was smiling instead of sneering. "And creative too. I mean, thinking up designs for all those shark earrings and stuff. You must have a real gift."

I stared at her for a moment, wondering if she was teasing, then decided she wasn't.

"It is fun—"

"Are you doing social satire?" Travis asked through a mouthful of food. His brown eyes burned into mine for a long moment.

"Well . . ." I hesitated. I had certainly never thought of my business that way before.

"Of course, she's doing social satire," Carrie answered for me. "How can you poke fun at attorneys and not be doing social satire?" She laughed, then said more seriously, "Kate's also a beginning writer."

"So, what sorts of things do you write, Kate?" Mave asked.

I tried to take a deep breath, but my chest felt too tight. I hated to lie, but I wasn't willing to admit to writing poems right then and there, either.

"Kate writes short stories," Carrie lied for me. My chest loosened. Then she added, "And poetry."

Poetry? My pulse began to pound in my ears. Why the hell had she said poetry? I'd told her not to—Then I tried to remember. I knew I'd told her to say I wrote short stories, but had I specifically instructed her *not* to mention poetry?

"A poet!" Mave exclaimed before I could remember. "Well, bully for you, Kate. Not enough good poets around these days. How long you been writing?"

"Not long," I mumbled, looking down at the food on my plate. It didn't look delicious to me anymore.

"'There is a pleasure in poetic pains which only poets know,'" she quoted. She closed her eyes and sighed, before adding, "William Cowper."

"Oh, great," I said. I pulled my mouth into a smile in lieu of further follow-up. I had no idea what else to say.

The silence grew longer. And longer. Strangely enough, it was Slade who finally rescued me.

"Why does everyone bring vegetarian food?" he demanded. "A man needs red meat, red wine and red-blooded women." He turned to Mave. "Bet you don't know who said that," he challenged her.

She wrinkled her already wrinkled brow a little further for a moment, then gave up.

"Who?" she asked.

"Me," he announced, then hooted with laughter.

Nan was the only one who laughed with him. Mave chuckled a little, but no one else seemed to think Slade was very funny.

"What's this?" he said, once he'd finished hooting. He speared one of the suspicious-looking brown chunks on his fork. "Tofu?"

"Seitan," Joyce murmured.

"What the hell is seitan?" he demanded.

"A meat substitute made from wheat gluten—" Joyce began.

Slade put up his hand. "No, don't tell me. Why you people seem to think there is anything inherently appealing in this garbage is beyond me. . . ."

He complained about the food for a good ten minutes more, both generally and specifically, with insults for each individual dish. At least his tirade gave me a chance to sample the dishes he was criticizing.

"Maybe if the food was better," he finished up, "Vicky might consider eating it."

Vicky clutched her plate of green salad so hard that the veins stood out on her thin arms. But she didn't say anything. I wasn't too surprised, though. I had yet to hear her utter a word.

"Speaking of better food," Nan said. "What's for dessert?"

"Coconut-honey-date bars," said Russell Wu, his mild, soothing voice a welcome change from Slade Skinner's loud haranguing one.

The coconut-honey-date bars were good, too. Even Slade didn't criticize them. Once they were gone, Nan licked the last crumbs from her fingertips and got up from her chair.

"Past four o'clock, time to toddle on home," she said, reaching for her purse. "A friend and I are going to that fabulous new Japanese place on Morton for dinner tonight. And I have to get up hideously early tomorrow to sell some red-hot real estate."

One by one, everyone began to stand then, shuffling, stretching and reaching for belongings. Travis and Donna turned toward the kitchen.

"The next group meeting will be at my house on Saturday afternoon," Carrie told us before anyone could leave the room. "We will be reviewing Slade's and Donna's manuscripts. Everyone should have received copies at the last meeting." She looked around. No one contradicted her. "And if each of you would please prepare to tell Kate a little about your own work at the next meeting, it would be appreciated."

I watched people nodding, wondering if I should speak up. I wasn't at all sure I was actually coming to the next meeting, but I couldn't think of a polite way to say so. And then it was too late. Everyone was moving and talking again.

"Mave, I brought you those pamphlets from the People for the Ethical Treatment of Animals," Travis said as he trailed the older woman into the kitchen.

"Need a ride?" Russell asked Joyce.

"No, I'll take the bus," she answered.

"You'll be wanting a copy of my manuscript," a voice whispered, very close behind me.

I jumped and turned to see Slade, less than a foot away, smiling down at me. He shoved a sheaf of white paper in my direction. I caught it as it connected with my chest.

"*Cool Fallout*," he said with a wink.

"What?" I said back.

"*Cool Fallout*, it's my newest manuscript. Not many people get to see it in this form, Kate. You'll enjoy it. See how a real writer works."

"Oh, thanks." I turned to look for Carrie.

"What are you doing tonight?" he asked.

"Doing?" I repeated, looking back at him. The smile was still on his weasely face. The man wasn't asking me out, was he?

"Know a great place for a late dinner," he said. God, he *was* asking me out. I wouldn't have thought short, dark and A-line would be his type. "California cuisine—"

"I have to work tonight," I cut in.

"But you're your own boss—"

"We're the worse kind," I assured him, looking around for Carrie in earnest now.

She came striding over from the direction of the kitchen, Tupperware in hand. And I was glad to see her. But before we could leave, Slade asked *her* out to dinner. Right in front of me. And he kept on talking after Carrie had politely refused his offer.

"I had a little talk with my agent about your sci-fi novel," he told her. "She might be interested in shopping it around. I thought we could talk about it over dinner."

I waited for Carrie to tell him off. But she didn't.

"Perhaps, since everyone else is gone, Kate and I could stay a little longer. Then you and I could discuss the idea," she suggested quietly.

The hair on the back of my neck prickled. Why was she so compliant? This wasn't Carrie.

"Sorry," Slade told her, not looking sorry at all. "You can't stay. I've got a secret meeting at five. It's with someone in the group. Wouldn't you like to know who?"

"It wouldn't be a secret then, would it?" Carrie replied sharply.

Finally, the smile left Slade's face.

"But I do appreciate the trouble you have taken to speak to your agent on my behalf," Carrie backpedaled quickly. I could tell by the way her fingers were wiggling what an effort the courteous words were for her. "Perhaps I could visit for a short time after your other meeting is over."

"Come back at six-thirty," Slade ordered. He was smiling again.

"Ye gods and goddesses, that man is arrogant," Carrie fumed as she pulled away from the curb into the wide, tree-lined street.

Slade Skinner was lucky enough to live in Hutton, the most expensive town in Marin County. And that's saying a lot. Hutton's streets were not only wide and tree-lined, they were quiet. I couldn't see another car or person in either direction. Not even a cat or a dog.

"Sometimes I find it very difficult to treat Slade as a fellow human being," Carrie went on. "Sometimes I wonder if he *is* a fellow human being. Do you believe the man actually writes in red ink with a quill-tipped pen? From a crystal ink well, no less?"

"Then why did you agree to see him?" I demanded as I snapped on my seat belt.

"His agent is Hildegarde Tucker," Carrie answered in a whisper.

"And?"

"Hildegarde Tucker is one of the best agents in New York. If she agrees to represent me, I'll probably have a real career in writing. If not . . ." She took one hand off the steering wheel and waved it dismissively.

"Can this woman really make such a big difference in your career?" I asked.

"Yes," Carrie answered simply.

She drove a few more scenic blocks in silence, then added, "Hildegarde Tucker only represents the best writers. And the best-selling ones. Kate, it could mean everything."

I looked at her round, freckled face. Her brows were puckered into an expression that looked serious now, even desperate. My chest ached as I saw that expression. I wanted to tell her that it didn't matter who Slade's agent was. That she shouldn't kowtow to him. That she would do just fine on her own. But I didn't really know any of that.

"Is Slade a good writer?" I asked instead.

"Yes, he is. Actually he is a *very* good writer. His thrillers are literally thrilling, real page-turners. *Cool Fallout* is an extremely well-crafted and engrossing novel. But Slade himself—" She sighed and shrugged in one elegant gesture.

"If he's such a big-deal writer," I demanded, "then why's he in the critique group?"

"I believe he's lonely," Carrie answered after a moment's thought. "I would guess that he doesn't have very many friends, if any. And he is always on the lookout for women." She rolled her eyes. "Slade Skinner is such a Lothario. Sometimes I think his chief interest in our writers' group is to seduce its members. He's already seduced Nan. And he isn't interested in men. Or anyone over fifty. So that leaves Joyce, Donna, Vicky and myself. And he thinks Vicky is too thin."

"Vicky *is* too thin," I put in.

"Well, *I'm* certainly not too thin," Carrie said with a smile. "I almost wish that I were. That damn fool man asks me to have dinner with him every time I see him. And each time I say

no, he acts completely surprised—completely astounded—
that I don't want that kind of relationship with him." She
waved a hand. "If I were going to be in a relationship, it
wouldn't be with Slade Skinner. And I haven't been in a
relationship for years, anyway. My kids keep telling me to get
a life."

"How are your kids?" I asked on cue. I was tired of talking
about Slade Skinner.

"They're doing well." Her deep voice grew warm and
relaxed. Even her hands seemed to relax on the wheel as she
pulled onto the highway. "Thank the divine powers that be,
Cyril Junior only has two more years of school. Then I'm free
from the supporting role of Bank of Mom."

"Congratulations," I said.

"Thank you, Ms. Jasper." She flashed me a smile. Then her
face grew serious again. "Kate, do you suppose you could
come with me to Slade's tonight?"

"Well . . ." I considered the idea. "It might be a little weird.
I already told him I was busy working tonight."

"Never mind," she murmured.

"Hold on," I told her. "I'm not saying no. I just have to think
of some excuse—"

"Perhaps you could pretend you left the casserole dish
behind that you brought your noodles in?"

"Damn, I *did* leave my casserole dish!"

It took us less than two minutes to come up with a plan. I
would drive back to Hutton in time to reach Slade's at six-forty,
looking for my Corning Ware. Carrie assured me she couldn't
get in too much trouble in ten minutes. Then I'd sit in on her
discussion with Slade. Afterwards, Carrie and I would go out to
dinner. Her treat, she insisted. Once that was settled, she asked
after Wayne, a fond smile gentling her face.

I was pretty sure that fondness was as much for Wayne as it
was for myself. Carrie was one of the few people I knew who

was able to instantly engage my shy significant other in conversation. Extended conversation. The last time Carrie had visited us, she and Wayne had discussed the relationship of body chemistry, self-determination, virtue, angst, prescription drugs and reincarnation until two in the morning. I had lost the thread somewhere around midnight.

"Wayne's fine," I told her. "He's visiting with his uncle for a couple of weeks. He wants to work on some of his 'childhood issues' before we get married."

"But I thought he was eager to marry you," Carrie objected.

"Now he thinks he's unworthy," I told her. "You know Wayne." I leaned back in my seat, seeing his kind, homely face in my mind's eye. And his muscular body. I let out an involuntary sigh, then sat up straight again. "Now that I've finally agreed to marry him, he's going through these fits of self-consciousness and worthlessness."

"And you?"

"I love him more than ever," I admitted. I could feel my face redden as I said it, much as I told myself that love was nothing to be embarrassed about. But after Nan's reading—

"Anyway," I went on quickly. "Now my ex-husband's heard that we might get married, and he's trying to win me over again. He thinks he's being subtle, but he's not—"

"But Craig instigated the divorce!" Carrie interrupted indignantly. It was just as well Craig wasn't in the car with us subject to that indignation, I decided.

"Craig left me all right. But then he decided he shouldn't have. Which was too bad. We were actually friends for a while after we separated. But now he's determined to get romantic again." I stuck my finger down my throat and made gagging sounds.

Carrie threw her head back and laughed. The conversation got lighter after that. By the time she pulled into my driveway, she was talking about her kids again, bragging really, not that she'd ever admit it.

I gave her shoulder a quick squeeze and climbed out of the car.

"See you at six-forty," I told her.

She shot me a grin and a salute before backing out of the driveway, popping gravel.

I clumped up my front stairs, smiling.

My cat, C.C., greeted me with a deep-throated yowl of displeasure when I opened the front door. Then she tilted her head to stare at me. C.C. was a black, overstuffed sausage of a cat with beret- and goatee-shaped white spots that gave her face a certain rakish charm. Especially when she tilted her head. She untilted it and began yowling even louder. So much for charm.

I picked C.C. up with one hand and with the other dropped my purse and Slade's manuscript on the nearest pinball machine. Then I crossed the entryway to the dining room, which served as my office, rubbing my chin against C.C.'s silky fur on the way.

At least there was nothing on my answering machine from the Jest Gifts crew. Saturday or not, I had expected another call. We were having an employee crisis at Jest Gifts. The parents of my second warehousewoman, Jean, were getting a divorce. That might not sound like an employee crisis, but it was. Jean wasn't upset about the divorce, she was devastated. On Friday, she had cried all day and sent out two dozen hollow-tooth mugs to an opthalmologist instead of the eyeball mugs he had ordered. Among other things.

I gave silent thanks that there were no messages, then sat down at my desk and let C.C. get comfortable in my lap. Once she was blissfully purring and clawing my thighs, I took a deep breath and pulled out the file folder of poetry I had hidden beneath my desk blotter.

"We return home like magpies," I read. "Each of us bearing a brightly colored scrap of conversation. He said, she said, I said—"

Damn. That was awful! And I wasn't even sure if magpies were the right kind of birds. Why had I believed I could write poetry? I could just imagine Slade Skinner's sneering critique. I shoved the folder back under the blotter with a shiver. It was time to get back to gag gifts.

Design or paperwork? I ran my eye over the towering stacks of paperwork on my desk. Then I got out a pencil and began to sketch.

It was just six-thirty when I remembered my promise to interrupt Carrie and Slade's tête-à-tête.

I hurried down the stairs, hopped into my Toyota and drove to Hutton, rehearsing my excuse for Slade on the way.

But when I got to Slade Skinner's doorstep, the thick redwood door was swinging wide open. And there was no one in sight to listen to my well-prepared excuse.

"Slade," I called out softly. "Carrie."

No one answered.

I rang the doorbell and called their names more loudly, but still no one answered. Had they gone out somewhere and left the door open?

I walked into the living room, trying to make a lot of noise, clearing my throat and scuffling my feet. I wasn't too worried about intruding, though. After all, that was the plan.

The living room was empty. I just hoped they weren't in the bedroom. Maybe they're in the garden, I told myself, and made my scuffling, coughing way toward the glass doors.

But then I heard a noise from down the hall. A sob. Carrie's sob, I was certain. And then another one.

I sprinted down the hall toward the noise, picturing Carrie in Slade's muscular grip. She was strong, but she was so damn small. If he had done anything to her, I'd—

I was through the first doorway off the hall before I could finish the thought, my heart pounding from the sprint. And Carrie was there too, standing in front of a long wooden desk, her back to me. Her shoulders jerked in uneven sync with her sobs.

"Carrie," I called gently.

"Kate?" she cried and swiveled around to face me, her eyes wide with fright. My mouth went dry. I had never seen fear like that on her face, not in all the years I had worked with her. Not in all the years since.

"He's meat and bone," she whispered.

"What—" I began.

Carrie stepped away from the desk and pointed.

My eyes followed the direction of her finger.

And then I saw it, saw what was left of someone's head resting on a computer keyboard, a bloody dumbbell next to it. Slade's head, I realized. That red-stained hank of hair was his ponytail. My heart stopped, and for an instant the vision was bathed in light like an overexposed photo.

"Meat and bone," Carrie whispered again.

But she was wrong.

Slade Skinner wasn't just meat and bone.

He was meat and bone. And blood.

- Three -

I CLOSED MY eyes, but I could still see the wreckage of Slade Skinner's head against the darkness of my eyelids. Gravity sucked at me, telling me to lie down. *Ordering* me to lie down.

I drew in a breath so sharp it cut at my lungs, then forced my eyes back open. I didn't want to fall, didn't want to land on the rug. There was blood on the rug.

There was blood everywhere. Even without looking at what was left of Slade's head, I could see the bright red splatters on the desk. And on the crystal inkwell and pen sitting there. One end of the dumbbell was covered in blood. There was even a splash of red on the computer screen.

That wasn't all there was on that computer screen. A few amber lines of text glimmered against the black background as well. I took another sharp breath and stepped closer, refocusing my eyes. The lines became words.

"I never thought that someone in my own group—"

And then the amber words disappeared.

For a stunned instant, I couldn't figure out what had happened. Then I saw Carrie's hand pull back from the side of the computer.

I swiveled around to face her, shouting as I did. "You turned it off! Why the hell did you do that?"

When she didn't answer me, I peered angrily into her face. Her eyes were still wide and her mouth was slack. Slack with fear. And with shock, I realized. My anger dissolved, leaving me weak and dizzy.

"Carrie, why did you turn off the computer?" I asked her again. This time I didn't shout.

"Slade is dead," she answered, her voice as lifeless as Slade's body.

"Oh, Carrie," I whispered. I felt cold dampness on my cheeks and realized I was crying.

She threw her arms around me and held on. I could feel her small body tremble.

"Did you kill him?" I whispered. I had to know.

She pushed away and stared at me, still slack-jawed. Then slowly she closed her mouth. Intelligence returned to her eyes.

"I did not kill Slade Skinner," she stated, her voice low and clear. "You must believe me, Kate."

I told her I did believe her, and together we went to call the police.

Minutes after Carrie made the call—she insisted it was her responsibility—two uniformed officers burst through the still open front door. Carrie and I were in the living room, sitting silently on one of the coppery leather couches. The larger of the two officers came to a halt in front of us.

"Excuse us, ma'am, um, ma'am," the officer said quietly, nodding at each of us. "Did one of you call the police?"

I didn't answer. I couldn't. On top of the shock of finding a dead body, a polite police officer was just too much. Was it because we were in Hutton? Carrie didn't have any trouble answering, though.

"Yes, Officer," she said crisply. "I made the call. Let me show you the . . ." Then her crisp voice faltered.

"The deceased, ma'am?" the officer offered helpfully.

Carrie jerked her head in a curt nod and rose to lead the two officers down the hall, returning to the living room minus one of them minutes later.

Three more men arrived not long after that. But these men were dressed in business suits instead of uniforms.

"Police Chief Gilbert," said the gray-haired one. He stuck out a hand to be shaken by both Carrie and myself. "I'll be taking personal charge of this case," he assured us, his voice as hushed and respectful as a funeral director's. "Please let us know if you need anything."

We both shook our heads. As Gilbert and the other two men in suits disappeared down the hall, I wondered if Carrie was as dazed by the police chief's performance as I was. The whole scene was taking on a dreamlike quality. And when the men walked back into the living room some time later, I noticed something else strange. All three men looked alike. They all had lean, aristocratic features with long noses and high foreheads. They could have been brothers, including the African-American among them.

"Ms. Yates," Police Chief Gilbert said to Carrie. "If you wouldn't mind, we'd like to ask you a few questions in the kitchen." He gave me a pleasant nod, assuring me he'd speak to me very soon.

Carrie left with the police chief, her back straight and head held high. For some reason, the sight of her small erect body made me want to cry.

I closed my eyes instead and leaned my head back against the leather cushions, willing my mind to think of anything but Slade Skinner's death.

My mind began to drift, and pretty soon the memories came floating on by, memories of the mental hospital where Carrie and I had worked some twenty years ago. I caught glimpses of the faces of my favorite patients. And heard their voices too. George, who used to march the halls chanting "Johnny get up,

Jimmy get up, Peter get up!" all the time staring at his crotch. And Marion, who whispered wide-eyed for days at a time, "I was there when Egypt burned, in the body of a priest. I was in Atlantis too, as it sank. And in Greece . . ." All the way up the reincarnational scale. And old Simon who always pretended we were on a cruise ship, danced like Fred Astaire and asked me to marry him. He had actually escaped the hospital. I always liked to think that he just swam away.

And then I remembered the time that Carrie had saved my life. Or so I had believed.

I'd been working on the residential ward of the hospital all of two days when Rosie had picked me up and squeezed. That might not sound too bad. But Rosie was over six feet tall. And she had the muscles of a football player. Her real name was Roslyn, but we called her Rosie in honor of Rosie Greer. And when she picked you up and squeezed, she didn't squeeze you like someone testing the freshness of a loaf of bread, she squeezed you like she was making lemonade and you were the lemon. I tried to tell her to stop, but she was squeezing me so hard I couldn't get the words out. And then I began to pass out. Words buzzed around my head, and pretty soon the room joined in.

It was then that Carrie trotted up.

She had said, "Rosie, put that girl down right now," in a deep, calm voice.

And Rosie put me down.

I never forgot it. Even when I got good at handling the violent patients myself. Even when I realized that Rosie always put the people back down, even the cop she picked up one day—

"Ms. Jasper," came a voice into my consciousness. I opened my eyes and Police Chief Gilbert's lean, aristocratic face replaced the rounded face of the cop in my memory. "If you wouldn't mind following me?" he said, waving me ahead of him. A gentleman of the old school.

The police chief's questions must have taken me all of five minutes to answer.

"Probably an interrupted burglary," he assured me as he stood up from the kitchen table. "Please feel free to go. I believe your friend is waiting for you."

That was it, I realized as I left the kitchen. No one asked me anything about the computer. No one even asked if I'd been with Carrie when she discovered Slade's body. As opposed to coming in later. They just seemed to assume we had found him together. I was glad. I didn't want to tell them any of that. Or to tell them about the desperation I had seen in Carrie's eyes when she'd talked about Slade's agent. What if Slade had only been teasing her? What if—

But then a happy thought intruded. If Carrie had bludgeoned Slade Skinner to death, wouldn't she have been splattered with blood? And she wasn't. But she could have covered herself, a voice within me argued. She could have—

"Are you ready to leave?" Carrie asked from my side.

I jumped a little in place, then nodded and followed her out of Slade Skinner's house.

I sucked in the fresh air gratefully once we were back on the other side of Slade's front door. I heard children laughing somewhere, a mother calling, and then, for a moment, only the hum of distant traffic and insects.

"We need to discuss what has happened," Carrie said.

"Not here," I warned with a nod toward the house.

We walked in silence to the curb, where our cars were parked. I looked over my shoulder. There didn't seem to be any Hutton police within earshot.

"Why did you turn off the word processor?" I asked Carrie for the third time. This time she answered me.

"If we assume that Slade typed the message on the screen,

the message would seem to indicate that Slade had found out something about someone in the critique group, some secret." She sighed. "The words didn't specify who that someone was or what Slade had found out. They didn't even specify whether that someone was male or female. Still, I didn't want the police to see the reference to our group. I'm afraid I panicked. I'm sorry, Kate." She turned back toward Slade's house. "I'll go back and inform the police—"

"No, don't do that!" I whispered urgently. "It'll just look suspicious now."

She turned back to me, her mouth opening to speak, but I beat her to it.

"Did you tell them that you found Slade's body by yourself before I got there?" I asked.

"No," she answered, looking straight into my eyes. "Do you think I should have?"

"No, I guess not," I answered, looking down at my feet. It was probably best if the police assumed Carrie and I found Slade's body together, though I wished—

"Kate, I am not a murderer," Carrie said sharply.

Warmth flooded my cold hands as something inside of me decided to accept her words.

"But I think someone in our critique group is," she went on.

I felt like putting my newly warmed hands over my ears then. As long as Carrie hadn't killed Slade, I didn't want to hear any more about it.

"First, there is the message on the computer," Carrie pointed out. She stuck out a finger. "Second, Slade stated that he had a secret meeting with someone from the group." A second finger popped out. "That meeting was scheduled for five o'clock. I found his body at six-thirty."

She didn't have to stick out a third finger. I got the idea.

"The police believe the dumbbell is the murder weapon," she added more quietly.

I felt a new surge of nausea as I saw the bloody dumbbell in my mind.

"Kate, will you help me figure this thing out?" Carrie asked.

"Of course I will," I agreed without thinking.

Carrie's eyebrows shot up. Was she surprised by my easy capitulation? I certainly was. What had I agreed to?

"I don't mean I'll actually investigate or—" I began.

"You have before."

"I don't really know much about investigating," I told her. "All I know is blundering around into dangerous situations and practically getting myself killed. In fact, now that I've thought about it, we shouldn't—"

Her steady gaze pinned me. I remembered Rosie again.

"Well, it can't hurt to talk," I conceded.

"Good, follow me to my house," she ordered.

So I followed her, glad for the short time I had alone in my Toyota.

It was still light out as we walked up the path to Carrie's house a little before eight. And warm. A tenuous breeze rustled the leaves of a nearby apple tree before moving on, leaving a sweet scent in the air. I took a deep breath. Then Carrie stuck her key in the door.

An explosion of yips, howls and yowls erupted as if detonated.

The sounds quickly converged on the other side of the door and I heard Yipper's claws stripping the paint from the wood. Yipper was a young schnauzer, an aptly named animal. The howler was an old basset hound named Basta. And the yowl belonged to Sinbad, an ink-black cat with neon-green eyes. At least the animals were all guarding the door, more than my own cat, C.C., would ever consider doing.

Carrie opened the door and yelled, "CEASE AND DE-SIST!"

Taking orders is another thing C.C. would never do. But

Carrie's animals did. The cacophony ceased within seconds of her shout.

"After you," Carrie said.

I tried to lead the way to the living room, but the animals were all vying for the honor. Sinbad won. He was settled on a couch licking a black paw by the time I walked through the doorway.

Carrie's living room was a pleasant collage of well-organized chaos. In the center, a rose-colored easy chair and two cornflower blue couches loaded with colorful throw pillows were arranged around a wooden coffee table. The walls were almost invisible under shelves of books, art prints, paintings, and photos of Carrie's children and her late husband, Cyril. More tables and chairs were scattered around the room, the tables loaded with books, seashells, rocks and vases. And more framed prints and photos.

My eyes stopped at a photo of Cyril taken in the years before cancer had fastened onto him, changed him and finally killed him. I looked at that kind, smiling face and my chest hurt.

"Please, sit down," Carrie ordered brusquely. "I need to make a brief phone call."

I sat down on one of the mauve couches. And then craned my neck trying, and failing, to hear Carrie's phone conversation in the other room. The two dogs and the cat watched me with accusing eyes. I had to listen, I told them silently. What if the call had to do with the murder? What if Carrie had to do with the murder? I was ninety-nine percent sure she didn't, but that remaining one percent kept pinching me.

I hadn't seen much of Carrie during the fifteen years she had lived and practiced law in southern California. But nine months ago the appellate law firm she worked for had opened an office in San Francisco and Carrie had come home to Marin. We picked up our former friendship as if those fifteen years had never passed. Just like the old days. But did I still know her, really?

She had been standing over the body. She had turned off the computer—

"Well, Kate," came a voice from behind me, Carrie's voice.

"So," I said quickly, turning my head to disguise the way I had jumped in my seat. "You think someone in your group murdered Slade Skinner?"

"Yes, I do," she answered quietly. "Shall I tell you about the group members?"

I nodded as Carrie crossed the room and took a seat on the couch facing mine.

"Nan Millard acted as my real estate agent when I purchased this house," Carrie began, her eyes losing focus as she spoke. "She was quite friendly. We had lunch together. I mentioned that I wrote, that I was beginning a novel of speculative fiction. She invited me to the writers' critique group."

Carrie flashed a crooked smile at me.

"Now that I've gotten to know Nan better, I realize her interest in me was based primarily, if not entirely, on my status as an attorney. Nan is only interested in people who have status or money. Period. But at least she's an equal opportunity social climber."

I chuckled, but only for an instant before the guilt set in. How could I laugh so soon after seeing Slade's dead body?

Basta waddled up and took a seat on my toes, and the guilt seemed to dissolve under the warm pressure of his body. The old basset hound liked to sit on people's feet more than almost anything else. Except for bringing Carrie sticks. Carrie had a stack of Basta's gift sticks behind the couch. She was too soft-hearted to throw them away.

"Then there was Slade Skinner," she went on. "As you know, Slade could be a very, very difficult man to like."

"No kidding," I said, remembering his sneering face.

Basta rubbed his head on my leg. I reached down and gave him a pat.

"Didn't you say Slade seduced Nan?" I asked.

"I suppose I should have said that Nan slept with him upon occasion," Carrie answered carefully.

"Did they have a falling out?"

"Not so you'd notice." So much for that idea. "Slade was cordial to Nan, at least by his standards. He was still sleeping with her, after all. And Nan reciprocated that cordiality. Slade was a famous writer. Quid pro quo."

"Quid pro quo?"

"One thing in return for another," Carrie translated absently. "Then there's Donna Palmer. She's writing a *Mommy Dearest* about her family, a pretty nasty family if there is any truth whatsoever to her allegations. But she has the New Age to keep her company. She is so"—Carrie's voice rose in mimicry— "so incredibly involved in her healing process."

Carrie stuck a finger under her chin and took on a look of innocent vacancy as she spoke the last line. Right, Donna—I remembered. The one who had spilled something on her purple blouse. The one who thought I had a gift for gag gifts.

"What about the woman with the black perm?" I prompted.

"Joyce Larson. Doer of good work, started Operation Soup Pot. Have you heard of it?"

"One of the groups that gives leftover food to the homeless?" I hazarded uncertainly.

"That's correct. They not only distribute food to the homeless, but to the sick and old too. Joyce started the organization. Currently, she's the kitchen manager. A very quiet woman." Carrie steepled her hands together in an imitation of prayer. "Joyce is some sort of Buddhist. She is currently writing a cookbook with homey little anecdotes to raise money for the Operation. Only she's having a bit of trouble with the homey little anecdotes, having even less of a personal life than I."

I smiled. Carrie's tongue always got sharper under stress. At least that much hadn't changed.

"Then we've got Vicky Andros, who must be the skinniest woman alive. The woman just plain won't eat. She writes soft porn. And Russell Wu, he's another quiet one. He writes true crime. And Mave Quentin. She's a hoot, isn't she? Seventy-some years old and one of the most agreeable shit-kickers I've ever had the pleasure to meet. She's writing a historical biography."

"What did Slade mean about Mave not being a normal woman?" I asked, jolted by the sudden memory of his words.

"Mave is a lesbian," Carrie answered. Then she paused to take a big breath. I got ready for a major revelation.

"Then there's Travis," she said finally and paused again, wiggling her left pinkie. I was still waiting.

"Travis?" I repeated.

Carrie got up from the couch and began to pace.

"Travis is writing a survivalist manual for the coming fall of the United States," she said as she strode across the room.

"The fall of the United States?" I repeated. I was beginning to feel like a parrot.

"According to Travis Utrelli, the U.S. is going to collapse into chaos within the next five or ten years." Carrie turned and strode back toward the couch. "First the Government won't be able to pay its debts. Then all the banks will close down. No more credit cards. No more cash. No more groceries. Warfare on the city streets. You know the rhetoric."

Actually, I didn't. But I nodded anyway, all the time wondering what it was about Travis Utrelli that made Carrie get up and pace.

She sat back down. "Those are all the group members," she said softly. "Except that Slade Skinner is no longer a member, being deceased." She clenched her fists suddenly. "Damn it,

Kate. He said he had a secret meeting, and I had to be smartass and not allow him to tell me who he was supposed to meet."

"But Carrie—"

"And I turned off the computer. The police think it's a burglar, for God's sake! I tried to suggest to Chief Gilbert that it might have been someone in the group, but he wasn't interested." She got up and began pacing again. "And if the burglary theory doesn't work out, they have Slade's three ex-wives to investigate—"

"Carrie," I put in. "Maybe they're right. Maybe it was a burglar or an ex-wife. I mean, if he had three—"

"Maybe, maybe, maybe," she rapped out, cutting me off. At least she had stopped pacing. Now she was standing in place, waving her hands in the air. "But then again, maybe not." She dropped her hands and sighed. "Sorry, Kate."

"Carrie," I asked softly, "can you tell me what happened before I got there?"

"I went to his house a little after six-thirty," she told me, her voice racing now as she stood still. "I rang the bell. There was no answer. And the door was open. Just a few inches. So I pushed it open the rest of the way and went inside. He wasn't in the living room or the kitchen. I decided to check the study and then leave if I couldn't find him." Carrie gulped and I saw tears on her round, freckled cheeks. "I found him."

I jumped up from the couch.

"No," she said, thrusting an arresting palm in my direction before I could get to her. "I'm fine." She closed her eyes for a moment, then opened them again. "I promised you dinner. I'd better start cooking it."

And with that, she marched into the kitchen, the cat and dogs at her heels. I wasn't hungry and I doubted that she was either. But I followed her in without protest. If cooking would make her feel better, I wasn't going to argue.

Carrie's kitchen had as much color crammed into it as her

living room. Copper-bottomed pans hung from the wall and ceilings. Dishware in bright blues, pinks and yellows sat on open teak shelves. Floral art prints decorated the walls. And strings of brightly colored papier mâché vegetables hung alongside real garlic and herbs.

"I believe I should call an emergency meeting of the group," she informed me as she grabbed a copper-bottomed saucepan. "Speak to everyone. Find out if anyone will admit to meeting Slade at five. Find out—"

But the rest of Carrie's words were lost in the renewed racket of her animals. All at once, the three of them seemed to go crazy. With a deafening explosion of sound, they raced out of the kitchen and across the hall to the glassed-in patio that Carrie used as a study.

What the hell?

"The back door," Carrie explained. Then her eyes widened. She dropped the saucepan onto the counter. "The back door!"

- Four -

"BACK DOOR?" I repeated as Carrie went racing across the hall after her animals. Then my brain kicked in and I went racing after her.

I thought I could hear the pounding of running footsteps other than our own as I rushed toward the study. But it was hard to tell over the animal clamor. Then I heard a door slamming. I came through the study's nearest doorway in time to see a flash of brown, freckled legs as Carrie ran out the far door.

"Carrie!" I called out as I ran across the room to catch up with her. My mind told me there must be intruders here and I didn't want Carrie tangling with them.

Luckily, she wasn't fast enough.

I heard a car start and roar off as I sprinted across her backyard. Then the yipping stopped. And the yowling and howling. And Carrie came huffing and puffing back toward me, the now quiet animals dancing behind her. I could see drops of sweat shining on her face. And hear my heart beating in my own chest.

"Well?" I demanded.

She held a protesting hand up as she caught her breath.

"Who was it?" I pressed her anxiously.

"I don't know," she told me between breaths. "I only saw the back of their suits." She sucked in more air. "Expensive suits. Armani, I believe. They got into a car and drove off."

"What kind of car?"

"Big," she said, extending her hands outward. That was a lot of help. "American," she added. Then she shrugged. "I couldn't read the license plate."

Damn. We hobbled back into the study in silence.

Then Carrie looked over at her desk. With one last sprint, she ran toward it.

"The manuscript's gone!" she cried.

"Slade's manuscript?"

"No, Donna's." Carrie collapsed into her chair. "Oh hell," she whispered, looking at the empty surface of the desk. "Maybe Donna's family really is Mafia."

At first, the word "Mafia" just bounced off of my fatigued mind. But on the second bounce, it sank in.

"What!" I shouted.

Carrie looked up at me, her perspiration-drenched face apparently calm now that she had delivered her bombshell.

"Donna Palmer," she explained quietly. Then she raised her hands and started waving them in the air, belying that quietness. "I told you she's writing a *Mommy Dearest* about her family." She took a deep breath, then went on. "Well, she claims her family is 'da Family,' if you know what I mean."

"Organized crime?"

She nodded.

"And you think those guys in Armani suits are part of the family?" I whispered. My sweaty shirt felt cold against my skin.

Carrie nodded again solemnly. She wiped the perspiration from her forehead with the back of her hand.

"Why do you think so?" I asked her, my voice too high even in my own ears.

"Because Donna warned us they might show up."

"Donna warned you?" I said and slumped down onto the desktop. Its sharp edges weren't very comfortable, but Carrie had already taken the only chair in the room. "You mean you knew these guys were going to show up?"

"Not exactly," Carrie said.

"What the hell do you mean by 'not exactly.'"

"Let's go make dinner," she suggested. "And I will tell you about Donna."

"Wait a minute," I protested. "Aren't you going to call the police?"

"Do you think it would do any good?" she asked back, tilting her head as she looked up at me.

"Of course it would," I answered. "You know who the guys were—"

"Not specifically," Carrie corrected me. "Donna never named anyone specifically. And I didn't see the men's faces just now, only their backs. And I would doubt that they left any fingerprints." She took one last swipe at her damp forehead, then stood up and straightened her shoulders. "Let's talk about it in the kitchen."

"But what if these guys murdered Slade?" I objected.

Carrie frowned for a moment, then said, "I doubt it," and turned to leave the study.

I opened my mouth to argue. But I knew from experience it did no good to argue with Carrie. So I closed my mouth and followed her as she made her way back to the kitchen at a far more leisurely pace than she had left it. So did Basta, Yipper and Sinbad, each one returning to his own individual bowl like nothing out of the ordinary had happened. And for them, nothing probably had. Seen through their animal eyes this latest example of human behavior had to be incomprehensible at best. But *I* needed to know more.

"Tell me everything," I ordered as Carrie opened the refrigerator and pulled out a bulb of garlic.

"If you wish," she murmured, carefully peeling a section of the garlic bulb. "Donna claims her family made their money originally through gambling, prostitution and loan-sharking activities. A very enterprising clan." She began mincing the garlic. "She also says her family subjected her to neglect, 'verbal abuse' and various kinds of 'emotional oppression.'" She glanced over at me, as if for comment.

"Well, that part sounds pretty normal," I obliged.

I'd lived in Marin long enough to figure "neglect" could mean not getting your parents to give you the money for that new pair of sunglasses, "verbal abuse" might be your parents explaining why, and "emotional oppression" was the result when they asked you to go to your own room to scream about it.

On the other hand, I knew all three descriptions could stand for truly cruel acts.

"Do you think her family was really mean to her?" I asked.

Carrie shrugged. "It's hard to tell with Donna," she muttered. She splashed a little sesame oil in the saucepan and turned the stove on. "Would you like to slice the bread?" she asked me over her shoulder.

I nodded. I needed something to do with my hands. My earlier rush of adrenaline had left them twitching. Not to mention the rest of me.

Carrie pulled a loaf of Alvarado Sprouted Sourdough from the refrigerator and handed it to me. Then she tossed the minced garlic into the sesame oil with a pinch of herbs from a jar near the stove. I sliced the bread while the garlic and herbs began to sputter. The aroma filled the room and I began to salivate. I was actually hungry, I realized. Then a vision of Slade's mangled head intervened and my mouth went dry again.

"Donna gave each of us group members a hard copy of her manuscript at last Saturday's meeting," Carrie said. "She was afraid her father's business associates—read 'hoods'—would steal her own copy. They have before. She also warned us that they might attempt to retrieve the copies she gave to each of us."

"And you think those were the guys in the Armani suits?" I said slowly. "Are we really talking Mafia?"

Carrie didn't answer me right away.

Instead, she dipped the slices of bread in the garlic mixture one at a time, then put them all into the microwave to heat. After that, she minced some fresh basil and added it to what was left in the saucepan, then poured in a can of minestrone soup and a splash of sherry.

"I'm not certain that the men in the suits are actually members of a specific crime organization. Or even that they are connected to Donna's family," she answered finally. "But the latter does seem probable if we assume Donna is telling the truth about her family. How many other men would come to steal her manuscript?"

"But you don't think they murdered Slade."

"No, I don't believe so," she said briskly, opening the refrigerator door again with a hard yank that shook the bottles on the shelves. "Wouldn't our visitors have roughed me up at the very least if they were that violent? They just ran, Kate. I couldn't have scared them that much." She looked into the refrigerator for a moment. "Not to mention the fact that Slade said he was meeting someone at five from our group, someone who probably killed him. The two men in the Armani suits were not in our group, I can assure you."

"But—" I began.

"On the other hand," Carrie went on, "one of the many questions I would like to ask Donna is whether she thinks her father's hoods are capable of murder."

"After you ask her if they've been out retrieving manuscripts," I said. I still wasn't sure that we had established that fact. My stomach began churning. Anxiety or hunger? Both, I decided.

Carrie pulled a bunch of butter lettuce, some tomatoes and a glass jar from the refrigerator.

"Marinated green beans, capers, kidney beans, onions, olives and mushrooms," she told me. "My own recipe."

I rinsed the lettuce and tomatoes quickly as Carrie stirred the soup. I chopped them up in an even bigger hurry once the microwave *pinged*. In spite of the shocks of the day—or maybe because of them—I was really hungry now. Even thinking about Slade couldn't quell my yearning for food.

In a few more minutes the meal was on the table. I crunched into a piece of bread, burning my lips. The burst of garlic, sesame and herb flavors was worth the pain. I chewed happily, then opened my mouth to ask Carrie what herbs she had used. But her mouth was faster than mine.

"So, what do we do now, Ms. Jasper?" she asked me, her tone light. The tone didn't fool me for a minute. I could see the way her hands were clenched together on the tabletop. And she hadn't touched her food yet.

"Eat?" I hazarded.

"About the murder," she added in a heavier tone. A much heavier tone.

"I don't know," I told her defensively. "I'm not a detective. I'm just a gag-gift maker."

"Well, *I'm* just an attorney and not a criminal attorney at that," she shot back. Her hands came apart and fluttered around like crazed butterflies. "And it appears that *I* am in this situation whether or not *I* like it." Then she leaned forward, crossed her arms and stared at me without blinking.

I hate that. It even works when my cat does it.

"How about asking the group members if any of them visited

Slade at five o'clock?" I suggested after another minute of the treatment.

"That's exactly what I plan to do," Carrie said, leaning back in her chair. "At least if I can reach each of them on the telephone to schedule an emergency meeting."

I took a bite of salad as I tried to think. It was perfect, full of vegetables dressed with a tart marinade flavored with more garlic and herbs. Mentally, I identified chervil and tarragon. I looked back up to ask Carrie if I was right.

She was staring at me again.

"So tell me more about the group members," I said quickly. "Anything weird or suspicious, aside from Donna's family?"

Carrie looked up at the ceiling for a moment. That was a good start. She wasn't staring at me anymore. I ate another forkful of salad and took a bite of bread while she was occupied.

"I can all too easily imagine Nan Millard killing someone for a good deal of money or status," Carrie said after another couple of bites. Mine not hers. "But how would killing Slade get her either? In fact, she has actually *lost* status now that her famous lover is dead."

I nodded my understanding, my mouth too full to say anything.

"And as for Joyce—"

"She's the one that started Operation Soup Pot, isn't she?" I mumbled through my mouthful. "A quiet Buddhist, right?"

Carrie nodded. "Slade was always trying to date the poor woman. And she was no more interested in him than I was." Carrie grinned. "I believe Joyce found it a wee bit difficult to extend her infinite love and compassion to Slade Skinner. Not just because he was so individually obnoxious either. I get the distinct feeling that Joyce isn't sexually interested in men at all."

"Lesbian?" I asked curiously.

"I don't think so," Carrie answered slowly. She circled her fingers as if trying to pluck a description from the air. "Celibate is more like it."

I slurped a spoonful of soup. So that was why Nan had agreed that Joyce couldn't comment on the romantic angle of her story. Now it made sense. The soup tasted of more garlic and herbs. Not that I would have complained. The soup was as good as everything else.

"Russell Wu has the most obvious connection to crime," Carrie commented, looking back up at the ceiling.

"What connection?" I asked eagerly.

"I told you earlier, Kate. He writes true-crime books."

"Oh," I mumbled, disappointed. Somehow, I figured someone analytical enough to write about true crime probably wasn't going to commit a crime. On the other hand—

"Tell me all about this Russell guy," I ordered.

"He's a published writer," Carrie obliged. "He has two books out. One that he ghosted for an illiterate mass murderer three years ago. Another about that nursing home aide who was helping his patients on to the great beyond." She wiggled her shoulders. "It gives me the creeps. I don't know how Russell can stand working with these people. Now he's working on the story of that musician in San Jose who was—or at least is alleged to have been—killing the groupies who hung around after his shows. Russell has to wait out the trial before he can do his last chapter. It won't work without a guilty verdict."

"Why is Russell so interested in mass murder?" I asked.

Carrie shrugged massively. "For what it's worth, I don't think Russell is a killer. He's very gentle, soft-spoken—"

"So are half the mass murderers they arrest," I interrupted. "You know, all the neighbors say what a nice, quiet boy he was after the fact. How they never suspected. It's classic."

"That's why I would like you to come to the emergency meeting," Carrie said. She jabbed a finger in my direction.

"You need to see these folks again for yourself. Then you can make your own judgments."

"I suppose so," I answered slowly, thinking it out. If I didn't get involved. If I only observed—

"I knew you would," Carrie purred, grinning now. She jumped out of her chair and ran around the table to put her arm around my shoulders. "Thank you, Kate," she added and squeezed.

Then she went back to her chair, grabbing a piece of bread as she sat down. She bit into it and I realized that the bread was the first food she'd touched. Damn, there was no way I was going to tell her I wouldn't go now.

Carrie swallowed and said, "Have any more questions, Ms. Jasper?"

"Do these guys all write for a living?" I asked back.

"Most of them aren't paid enough for their writing to make an actual living," Carrie answered. She looked down at her salad and picked up a fork tentatively. "So they have day jobs. Travis fixes video games. He's very bright. I have tried to convince him to go back to school and study computer programming, but . . ." She swiveled her head and massaged her shoulder with one hand. "It's no wonder he doesn't want to go back to school. He's working, writing, and spending most of his time on causes—"

"What kind of causes?"

"Animal rights. Freedom for Tibet. Fighting world hunger. Those are just the ones you would recognize. Travis can tell you about causes you've never even heard of." She let out a big sigh and put her fork back down.

"Russell's a technical writer," she went on before I could ask her what the sigh was about. "Vicky programs computers. Nan sells real estate. Joyce manages Operation Soup Pot's kitchen. And I argue appellate insurance cases." She sighed again. At least I understood this sigh.

"But I shouldn't complain about my work," Carrie went on. "Hazelwood, Hazelwood and Lau has paid for my children's education. I only wish I didn't have to practice law at all."

She picked up her fork again and took a bite of her salad.

"Mave doesn't have to work outside of her writing," she mumbled through the bite. "She's long retired from teaching. Lots of time for her historical biography. Donna doesn't work either. I'm not sure where her money comes from. Probably from her husband. Or perhaps from her family."

She sent me a significant look across the table as she said "family." I wished she hadn't. I'd almost managed to forget Donna's family.

"And Slade certainly didn't need a job. He made a fortune on his thrillers. And I believe he had inherited wealth to begin with."

"Tell me more about Slade's writing," I commanded. An idea was beginning to tickle the back of my brain. If Slade made so much money off his writing, maybe someone had killed him to steal his latest manuscript.

"As you know, he writes—or wrote—thrillers," Carrie said. "Often international. Thrillers with deep character development. I've always found it hard to believe that he could write such fully-realized fictional characters while remaining completely insensitive to any non-fictional characters, otherwise known as human beings. *Cool Fallout* was his new manuscript, the one he gave to you." She looked across at me. "Do you want to know what it's about?"

I nodded. Why not?

She leaned back in her chair. "You'll have to trust my memory on this," she cautioned. "Basically, it concerns a group of sixties radicals and what became of them. During the late sixties, these radicals sold dope to support a sort of underground railroad for Vietnam draft evaders. Then a sheriff is killed and they're forced to disband." She circled a pointed finger in the air. "Flash forward to the nineties. Now the members of this group are all being contacted by someone who wants to use their particular services. A mysterious someone. That's the suspense component—Who is this someone?" She paused.

"Who does it turn out to be?" I asked, caught up in her secondhand recital.

"I don't know," she answered. "I haven't finished it yet."

I was surprised at my own disappointment. I really wanted to know. Either Slade had been a good writer or Carrie was a good storyteller. Or both. I took another piece of bread as a consolation prize.

"So, is it well written?" I asked with my mouth full.

"Hell, yes," Carrie grumbled. "That is what's so aggravating—or was so aggravating—about Slade. He was a damn good writer. His *Cool Fallout* characters are wonderful. A man who did the wheeling and dealing in the sixties is a banker now. And Slade makes you believe it. And the woman who killed the sheriff has become a Catholic nun. Then there's the firebrand leader who became an actor and is now dying of AIDS." She shook her head ruefully. "Good stuff."

"It sounds like it," I muttered. "Now I want to read the damn thing."

"Well, you've got a copy," Carrie pointed out. "And Slade—"

But then the dogs and the cat went crazy again, exploding into a bedlam of sounds that drowned out the rest of her words. They yowled and howled and yipped as they ran from the kitchen. But this time they didn't head for the back door. They headed for the front.

I looked at Carrie. She looked back at me. And her eyes were wide again.

- Five -

CARRIE CONTINUED TO stare across the table at me as the pounding of my pulse joined in a rhythmic counterpoint to the raucous animal sounds. Who the hell was at the door this time? We'd already had the Mafia.

Carrie stood up, shaking her head violently. Was she shaking away her own fear? Then her eyes contracted to normal size once more.

"Ye gods and goddesses," she murmured, trying on a smile. "I certainly am popular tonight."

I started to get up, too.

"No, Kate," she said, straightening her spine. "It's just someone at the front door. In any case, it is *my* door. You stay here."

Before I could argue, she had left the room.

I snuck into the hallway on tiptoe, holding my breath. I wasn't going to stay glued to my chair if there was a possibility of danger to Carrie. But I didn't want her mad at me either. She was mighty formidable for a small woman. In fact, she was mighty formidable for a woman of any size.

After she had ordered the animals into silence, she opened the door. I couldn't see her from my spot in the hallway, but I could hear. First there was a rustling and clicking as she unlocked the door, then the creak as she swung it open.

"Travis," Carrie said then. Her voice sounded funny, but not afraid funny. It was something else.

"Got your message on my machine," came a brusque male voice. "Did someone really murder Slade?"

Silence. I wondered if Carrie was nodding. I wondered why she'd called Travis.

"Are you okay?"

"Of course, I'm okay," Carrie answered. "There was no need for you to . . ."

I scurried back to my kitchen chair, ashamed of my eavesdropping, then took a deep breath to replenish my depleted oxygen.

A few more breaths later, Carrie came back to the kitchen with Travis in tow.

"Kate, you remember Travis Utrelli," she said with a nod my way. Then she turned her back on me to look up at Travis, who towered over her by more than a foot.

I didn't blame her for resting her eyes on him rather than me. Travis was looking as handsome as ever despite the scowl that nearly converged his lush black eyebrows over his big brown eyes. I wondered how old he was. He didn't look more than thirty. His long black hair fell unfettered to his shoulders. His nose was straight, his cheekbones were high and his lips were full. Did his ancestors come from India? South America? Wherever roving gypsy boys came from?

"Hi, Travis," I piped up.

He took the time to meet my eyes over Carrie's shoulder and nod in greeting. But the frown never left his face while he did. And a moment later, he was gazing intently at Carrie again.

"Is everything really cool?" he asked urgently. "I can hang out here if you need me—"

"I'm fine," Carrie assured him, putting her hand on his arm.

I wished I could see the expression on her face. Was that just the touch of a friend? Or a lover?

He clasped her hand. She didn't pull away.

"If anyone ever hurt you, they'd have me to answer to," he muttered. His frown deepened. He looked even more handsome. And dangerous. A chill prickled the hair on my arms.

"There is no call to be so protective, Travis," Carrie said a beat later. And then she did pull away. "I assure you I am not in any personal danger."

She turned back to me, a weak smile on her face. I looked at her, wondering what Travis meant by "they'd have me to answer to." Under the circumstances, the phrase sounded frightening. But then the male of the species is given to those kind of pronouncements, I told myself.

My thoughts must have shown on my face.

"Don't worry, Kate," Carrie said. "Travis is a friend. I'll be safe with him for the evening."

Was I being dismissed?

After a few more moments of awkward silence, I was pretty sure I *was* being dismissed, but I dragged Carrie into the hall with me to make sure.

"Are you all right alone with this guy?" I whispered.

"I am perfectly capable of defending my virtue, such as it is," she whispered back with a grin. "I don't need a chaperon." Was she misunderstanding me on purpose? Or was I misunderstanding her?

"Carrie, you think a member of your group is a murderer," I reminded her impatiently. "What if it's Travis?"

Her grin disappeared.

"No, not Travis," she said. Her hands rose suddenly, palms out. "Not Travis," she repeated, jerking them awkwardly, Richard Nixon-style.

"But—"

"I will be perfectly fine," she insisted, dropping her hands and pulling back her shoulders.

She led me to the front door at a brisk pace, then turned to enfold me in a tight hug.

"Thank you, Kate," she whispered and released me.

"I'm not sure if—"

"Don't you worry," she ordered and opened the door.

I stepped out through the doorway, trying to think.

"I'll let you know when I schedule the emergency group meeting," she added.

The door closed before I could respond.

I drove home through the dark, my shoulder muscles aching with tension as I gripped the steering wheel, wondering all the way about Carrie's relationship with Travis. It was better than remembering Slade's battered head. Were Carrie and Travis lovers? And if so, so what? It was about time Carrie found someone to love. As far as I knew, she hadn't been serious about anyone since her husband Cyril had died. But what if Travis was a murderer? What if Carrie was? I shook my head hard. I wasn't going to even let myself think that.

As I pulled into my driveway, popping gravel, another thought hit me. Maybe Travis was the one Carrie really suspected of murder, despite her protests. Was that why she had turned off the computer? Was that why she wanted so badly to investigate?

I didn't have any answers to my questions by the time I climbed the stairs and opened the front door.

C.C. was waiting for me in the entry hall, on the other side of the door. She meowed in disapproval. Where had I and my lap been when she needed us? Not to mention the fact that she was starving. C.C. was always starving.

"Cease and desist!" I shouted.

C.C.'s eyes widened. She silently tilted her head for a

moment. A smile twitched my lips. Then she started yowling in earnest.

"All right, all right! It's dinner time," I conceded.

I dropped my purse next to Slade's manuscript on the pinball machine and trotted into the kitchen to feed her, turning on my answering machine on the way.

"Hi, this is Judy," the machine said as I scooped Friskies Senior into C.C.'s bowl with an old pie server.

Judy was my senior warehousewoman. I hoped nothing was wrong. "I didn't want to call from work yesterday," she said, "but I thought I'd call from home. Jean's brother came in yesterday to hassle her. Right after you left. He's this born-again geek and he's real uptight about their parents getting a divorce. I mean, more than Jean even! Jeez, what a jerk! Got Jean all uptight again. She even managed to screw up the big order for the chiropractor's convention." There was a pause, then Judy finished cheerfully, "Just thought you'd want to know."

"Thank you for sharing," I told the machine.

C.C. looked up at me suspiciously. She must have caught the sarcasm in my tone. Then she looked back down and pulled a chunk of Friskies out of her bowl onto the floor. I pretended not to see her and threw the pie server into the sink.

The next voice on the tape was my ex-husband, Craig's. It sounded forlorn as it came out of the tinny speaker.

"Just wanted to know if you'd like to go out to dinner with me tonight," he proposed. "Maybe tomorrow night. Or the next—"

"No, I wouldn't!" I snapped. I ran to the answering machine, shut off the tape and hit rewind. "Not now. Not ever."

No matter that Craig was the one who had left me. His pleas could still trigger an explosion in me composed of anger and guilt in equal parts. And the guilt was getting weightier now that I was ready to marry Wayne. It wasn't logical, but then, guilt rarely is.

I sat down at my desk. It was late, after ten, but the day's events had left me too keyed up to read. Or to go to bed. I needed to get to work.

At least I had a short commute. I put in most of my sixty hours a week for Jest Gifts from my home office, dropping in at the Oakland warehouse periodically to issue paychecks and take care of crises. I contracted out the actual manufacturing of the gift items.

Unfortunately, designing the gag gifts was the least of my work. Checking over the hundreds of mail orders a week, producing and correcting advertising copy, and keeping an eye on work orders took far more time. And payroll, miscellaneous paperwork and general bookkeeping took an equally big chunk. Taking care of disasters took the biggest chunk of all. My disaster correspondence alone could have kept a hired secretary busy. But I had a hard enough time paying Jean and Judy their salaries, not to mention mine.

I ran my eyes over a stack of paper containing questionable orders, a leaning white tower of unpaid bills and a shorter pile of ledger sheets which I needed to transcribe for my accountant. Then I grabbed the sketch I had made earlier of a computer necktie and computer-bug tie tack. I had drawn the computer as an elongated screen atop a box atop a keyboard. What if it could be represented as a keyboard hanging sideways instead?

By Tuesday afternoon, I was working on the stack of unpaid bills. Over the previous three days I had wondered who killed Slade Skinner, reviewed the members of the critique group in my mind continuously, and come up empty every time. But I hadn't called Carrie. I hadn't wanted to encourage her. I had even begun to hope she had given up the idea of investigating.

The Hutton police hadn't talked to me since Saturday either. Maybe they had arrested their hypothetical, interrupted burglar.

The phone rang just as that happy thought occurred to me. It was Carrie.

"No, Kate. No one has been arrested," Carrie assured me when I proposed the idea. "It is still up to us to pursue this matter. I apologize for taking so long to get back to you. It took some time to convince everyone to come to an emergency meeting. The others have agreed to Thursday evening." She paused as my stomach turned over. "You will be able to attend, won't you?"

I thought about lying, but despite my stomach's vote, I couldn't get my mouth to say no. Carrie told me she'd pick me up Thursday evening, and hung up.

By Thursday evening, I had lowered the unpaid bills stack by two-thirds and was reviewing a new stack of questionable orders. The doorbell chimed.

I grabbed my purse off the pinball machine on the way to the door, expecting Carrie. She had never told me exactly what time the emergency meeting was supposed to be. I opened the door, ready to ask her.

"Hey there, Kate," the man in the doorway greeted me. He was a long, lean, handsome man with large puppy-dog brown eyes. My ex-husband, Craig. "Thought I might drag you off to dinner."

He walked quickly through the doorway into the entry hall and peeked into my office. "Or maybe we could go to a Workaholics Anonymous meeting," he finished with a laugh.

He stopped laughing abruptly when he noticed that I hadn't joined in. Then he opened his puppy-dog eyes even wider. He turned to survey the living room.

"Still looks the same," he whispered sadly.

Guilt twinged in my chest before I could harden myself.

Then I remembered that Craig had once described this living room as a "goddamn jungle complete with library." And he was wrong anyway. It didn't still look the same. The rug was still beige and the walls were still white, but the potted plants had grown even taller and wider, more books spilled from the floor-to-ceiling bookcases, and the hanging chairs hung lower with age. And there were only two pinball machines in the living room now to commemorate our long-gone business. Craig had taken the other four when he moved out, and kept them as part of our divorce settlement.

I crossed my arms and tightened my lips into a frown.

Craig looked down at the floor for a moment, then reached into his pocket.

"I brought you a model," he said softly and pulled out a computer chip. "For your bug design."

He smiled hopefully at me. I took a breath and reminded myself that encouraging him was cruel in the long run. Then I thanked him for the chip and said goodbye.

"But—" he began.

"Goodbye," I repeated firmly.

"Have you heard the new joke about the computer programmer and the nun—" he tried again.

The third goodbye did the trick.

I leaned against the front door and listened to Craig's footsteps going down the front stairs, suddenly remembering another time when he had left. When he had left for good. My gut tightened. Then the doorbell rang again.

I jerked the door open, ready to shout.

But this time it really was Carrie. She gave me a quick hug, then hustled me out the door and into her Honda Accord without further ceremony. She told me the emergency group meeting was going to be held at Mave's house in the town of Hutton. The same town where Slade had lived. And we were running late.

"The theme of Hutton is money," she lectured as she zipped

up the highway. "Class comes into it too. And of course, beauty
and the very best of taste. . . ."

She was still lecturing ten minutes later as she guided her
Accord down the wide, nearly empty, tree-shaded streets of
Hutton. "According to Police Chief Gilbert, there is no crime
problem here. Hutton's citizens are certainly the wealthiest in
Marin County, which is saying a lot. I understand you can't buy
a house in Hutton for less than a million these days." She
slowed the car as we passed Slade's house, then pointed. But
she was pointing at the other side of the street.

My eyes followed her finger to a rambling, two-story
redwood home set back tastefully behind a lush green sea of
lawn and flower beds where immense dahlias bloomed in strict
rows. A much smaller building sat off to the side, surrounded
by more dahlias.

"Nan rents the former maid's quarters," Carrie went on, and
I realized she had been pointing to the smaller building. "She
pays more than two thousand dollars a month for the privi-
lege." I looked more closely at Nan's home as we passed.

"Two thousand for that tiny place?" I breathed. "It can't be
anywhere near half the size of my house. And my house isn't
all that big."

"The prestigious address is worth it to Nan," Carrie informed me. "Not to mention the proximity to Slade's house. I'll
bet she kept an eagle eye on him from her ever-so-tiny but
well-furnished living room."

I turned to Carrie again. "If Nan was this close, do you
suppose . . ."

Carrie shrugged as I let the question peter out.

"I spoke to Donna," she said. "Donna tells me she is glad she
gave everyone a hard copy of her manuscript. Apparently, the
family's hoods broke into her place Sunday and took all of her
papers. She's certain they are the same men who visited my
house on Saturday evening. However, she still has the text of

her manuscript stored on her computer. She will be handing out floppy disks this evening."

That was the end of Carrie's lecture. She didn't say anything more as she took the last few turns of the road and then pulled her car over to the curb to park neatly behind a Honda Civic.

But she gave my shoulder a quick squeeze before she opened the slatted gate in front of Mave's house. I wasn't sure if the squeeze was for my benefit or hers, but I appreciated it. We walked side by side up the flagstone path to Mave's front door. The house itself was a modest Victorian box set in the center of its modest quarter-acre lot. I was admiring a bed of begonias near the front door when I suddenly wondered how Mave could afford even this relatively small hunk of Hutton.

"Inherited," Carrie whispered, as if I'd voiced the question aloud.

Then the front door flew open and Mave peered out at us. For all her wrinkles and gray hair, there was something childlike about her gaze. Maybe it was the roundness of her eyes under her violet-rimmed glasses.

"Hi, Mave," I greeted her self-consciously. My mouth felt dry suddenly. Did she know I was here as a spy?

"Howdy there, Kate," she returned my greeting, her voice rasping pleasantly. She reached out and clasped my hand in a firm grip for a moment.

Then she told Carrie "Howdy" too and led the way through the doorway and down the hall to a living room decorated in shades of lavender, mauve and pale yellow. Black and white photographs covered the far wall. I would have liked to examine them but my eyes were drawn to the members of the critique group who stood in two small clusters in front of us. Nan Millard was the closest.

"The condo in San Ricardo is just adorable. And it has oodles and oodles of space for a writer," she was telling Russell Wu. She waved a tan hand in his expressionless face, clanking chunky gold bracelets as she did. "Why you stay in that dumpy little apartment when you could . . ."

"Nan's trying to sell that poor critter real estate again," Mave whispered in my ear.

I chuckled, then swallowed uneasily. Was Nan a murderer? Was Russell?

I turned my eyes to the other little group. Vicky Andros and Joyce Larson stood quietly listening to Travis as he ranted and pounded a fist into his palm.

". . . these fascists from the California Beef Council are telling ignorant little kids that meat's good for you!" he told them.

Joyce nodded thoughtfully. I watched her and wondered if she actually paid someone to perm her hair and dye it that ghastly shade of black. It certainly didn't look natural, especially with her pale blue eyes. But then her blue eyes were covered by the oversized glasses she wore. I chided myself. This was a good woman. She didn't have to be good-looking too.

"It's time to do something!" Travis ranted on. "We can't let those poor little kids listen to lies." He turned his head to include Vicky in his broadcast.

Vicky didn't nod thoughtfully. She just wrapped her arms around herself and hugged. She was so thin, she could have wrapped them around twice.

"I say we picket supermarkets," Travis went on. "Hit them in the pocketbook—"

But the sound of running footsteps behind us interrupted his harangue. I turned in time to see Donna Palmer come galloping through the doorway. She wore a white peasant blouse and swirling skirt topped by a multicolored hand-woven sleeveless vest that hung all the way to the floor. She was smiling and brushing her dark, tangled hair with her fingers as she rushed toward us.

She was only a yard away when her body jerked suddenly. And then she fell to the lavender carpet with a muted thud.

– Six –

MY HEART JUMPED in my chest. And in the same microsecond, my mind screamed at me, telling me that the woman who had just fallen face down on the carpet was Donna Palmer, beleaguered daughter of organized crime. Had they shot her? I hadn't heard a shot. But maybe they'd used a silencer.

In the next microsecond, I was on my knees next to her body. I reached to take a pulse, hoping I would find one. Hoping she was still alive. But just as my hand made contact with warm flesh, the body rolled over and sat up in a tangle of swirled skirt and sleeveless vest. With a smile on her face, the woman I had been afraid was dead extricated an arm and stuck out her hand.

The smile couldn't overshadow the red patch on her forehead however. I'd have bet it would be a bruise soon enough. I ignored her outstretched hand.

"Are you all—" I began.

"Jesus, not again," I heard someone say from behind me. I turned in time to see Nan Millard shake her head, gold earrings flashing.

When I turned back, Donna was running her hand along the top of her peasant blouse. Her hand snagged in the chain that one of her many crystals was hanging from.

"Do I still have my ribbons?" she whispered.

I nodded. There were two ribbons pinned to her blouse, one red and one blue. I knew the red one was for AIDS awareness. I wasn't sure what the blue one was for.

Then I swiveled my head to look around the room. What was wrong with everyone? Nobody but me seemed to be so much as looking at Donna.

"I can be so incredibly klutzy sometimes," Donna confided. She jerked her hand through her tangled hair and winced. "But the benevolence of the universe always protects me from harm." She stuck out her hand again. "I'm Donna," she told me.

"I'm Kate Jasper," I answered and this time I reached out and shook her hand. "I met you last Saturday."

"Oh, that's right," she giggled. "The gag-gift maker." Her hand felt small and soft in mine.

"What the hell just happened?" I asked.

"She tripped over her skirt," Nan explained in a drawl from behind me. "It's so damned long, it's a wonder she didn't strangle herself in the process. But we can only hope for so much."

Donna stared up at Nan without any visible sign of rancor in her soulful honey-colored eyes. Or any comment.

I could have made a comment, though. Donna's skirt may have been too long, but Nan's beige linen one was close to nonexistent, barely skimming the top of her tan thighs. I shook my head to clear it. I wasn't here to observe relative skirt lengths.

"Do you need help getting up?" I asked Donna.

"Oh, no. But thank you, anyway," she said with a sweet smile. In fact, her whole face had a sweet innocence to it. She must have been at least thirty, but when she smiled she looked all of ten years old.

We both stood up together. Donna's rise was a little shakier than mine though, since she was still standing on the hem of her skirt. I turned away when she tried to pick up her purse by its long strap, which was tangled up with her vest now. It was too damned painful to watch her struggle. Now I realized why no one else would look at her.

"Well, no harm done," said Mave briskly once we were standing. "How's about using the dining room table for the meeting? I think I've got enough chairs."

She began counting us, using her fingers to keep track. When she got to nine, she squinted her eyes for a moment, then smiled. "Oh, that's right," she said cheerfully. "We've still got the same number. Lost one. Gained one."

Mave certainly didn't seem unduly upset by Slade Skinner's murder. As we walked into the dining room, I wondered if anyone in this group had really liked the man.

Mave's rosewood table was long enough for a board of directors. It filled the space in the pale yellow dining room with exactly enough room to push back its matching upholstered chairs and walk two steps to the sideboard, almost as if each item of furniture had been built to fit. They probably had been, I realized. We were talking Hutton here, after all.

"Carrie," Mave instructed, "you take your place at the head of the table, since you called this here meeting. And you, Kate, why don't you take Slade's place next to Carrie?"

I nodded politely, wondering if I really wanted Slade's place, metaphorically or otherwise, and took the seat. Travis quickly claimed the chair on Carrie's other side. Everyone else shuffled and rustled until they were seated, Donna, Joyce and Mave along with Travis across from me and Nan, Vicky and Russell filling in my side of the table.

"Slade Skinner's death raises some very important issues," Carrie began once we were all quiet in our chairs. She paused and ran her dark eyes slowly over each of us in turn. It was a good technique. I was ready to confess. "Issues that need discussion and consideration."

"Like what exactly?" asked Nan, her voice loud and bored as if to say that she for one was not intimidated.

Carrie turned to her and stared until Nan shifted in her seat, then answered. "The first issue, as I see it, is whether the group members will choose to continue *as* a group without Slade's presence."

"We're cool by ourselves," Travis answered, his voice low and angry. "We don't need Slade Skinner to push us around." Then he crossed his arms across his chest and glowered across the table. Heathcliff, I realized. He looked exactly like I had imagined Heathcliff while reading *Wuthering Heights* as a teenager.

Mave raised her hand. Carrie nodded at her.

"Joyce Grenfell said it best," Mave told us with a smile that half-closed her round eyes. " 'If I should go before the rest of you, break not a flower nor inscribe a stone,' " she recited. " 'Nor when I'm gone speak in a Sunday voice, but be the usual selves that I have known—' "

"I vote to keep going," Vicky interjected in a surprisingly high-pitched voice. I took a better look at her bony face. It wasn't a bad face, just thin. Her mouth looked oddly heavy and sensual against the backdrop of scarcity.

" 'Weep if you must, parting is hell.' " Mave continued her eulogy, putting a hand on her chest for emphasis. " 'But life goes on, so sing as well.' " Then she smiled broadly, wrinkling her face even more deeply, and bowed her head.

I gave Mave a little round of applause. Donna was the only one who joined me, though.

"Shall the record show a 'yes' vote?" Carrie asked, her tone transforming the formality of her words to a teasing affection.

"You betcha," Mave confirmed with a wink.

"Me too," Donna chimed in. "Slade wasn't always, well,

exactly in harmony with everyone, but he had, well, integrity. He'd want us to validate our own experience, I'm sure—"

"I vote yes, too," Nan put in brusquely.

"Joyce?" asked Carrie with a look at the brunette.

"I suppose we should go on," Joyce answered softly, her pale skin pinkening as she spoke. Debilitating shyness, I guessed. No wonder the poor woman had less of a life than Carrie.

Carrie turned her eyes to Russell.

"I'll go with the consensus," he said, nodding ever so slightly. I had forgotten how pleasant his voice was to the ear, deep and melodious. I would have expected a harsher tone from a true-crime writer.

"Then we are all agreed to continue as a group," Carrie concluded. "Which brings us to the second issue for discussion."

"Now what?" Nan demanded with a toss of her blond hair.

"I'll make it very simple," Carrie answered, her round, freckled face deadly serious. Once again, she ran her eyes over each of us in turn. "Does anyone here have any information that might be relevant to the identity of Slade Skinner's murderer?"

Her question was greeted with absolute silence. Even Nan kept her mouth shut. Travis jutted his head forward as if he were going to say something, but then seemed to think better of it and leaned back again with his arms crossed.

"Slade told me he had a date with someone last Saturday after our regular meeting." Carrie's voice was stern as she went on. "He said that 'someone' was a member of our group. I have asked you each individually, and I will repeat the question once more to all of you. Did one of you have a five o'clock date with Slade Skinner last Saturday?"

Still no one answered. I looked around the table, Nan was staring up at the ceiling with an expression of strained exasperation. I couldn't tell if it was real or feigned. Vicky was concentrating on a cuticle she was chewing. At least she was eating. Russell sat perfectly still, his eyes resting lightly on Carrie. Mave's head was tilted, her eyes wide with what looked like rapt interest in the proceedings. Joyce's eyes were closed, her hands clasped in front of her. Maybe she was meditating. Donna was smiling sweetly as she twirled a piece of hair around her finger. And Travis was still glowering across the table.

I had no idea if any of them was harboring guilty thoughts about meeting Slade and/or killing him. Neither did Carrie apparently.

She sighed deeply, then asked if anyone had any ideas at all about Slade's murder. At least this time there was a response.

"Well, uh," Donna began. "There is my family."

"And . . ." Carrie gently encouraged her.

"They don't think it's appropriate for me to write my autobiography and include them in it," Donna went on. "They're in, like, complete denial about their roots, how they made their money and stuff. Especially my dad. He's been very abusive about the whole thing. Yelling his head off. Not really trying to communicate at all—"

"What does this have to do with Slade's murder?" Nan cut in. "If anything."

"Uh, I'm not sure," Donna admitted. "But my dad did send his men out to get the manuscript back from everyone I gave a copy to." She smiled suddenly. "See, he thought they had all my copies, but they didn't. Oh, they took my computer and all my papers and everything from my house. But they don't know that I've rented a work space. Everything they took from my house is duplicated there." She giggled, her face looking more like a ten-year-old's than ever. I wondered for a moment if she was mildly retarded, then decided against it. "So it didn't them one bit of good," she finished up triumphantly. Maybe she was just emotionally backward.

"I believe I was visited by your father's men Saturday evening," Carrie said, her tone as serious as Donna's might have been. Carrie wiggled one finger, then another. "They took my copy of your manuscript."

"Mine's gone too," Russell added quietly. "Although I didn't see who actually took it."

"Good golly!" yelped Mave. "I couldn't find my copy, but I just thought I'd put it somewhere goofy." She swiveled her head around abruptly to look behind her, as if to catch the thieves here and now. "Those donkey bottoms better not come back again," she declared fiercely.

"Listen, Mave," Travis put in, jutting his head forward. "If it'll make you feel better, I'll come and stay with you. I've still got my copy. I checked."

"Don't you worry about me, you sweet boy," Mave answered, straightening in her seat. "This old woman's got ways of dealing with these kind of critters."

Oh great, I thought. She's probably got a shotgun somewhere. And I'd have bet she knew how to use it too.

"Wait a minute," Nan said, glaring across the table at Donna. "Are you telling us you gave our addresses to these goons?"

"Well, not exactly," Donna replied, her smile disappearing. Her face colored under Nan's glare as she spoke. "But I did tell Dad that the group members had copies, and I guess his men found my address list when they took all my other stuff."

"You guess?" demanded Nan. She shook a well-manicured finger at Donna. "Jesus, you're an idiot! Don't you have any sense at all? Are you trying to get us all killed?"

"Now hold your horses there, Nan," Mave objected. She held up a hand, palm facing outward. "Donna didn't know that those burro's behinds were gonna steal everything."

Nan reared up in her chair and opened her mouth again.

But Carrie's tongue was faster. "Is anyone else missing their copy of Donna's manuscript?" she asked.

"How do I know?" Nan replied, brushing her blond bangs out of her face with the back of her hand. "I didn't know anyone was after the damn thing until today. The whole situation is totally absurd."

"I'm not sure either," Vicky threw in.

"I don't know if my copy is gone," Joyce murmured. "I'll check as soon as I go home." She took a deep breath before going on. "But I think our real concern here should be whether these men are actually violent."

"They haven't proved themselves violent yet," Carrie put in. She paused before adding, "As far as we know, that is."

The table went silent as the group considered her addendum. Finally, Donna spoke up.

"I don't think my dad lets his men do any of the violent stuff anymore," she said thoughtfully.

"Donna, this is important," Carrie said. "Do you think any one of your father's men is capable of murder?"

Donna frowned and chewed on her upper lip for a few moments.

"Are you thinking or in some kind of coma?" Nan demanded.

"Thinking," Donna answered slowly. Then she sat up straight and smiled again. "No," she concluded. "I don't think any of his men are capable of murder. I mean, they are kind of ethically challenged. But they're not *that* ethically challenged!"

I groaned aloud. But no one seemed to notice. Maybe everyone but Donna was trying to figure out what "ethically challenged" meant.

"I agree with Donna," Russell said after a moment. A hint of a smile touched his even, Asian features. "Though I might not have used quite the same description." He paused, then went on, his deep voice as reassuring as his words.

"I've got a few buddies on the police force," he told us. "Even one with the FBI. After my copy of Donna's manuscript disappeared, I talked to each of them informally. I asked if someone working for Donna's father might have panicked and killed Slade while trying to retrieve Donna's manuscript. But none of the guys I talked to thought it was very likely. Donna's father and his business associates are respectable now. And more important, they're trying to keep a low profile. They don't want the cops climbing all over them in a murder investigation. They wouldn't want to risk even a hint of suspicion. At least that's the theory."

"Are your friends on the police force investigating the possibility?" Carrie asked.

"They're looking into it informally," Russell assured her. "And they've talked to the Hutton police about it. But who knows?" He shrugged his shoulders.

"Oh, I forgot!" Donna piped up. "I've got floppies to give to everyone."

Nobody looked thrilled by the prospect. But she pulled them out of her purse and handed them out to everyone anyway. Including me. I just hoped she wasn't going to give her father's friends an updated list of group members.

"This has my latest draft," she told us cheerfully. "It's even got a new title."

I looked down at the label on the computer disk. It read "MY FAMILY, THE FAMILY—by Donna Palmer."

"Catchy," Mave said approvingly. Then she set her floppy down on the polished surface of the rosewood table. Keeping her eyes lowered, she spoke softly. "Been thinking of what Carrie said about Slade having a date with one of us after the last meeting. Wouldn't want to think there was a murderer among us, but I can't help but wonder if, well, if the son-of-a-gun wasn't killed 'cause someone was real hot under the collar over one of his critiques. He gave one heck of a nasty critique, that's for sure—"

"That is an absolutely ridiculous idea," Nan interrupted. "Slade was a professional. And so were his critiques."

Did the lady protest too much? Nan certainly hadn't appeared to have enjoyed Slade's critique of her own work on Saturday. Though I seemed to remember her trying to act as if she didn't mind his comments. And Slade was sleeping with Nan. He might have been even harsher with the others.

"I had another idea too," Mave went on, apparently unfazed by Nan's interruption. "What if someone got a burr under their saddle reading *Cool Fallout*? If you ask me, Slade drew some of his characters straight from real life—"

"That's right!" shouted Travis. He leaned forward and hit the table with his fist. "The scheming, social-climbing real-estate agent is obviously Nan."

"I resent that remark," Nan announced coolly. Her voice wasn't loud, but the way she narrowed her eyes as she spoke gave me goose bumps. She sat up straight in her chair and glared across the table at Travis. "I may be a real estate agent, but that's where the resemblance ends. I have had lunch with Martin Cruz Smith. And Joe Gores. I am an author. I am not anything like the character in *Cool Fallout*."

Travis opened his mouth again, but Russell headed him off with his own admission.

"Well, I certainly recognized myself as the stereotypical Chinese-American nerd," he said without a sour note in his melodious voice. "Though at least Slade had the decency to make me an artist and curator instead of a writer—"

"I never noticed!" Joyce exclaimed. Her blue eyes were wide under her oversized glasses. She raised a hand to her temple, then drew it back over her black, permed hair. "Of course, the nerd. And the real estate agent. How could I have missed them?" She seemed to be talking to herself.

"Russell Wu is no nerd!" Travis protested hotly. "If anyone was a nerd, it was Slade. Sitting in his fancy house and thinking up nasty things to say about the rest of us. That's not how a real man acts. . . ."

I glanced at Russell as Travis continued his tirade. Russell's face was stiff. With embarrassment?

"Did Slade ever do anything really *important* with his writing?" Travis demanded. He threw his arms into the air. "Did he ever care about the effect it had on others? No, he just blabbed on and on without a conscience. And to make fun of Russell—"

"Travis," Carrie interrupted gently. "Maybe we could move on now."

"Oh," Travis said blankly. He sat with his mouth open for a moment, then waved a hand at Carrie. "Sure, go ahead."

"Does anyone else have any other ideas about Slade Skinner's murder?" Carrie asked.

No one spoke up.

"Then I'd like to ask the group's permission to add a new member to our permanent roster," Carrie proposed, a grin splitting her round face. Damn. I wished she'd asked me first. "I introduced you all to Kate Jasper at last Saturday's meeting. Kate is my long-time friend." She paused, then added, "And she writes short stories."

"And poetry to boot," Mave reminded everyone.

– Seven –

I SMILED WEAKLY as eight pairs of eyes stared my way. Then I asked myself why I had ever agreed to come to this group. And why I had ever mentioned poetry to Carrie.

"Oh, I'm a poet too!" Donna exclaimed happily.

A soulmate. I should have guessed. She closed her eyes and then clasped her hands together, knocking one elbow on the rosewood table as she did.

"God save us," drawled Nan. "She's going to recite her work again."

"Red on white," Donna whispered. Then her voice grew stronger. "My mother!" she boomed. "My grandmother. Blood ties. Blood spilled."

She paused for a breath and finished in a shout. "Blood shared!"

Donna opened her eyes again and looked across at me. I arranged my features into an expression I hoped looked encouraging, wondering just whose blood had been spilled. Was this an example of organized crime poetry?

"That was real nice, Donna," Mave praised. I turned to her, grateful for the intervention. "What kind of poetry do you write, Kate?" she asked.

"Uh," I replied, startled. "Nothing really. Nothing I'd want to share."

"Aw, bull-chips," Mave chided, but her face was friendly enough. "Don't you worry. We'll get you over that in no time, Kate. Poetry is for reciting. That's what I always say. . . ."

Maybe I could claim laryngitis. I could almost feel my throat closing up already.

"I grew up when poetry was important," Mave went on. "We read it, memorized it, recited it. I know free verse is all the rage now, but I love a poem with traditional meter all the same." She looked my way as if for agreement.

I nodded and smiled. My jaw muscles were beginning to twitch with the effort. Why is it that a false smile takes so much more effort than a real one?

"Some good new poets out there, though," she admitted. "You read Margaret Atwood?"

I shook my head. "So, do you write poetry too?" I asked, hoping to derail her.

"No, no," she answered. "Only wish I could. Never had it in me, I guess. But I do dearly love reading it. And hearing it. I'd love to hear you recite something—"

"Oh please," Nan groaned. "No more poetry!" I could have kissed her. "Carrie, come on," she whined. "Let's get on with it. What's next on the agenda?"

"I thought we could each give Kate a brief synopsis of our work, since she will be a permanent member of our group," Carrie replied. "That way she could get to know us all a little better."

"Hey, I'm hungry," Travis announced from across the table. He was wearing a smile now. It looked good on his handsome face. But then everything did. "Can we eat while we talk?"

"Good golly, yes," seconded Mave. "I'm more than a mite hungry myself."

My own stomach was pretty empty too, I realized. But this meeting wasn't a potluck, was it?

"I made sweet-potato bread," said Carrie, rising from her chair. "But I left it in the car. I'll go get it."

"I did a fruit salad," Nan said lazily. "Vicky, can you get it out of the refrigerator for me when you get your own salad?"

Vicky nodded stiffly as she stood up. Her thin face looked drawn and unhappy. I wasn't feeling so great myself. I hadn't thought to bring any food.

I looked at Mave. "I didn't realize this one was a potluck. I—"

"Aw, don't you worry," Mave interrupted. She pushed back her chair. "We usually have enough grub to slop an army of hogs anyway. Plenty to spare."

Then everyone besides Nan seemed to stand up and leave the room just as Vicky got back with two bowls in her hands. She put both of them down on the rosewood table and removed the Saran Wrap from one, keeping her eyes averted from its contents.

Within ten more minutes there was a feast spread out on the table in bowls and covered casserole dishes. Mave handed out her offering: lavender paper napkins and paper plates, and silverware that looked like real silver. Then finally, people began passing the bowls and dishes around. Vicky's bowl turned out to contain a green salad, lightly dressed in lemon juice. Nan's fruit salad looked good, full of melon and strawberries. And Carrie's sweet-potato bread smelled wonderful.

The next dish that came around the table looked like a vegetable ratatouille, but it was hard to tell. I hesitated before dishing some out. Could there be meat lurking among the vegetables?

"Kate's a vegetarian," Carrie announced from beside me.

She was getting as psychic as my friend Barbara. "Is all the food vegetarian tonight?"

"Mine sure is," Travis declared loudly through a mouthful of bread. Then he swallowed. "Tofu-stuffed potatoes with pepper and tahini."

"The ratatouille is completely vegan," Joyce assured me.

Russell said he'd brought a berry pie for dessert and he'd brought the label from the package too. Then Donna started in on the recipe for her multigrain pilaf. All the food had been passed around the table by the time she finished. And I had a little of everything on my paper plate. I took a bite of Carrie's bread. It tasted as good as it smelled, sweet and full of raisins and nuts.

"Joyce and I are vegetarians too," Travis announced a few minutes later. He had finished his first plateful of food and was reaching for more. "I don't see how anyone with a conscience can be anything else." He scooped about a pint of ratatouille onto his plate and grabbed five or six more slices of bread. "People have to realize that animals are on this earth too, just like you and me. You don't kill your neighbors for food just because they're a different species!" He stuffed a whole slice of bread into his mouth and spoke through it with muffled passion. "And fish. People say fish don't count. Well I say, how'd you like to be pulled outa the water and suffocated?"

"The violence done to animals in the name of nutrition is terrible," Joyce whispered, her hand arrested over her plate. "Really terrible. I just wish we could serve all vegetarian food at Operation Soup Pot, but we rely on handouts." She sighed. "We have to use what is given."

"Carrie tells me you're the moving force behind Operation Soup Pot," I said, hoping to encourage her. And to discourage Travis at the same time. Vegetarian though I was, I was certain I could live the rest of my life quite happily without another animal rights lecture.

"Oh, I'm just the kitchen manager," Joyce objected, her pale skin suffused with a pink tide that went all the way up to the roots of her black hair.

"Come on, Joyce," Travis said affectionately. "If it weren't for you, there'd be no Operation Soup Pot."

Joyce's blush deepened even further with the compliment. "Oh, no," she mumbled, shaking her head. "Other people have done similar things. It doesn't take much thought to realize you can use leftovers to feed the needy."

"But you—" Travis began.

"Excuse me," Joyce cut in, rising from her chair. "I have more ratatouille in the kitchen. I'll bring it in."

"She's kinda shy," Travis explained once Joyce had left the room. "She does all this good stuff, but she won't talk about it."

"Isn't that nice?" Nan drawled next to me. "Some of us could take a lesson from her."

"You know what's even crueler to animals?" Travis went on, ignoring Nan completely. Maybe he hadn't even heard her. "Animal research. And what has it gotten us? Bigger and better drugs for the pharmaceutical companies to push. Cosmetics that we don't need—"

"Oh please," Nan interrupted. "Haven't we heard this tirade enough times already?"

Travis crossed his arms and glared across the table at her. But his reaction didn't seem to bother Nan. She speared a piece of watermelon and lifted it to her mouth with a languid hand.

As I watched Nan, I noticed Vicky on her other side. Vicky's eyes were on that fork. As the watermelon disappeared into Nan's mouth, Vicky blinked her eyes and swallowed. Vicky didn't appear to be eating anything more than she had on Saturday. Once again, all she'd put on her plate was a small portion of her own green salad. And even that was untouched. Nan took another leisurely bite of melon, and again Vicky followed its progress with her eyes.

If she hadn't been so thin, I would have sworn Vicky was on a diet.

"Vicky, why don't you tell Kate about your work," came Joyce's quiet voice from the doorway.

Vicky's head jerked, startled. I was startled too. I had become lost in her surveillance of Nan's fork. Joyce set another dish on the rosewood table and sat back down.

"Soft porn," Vicky said brusquely, brushing her short brown hair away from her face with a twitch of her hand. "I write soft porn."

"Oh," I said, smiling politely. "That must be fun."

Vicky lifted her shoulders in a quick shrug without smiling back. I picked up what was left of my slice of sweet-potato bread and brought it to my mouth. Her eyes followed the movement of the bread. Suddenly, I didn't feel like eating it. I set it back on my plate, looking at her bony face and thinking of starving children.

"Vicky's writing is incredibly sensual," Donna said, flinging out a hand in her enthusiasm. I was glad I wasn't sitting next to her. "And it isn't just porn. It's like . . . like a metaphor. You know, a higher communion. Male and female aspects of the godhead."

"Is that what they call screwing these days?" Nan asked, her voice a passable imitation of Donna's higher, childlike one.

I chuckled before I could check myself. Nobody else laughed. I had a feeling Nan's particular brand of humor got old fast.

"Perhaps you can talk about your own work, Nan," Carrie suggested in a stern voice. But Nan responded to the content of Carrie's words rather than the rebuke in their tone.

"I'm writing another historical novel now," she said, her voice serious now that she was discussing her own work. "A different one than I read from last week. This one takes place in Canada during the seventeen hundreds, when the French

Acadians were forced to leave Nova Scotia. Antoinette is an Acadian woman who's in love with an English soldier. It's going to be a classic story. My agent thinks it could make the best-seller list." Her voice deepened with desire. "Not to mention oodles and oodles of money."

"What's it called?" I asked.

"*Love's Passionate Embrace*," she replied with what looked like a genuine smile in my direction. "Isn't that an adorable title?"

I nodded and smiled back. Who was I to judge?

"The title is real catchy, but it seems to me I've heard it somewhere before," Mave said slowly. She frowned and shook her head. "Can't say where, though."

"Well, maybe someone *else* has used it before," Nan replied with a shake of her blond bangs. "But *I* haven't. So who cares?"

I didn't want to get in the middle of that one. I returned my attention to my plate and took a bite of Travis's tofu-stuffed potato. I resisted looking over at Vicky to see if she was watching me eat.

"The Acadians sure got dumped on by the British," Travis told us a few minutes later. He glared in solidarity. "But the Native Americans—or Canadians or whatever—got dumped on worse. You gonna put anything in your book about them?"

"*Love's Passionate Embrace* is an historical novel, not a thinly disguised political diatribe like some people's work I could name," Nan replied. Her tone didn't seem to hold any real malice, though. "But don't worry, there'll be some Indians in there somewhere."

"Huh," Travis snorted, looking down at the table. I wasn't sure whether the sound was a comment on Nan's words or on the emptiness of his plate. "Hey, can you pass the pilaf down here?" he asked. "And some more fruit salad."

Russell complied silently, stretching his arm across the table to pass down the food. Travis filled his paper plate for the fourth time. I wondered how soon the paper would wear through to the table as I tasted my own serving of ratatouille. Yum.

"My work isn't a political diatribe," Travis announced after he'd inhaled another half a plateful of pilaf and fruit salad. Maybe Vicky could take eating lessons from him. "It's a practical manual. If you're living in a city when the United States collapses, you're gonna be glad to know how to survive. No electricity. No plumbing. No heat. No food." He shoveled in a few more mouthfuls as if to protect himself from that terrible fate. "People killing each other in the street. You gotta be prepared."

"If I was a betting woman, I'd bet on you to whup the apocalypse," Mave commented. Her eyes were creased with affection as she looked at Travis.

And so were Carrie's, I noticed. I hadn't seen an expression that soft on her dark, freckled face since her children were babies. Just what was her relationship with Travis?

"Guess it's my turn to talk about my work," Mave said. "You could say I'm writing something historical too, though mine's not fiction like Nan's. Never got a yen to write fiction, myself. Though I sure do love to read it. Marge Piercy, Carolyn See—"

"*Your* work, Mave," Nan cut in.

"Now, don't you jump out of your britches," Mave admonished gently. "I'm getting there at my own pace." She took a bite of something and swallowed before going on. "I'm writing the biography of one Phoebe Mitchell. Lived 1830 to 1920. And she was one helluva woman, if you'll pardon my language."

"What did she do?" I asked, curious now.

"Phoebe was an American painter," Mave answered. She sat back in her chair, her eyes drifting out of focus behind her glasses. "And a lover of women like myself. And did she have herself a life?" Mave shook her head and laughed.

I nodded encouragingly, wanting her to go on.

"Phoebe painted nude women in scenes from classical Greek

mythology during the Victorian years, when that was just *not* done, especially by another woman. And she even worked from undraped models. Whooeee, did that get folks riled!" Mave laughed again. "Her portrait of the goddess Artemis—as naked as a jaybird along with all the other animals in the forest—got her some press all right. She was called 'shockingly indecent' and 'disgusting' and 'wanting in modesty,' just to name a few. And she wasn't only criticized for her work, but for her life.

"She lived like a man, people said. She never married and lived most of her days with one Emily Early, a 'lifetime companion.'" Mave winked largely here, then went on. I suspected the wink was meant to emphasize the sexual aspect of Phoebe's relationship with Emily, but I wasn't sure. "Phoebe rode horses bareback, set up her own art school for young women and lived her own life. Golly, did she live it! She was even known to cross-dress and visit men's clubs. She didn't stay too long in Minnesota, where she was born, though. The local citizens probably would have had her tarred and feathered if she had. So she went to Europe. Lived in Paris and earned herself quite a name as an artist there. Lived in Rome for a while too. Only wish I'd have been with her.

"Phoebe came back to the United States for the last twenty years of her life, though. And she lived those last years raising a ruckus just like she had before. Stumped for 'Red' Emma Goldman, the anarchist, and Margaret Sanger, the birth control advocate. Boy, you think the fundamentalists are donkey's bottoms now. Back then, they were meaner than polecats, and just about as intelligent. But all their conniptions didn't bother Phoebe a mite. She did illustrations for Sanger's pamphlets and a cover for Goldman's *Mother Earth*. Good golly, what a woman she was! I was lucky enough to meet her as a child—"

"Wait a minute," Nan interrupted. "Slade said you weren't old enough to have met her. Remember?"

- Eight -

"Aw, FIDDLESTICKS!" MAVE snapped. She slapped her hands palms down on the rosewood table and leaned forward, scowling through her glasses at Nan. "Maybe I'm not old enough to have met Phoebe Mitchell, but my mother talked about meeting her so often it was as if I had too. And that's enough, I think, for this old woman."

I wondered how much Mave cared about her claim to have met Phoebe in the flesh. She was obviously in love with Phoebe in spirit. Just how angry had she been when Slade exposed her cherished memory as fiction?

Mave leaned back again, her face softening.

" 'The Fancy is indeed no other than a mode of memory emancipated from the order of time and space,' " she recited softly. "S. T. Coleridge wrote that. Mighty fine words and a mighty fine meaning in my opinion."

"Bravo," Joyce cheered quietly.

"Right on!" Travis boomed, raising a clenched fist into the air.

"Oh, I know exactly what Coleridge meant!" Donna added her unconditional support. "It's like reality has all these incredibly different continuums, you know. Who's to say which one is real? I feel like I know the Yogananda too, like he's my friend, but he died in 1952 before I was born. I've got his picture on the wall so my kids will feel like they know him too. It's a real gift from the universe!"

"Thank you, dear," Mave said, a rueful smile on her wrinkled face.

I was still absorbing the news that Donna apparently had children. It was a frightening probability. I wondered how often she had dropped them as babies.

"Listen, Mave," Nan said from beside me. "I didn't mean to rain on your parade about Phoebe. I don't care whether you met her in real time or not. I just remembered what Slade had said—"

"Aw, that's okay." Mave cut her off with the wave of a hand. "A tad of reality won't hurt me every once in a while." She picked up her fork again. "So who else wants to tell Kate what they're writing?"

"I suppose I could," Russell said, his low, soothing tone a pleasant counterpoint to Mave's rasp. "I write what's called true crime, documentary accounts of real-life crimes and criminals. Right now, I'm chronicling the events leading up to the alleged murder of six young women by Dobie Jay Johnson, also known as John Johnson. He played drums for The Dithyrambs. Hopefully, he'll go to trial next month on schedule. And hopefully, at least for me, he'll be found guilty."

Russell kept his gaze fixed unwaveringly on me as he spoke. His tinted glasses made it hard to see the expression in his eyes, if there was any expression. I felt like ducking under the table to avoid his scrutiny. But I only squirmed a little in my chair instead, not wanting to embarrass Carrie or myself.

"Dobie's pled not guilty, but he's still been willing to speak to me." Russell's lips twitched in a hint of a smile. "Much as his attorneys disapprove. Dobie likes to talk about music and criminal psychology mostly. He keeps it abstract. And he refuses to talk about the murders he's accused of. Or about his childhood, which is classic. His unmarried mother shuffled him off to various unloving relatives, most of whom abused him. He grew up a loner with poor grades in school, though he was above average intelligence. Dobie's a quiet man, especially for a rock 'n' roll drummer."

Russell paused for a moment, then went on. "The other guys in the band still say they can't believe he killed the women, even though they're going to testify against him. One of them actually saw him disposing of a body."

Goose bumps formed on my arms. Russell stopped speaking, but he was still staring at me. He was a quiet man, too. I wondered what *his* childhood had been like.

"That's about it," he finished up after a few more heartbeats. He shifted his gaze to the space above my head.

"Very interesting," I told him. My mouth felt too dry to say more.

I looked down and saw food I had forgotten on my plate. I took a bite of fruit salad to moisten my mouth. When I looked back up, I saw Russell's eyes on me again. At least his tinted glasses were faced in my direction.

"I think you're really brave to talk to Dobie Jay Johnson," Donna said. Russell turned his glasses toward her. "The poor guy sounds like he's had an incredibly painful childhood. I mean, it makes me almost physically ill just to think about it. Is he getting therapy?"

"Oh please," Nan objected. "This guy killed six women."

"He's still a human being," Donna replied, her soulful eyes widening. "He can still learn. We're all children of the same universe, after all. We need to take loving care of each other no matter what."

"Including your father?" Nan inquired, her voice dripping with false sweetness.

"Of course, including my father," Donna answered, throwing up her hands. Unfortunately, one of her hands still held a fork, which went flying, just missing Travis's head. "I may have . . . well . . . a complex relationship with my father, but love is still at the base of it."

"Then why are you trying to drive him crazy writing a book about his mob connections?" Nan demanded.

"I'm not trying to drive him crazy," Donna retorted, her voice squeaking on the high notes. "Just the opposite. The truth will set him free. It's all part of the healing process. See, the thing is, my whole family is in this incredible state of denial. But if they can learn to communicate with real integrity, then they can learn how to be a real family again." She smiled broadly in closing.

"Oh sure," Nan drawled. "Right after they pull their bodies out of the bay."

Donna's smile disappeared. She frowned and looked at her plate. "Where'd I put my fork?" she murmured.

Travis picked it up from where it had landed on the floor and handed it to her without comment.

Everyone was quiet after that. I was surprised that no one jumped in to defend Donna, not even Travis. But maybe they were all considering Nan's suggestion. I certainly was. Could Donna's exposure of her father's organized crime connections amount to a form of murder? His business associates weren't going to be real happy about it if they were mentioned, that was for sure. No wonder he was so frantic to retrieve the copies of her manuscript.

When Carrie broke the silence a few minutes later, both my mind and my body were full. Only my plate was empty.

"As most of you know, I am endeavoring to write a novel of speculative fiction," she said to the table at large. "I've written a few short stories. Two have been published. But this is my first attempt at a novel-length work. It's set in the not-so-far future. The AIDS virus has infected the animals of the world." She winked largely at Travis. "Everyone is a vegetarian now, of necessity. But there is a new plague upon the earth. One that affects the mind as well as the body. One that affects the spirit." She opened her mouth to go on, then seemed to change her mind. "I don't want to give too much away."

"Carrie!" I yelped. "You can't leave it there. I want to know what happens."

"You'll be the first to read a copy of my manuscript once I'm completely finished," she promised.

"That's what she told us," Mave said with a chuckle. "Gotta admit she's whet my appetite. Great build-up."

"It's an age-old technique," said Nan. "Fictionus Interruptus."

This time I wasn't the only one who laughed at Nan's words. She was a funny woman, even more so when she left the cruelty out of her jokes.

After the laughter had died away, Joyce told me she was writing a cookbook to raise funds for Operation Soup Pot.

"The recipes are easy," she said, "but I'm supposed to insert little human interest pieces between them. About the people that work at the Operation and about some of our clients." She sighed. "I'm not very good with that part, but the group here is helping me a lot."

That seemed to end the tell-Kate-about-your-work phase of the meeting. Russell got up and brought in his berry pie. I didn't have to look at the label to know it wasn't something I ought to eat. A sniff told me its first ingredient was sugar. But I had an inch-wide sliver anyway. I knew it had to be vegetarian, since Travis had already served himself a quarter of the pie as it passed his way. I sat, along with Vicky, watching him gobble it down, and wondered if it were possible to receive a metabolism transplant from a willing donor as he took his last bite.

The meeting ended not long after that. Carrie and I helped Mave clean up the dining room and wash the silverware, then said our thank-yous and goodbyes. The sky was luminous with twilight by the time we left Mave's house.

"Well?" asked Carrie once we were alone in her car again. She stuck the key in the ignition without waiting for my answer.

"Well, what?" I asked back.

"Did you reach any conclusions?" she specified, her voice steady as she turned the key with one hand and gestured with the other. "Did you discover any clues? Do you have any suspicions?"

"I suspect I'll gain a lot of weight if I keep coming to your meetings," I answered, patting my stomach.

"Everyone's a comedienne," Carrie grumbled as she pulled away from the curb.

"Nan certainly is," I put in. "Is she a good writer?"

"I suppose she is a good writer in her own way," Carrie answered carefully. "Although the only examples I've read of her work are her romance novels. And I don't have a real appreciation of the genre."

"Did Slade really challenge Mave about meeting Phoebe Mitchell?" I asked next.

"Oh, he did indeed," Carrie replied. "The Saturday before last, he even wrote out the math to disprove Mave's claim. As Mave would have put it, she was madder than a wet hen. But her anger appeared to be short-lived. She was friendly to Slade, as well as to everyone else by the time we left that day." Carrie sent me a quick frown. "Kate, do you really think Mave had a motive?"

I shrugged my shoulders and stared out the window. Hutton's tasteful gardens and trimmed hedges looked even more beautiful now, in the twilight.

"Do you think Slade really based his characters in *Cool Fallout* on members of your group?" I asked after a few more glimmering blocks floated by.

"You mean, I presume, the scheming, social-climbing real estate agent and the Chinese-American nerd?" Carrie said.

I nodded. She thought for a moment.

"Yes, I believe so," she answered finally. "Although I can't say I actually noticed the resemblance while I was reading the manuscript. I suppose I might have done so had it featured a short, plump African-American attorney." Carrie let out a loud, full-bodied laugh. The car veered to the left in appreciation.

"It is an appropriate comeuppance for Nan, in any case," she said, giving the wheel a compensatory jerk to the right. "Nan thinks she's immune to satirical treatment. Perhaps Slade wanted to prove that she wasn't."

"Do you really think so?"

"No, not really." Carrie sighed, serious again. "He probably used Nan simply because he needed a character and hers was handy. I would imagine he didn't even stop to think the similarity might be noted and objected to. The man was not sensitive to others."

"Do you think Nan—"

"Killed him because of the characterization?" she finished for me. "No, I don't. Nan can be a grade-A bitch sometimes, but I don't believe she's a murderer."

That took care of that theory. But I had another one. Actually, I had two or three more.

"How about Russell?" I asked for a start. "Did you see the way he stared at me?"

Carrie turned to look at me herself for a moment, then looked back at the road. "Yes, I did," she said slowly. "You've never met him before?"

I shook my head vehemently.

"Maybe he's attracted to you, Kate. You're not an unattractive woman."

"But I already have a sweetie," I objected.

"Russell doesn't know that," Carrie pointed out.

I groaned. She was right. I was so used to being with Wayne, I imagined our relationship was tattooed on my face.

"Russell can seem a wee bit strange, I know," Carrie said. "But he's a very bright man, a really keen observer of human nature. In fact, I've often thought that he seems odd precisely because his focus is so absolute. Very few people are able to concentrate so intensely, to be so still."

"Well, I don't want him concentrating on me," I said sullenly.

"Don't worry, Kate," Carrie chuckled. "I'm just thinking aloud. I am not proposing that you date the poor man."

"Do you think Slade's book was good enough to steal?" I asked, more than ready to change the subject.

"Now *that's* an interesting question," Carrie murmured.

It must have been a *very* interesting question. Carrie didn't give me an answer until we were out of Hutton and on the highway headed home, five minutes later.

"The issue isn't really whether *Cool Fallout* is good enough to steal," she told me as she switched lanes. "It is a well-written book, and likely to be a real money-maker for his publishers. But the real issue is whether anyone else but Slade could sell it for the money it deserves. Now, I don't know if his publishers have seen it or bought it yet. But if they have, it seems likely that they would spot any duplicate on the market. And there's yet another obstacle for our hypothetical thief, the simple fact that Slade had a name. When Slade sold a book, he could ask for a six-figure advance and receive it. But the offer of a commensurate advance to an unknown author would be highly unlikely, no matter how good the manuscript."

"Oh," I said, disappointed.

"But don't be too quick to give up the idea," Carrie added. "What if someone in the group knew or thought they knew that the publishers hadn't seen the manuscript yet? And what if he or she wasn't sufficiently sophisticated to realize that the book would be devalued without Slade's name?"

"Who?" I asked quickly.

"Joyce," she answered just as quickly. But then she shook her head. "I can't imagine money being a temptation to Joyce. The woman lives as if she's taken a vow of poverty. She gives the lion's share of her income to charity, anyway."

"What if she wanted to raise money for Operation Soup Pot?"

Carrie shook her head. "No," she said, taking one hand off the steering wheel to wave away the suggestion. "Not Joyce. Not even for the poor."

"How about Travis?" I proposed.

Carrie's hands tightened on the steering wheel. She straightened her shoulders against the fabric of the car seat.

"No," she answered brusquely. "Not Travis."

"Why not Travis?" I pressed.

Carrie didn't answer. She just gripped the wheel and pressed her lips together into a tight line.

"Carrie, what's the deal between you and Travis?" I asked. "Are you in love with him or what?"

"That's none of your—" she began. But then she shook her head. Her shoulders slumped away from the seat. "Of course, it is your business. I have made it your business, haven't I?"

I was glad she'd taken care of both sides of the argument herself. I wouldn't have stood a chance arguing against her.

"I do have certain . . . feelings for Travis," she admitted.

That was a big help. Suddenly, Carrie's verbal precision seemed to have disappeared.

"Travis has told me that he's in love with me," she went on after a moment. One brown, freckled hand pulled away from the steering wheel to make chopping motions in the air. "But he's so young, Kate. He's more than ten years my junior. And . . ."

"And what?" I prodded.

"I don't know if I really want to love another man," Carrie finished in a rush. "Not after what I went through with Cyril. He was such a good man. To watch him die like that . . ." She shook her head, then closed her eyes.

For one long second, I was torn between sympathy and visions of us crashing on the highway if she didn't open her eyes again.

"Carrie?" I prompted nervously.

She opened her eyes again. My heart settled back down into my chest.

"Travis isn't going to die like Cyril," I declared emphatically. What the hell, it was almost certain to be true. Especially since Carrie was ten or fifteen years older than Travis. If anyone was going to die first—

"Travis is awfully sweet, isn't he?" Carrie said dreamily, interrupting my morbid train of thought.

"He is gorgeous," I offered. As far as I was concerned, Travis wasn't "sweet" at all. Brooding and belligerent was more like it.

"It's not only his appearance, Kate," Carrie told me. "It's his innocence, his belief that he can make the world a more just place. His untarnished kindness. He makes me feel young again."

Damn. She really was smitten.

"Not that I've committed myself to him in any way," she assured me. "But maybe, once all this is over . . ."

She never finished that sentence. And by the time she pulled into my driveway, popping gravel, I still hadn't worked up the courage to ask her specifically if she suspected Travis of Slade's murder.

She stopped the car, put it in Park and turned to me expectantly.

"Listen, Carrie," I said, telling myself it was time to be

assertive. Or at least to be something close to assertive. "I'm afraid I'm a failure as a sleuth and as a writer. I'm not going to share my poetry with the group, and I can't finger the murderer either. I'm sorry, but that's all she wrote."

A brief frown crossed her face, but then she threw her hands into the air and grinned. "Don't worry, Kate," she said cheerfully. "We've barely begun our investigation."

I took a deep breath, trying to dispel the sudden tightness in my chest. "I think we've, or at least *I've* done enough investigating," I told her in my firmest voice.

"We'll both sleep on it," she declared. Then she reached over and put her arm around my shoulders. "You're a good friend," she added softly and squeezed.

I took another deep breath. And let it out again. I wouldn't try to argue with her now. I got out of the car instead and said goodbye.

"Don't forget your floppy," Carrie called as I was about to slam the car door. She handed me Donna's computer diskette. MY FAMILY, THE FAMILY, black letters on a white label, stared up at me in the failing light.

"Oh, thanks," I said automatically as Carrie backed out of the driveway. Right, thank her for making you a Mafia target, I chided myself.

I turned and climbed my front stairs, holding the diskette as if it were dynamite. Which, of course, it was.

C.C. was waiting for me when I opened the door, yowling her whiskers off. She wanted food, damn it. And not that dry stuff in her bowl either. She wanted that good stuff in the little expensive cans. I put Donna's diskette on the pinball machine next to Slade's manuscript and trotted into the kitchen to open a can for C.C. I didn't feel like arguing with her either. At least I was consistent.

C.C. attacked her kitty pâté with one last meow and then the house was silent except for the faint sound of slurping and chewing. I walked into my office in that silence and heard the sound of footsteps on the driveway gravel. The sound was unmistakable. I had long ago trained myself to hear the approach of solicitors before they reached my door. I stood up straight, holding my breath. Then I heard it again. A shoe on gravel. Not a paw. Not a tire. A shoe.

My mouth went dry. Who the hell was walking up my driveway at this time of night? Neighborhood kids, I told myself. Late-evening Jehovah's Witnesses. But my body didn't buy either explanation. It sent my pulse into overdrive and moistened my palms and armpits just in case I hadn't gotten the point. Someone was out there.

- Nine -

I TIPTOED TO the front window, then sucked in some much needed air as I slowly slid the curtain back to uncover an inch-wide sliver of glass. I pressed one eye against that cool sliver and peered out into the dark, unable to see much of anything at first. Moonlight was all that illuminated the driveway. Then I heard a foot scruff the gravel once more. Another jolt of adrenaline improved my vision dramatically. Finally I saw it, a dark figure standing stock-still halfway between my house and the street.

I strained my eyes to see more detail, but the effort was useless. I couldn't tell who that figure was. I couldn't even tell if it was male or female. Though I was pretty sure at this point that it wasn't canine.

A new feeling flooded my body along with all the adrenaline. Anger. God damn it, I wouldn't be afraid in my own house! I dropped the curtain and ran to the front door.

But the dark figure must have run too. It was gone from view by the time I made it down the stairs.

I heard the sound of a car starting as I ran the length of the gravel driveway. And then the sound of the same car accelerating. I got to the street just in time to see its rear lights disappear, and then all I heard was the hum of traffic from the main road.

I stopped running and stood panting in frustration at my mailbox.

Who had my visitor been? An organized-crime associate of Donna's father? But I had only seen one person. And two men had come to Carrie's. And how would they know I had a copy of Donna's manuscript so quickly anyway? Then another possibility jumped into my mind in full video. Russell Wu. Standing stock-still and watching me through his tinted glasses. I shivered in the warm evening air and told myself I had been right the first time, the visitor was just some neighborhood kid wandering in. Then I remembered that most of the neighborhood kids weren't old enough to drive yet.

I stomped back up the driveway, cursing my own fear. There was no reason to assume the figure had anything to do with Carrie's critique group. It could have been my ex-husband, Craig, for that matter. I paused as my foot touched the bottom step of the front stairs. It probably was Craig, I decided. I liked that theory. It was safe.

I walked back up the stairs and into the house, convincing myself of the nice, new, safe theory.

Twenty minutes later, I had decided it was too late to work on Jest Gifts anyway and settled down in my Naugahyde comfy chair with the copy of *Cool Fallout* in my lap. I turned the title page face down. Chapter One stared up at me.

"Peter Dahlgren looked at his watch and thought he saw death in the movement of the second hand—"

C.C. leapt, making a perfect landing in the middle of the page.

I had just persuaded her to sit under the manuscript rather than on top of it when the phone rang.

"Hello," I answered hesitantly, now afraid of who might be on the other end.

"Kate?" came a deep, concerned voice. Wayne's voice, I realized a second later.

"Sweetie!" I whooped, standing in my excitement and dropping both the manuscript and C.C. "I'm so glad you called!"

"You okay?" he asked, the concern still evident in his tone. Wayne could be too damn perceptive sometimes. For less than a heartbeat, I considered telling him all about the murder. And about Donna's family. And about the dark figure. It would have worried him right on home.

"I'm fine," I lied instead. He needed his time with his uncle. And I needed my time to snoop, I realized suddenly. "That is, aside from resisting Craig's not so subtle advances."

Wayne chuckled. The rough sound warmed me over the line like a favorite wool blanket. I snuggled back down into my comfy chair. "Poor guy's probably frantic," he growled. "I would be too if I was losing you."

"Do you feel sorry for him?" I asked, really curious. Craig was the one person who seemed exempt from Wayne's all pervasive sympathy.

"Maybe after the wedding I'll feel sorry for him," he answered. "Right now I feel sorry for me. I miss you, Kate."

"I miss you too," I whispered, suddenly feeling the separation as an ache in my throat and chest. I pulled my shoulders back sharply as an antidote. "How's your uncle?" I asked.

Wayne and I talked for close to an hour. I couldn't say what about. Only that we laughed and longed for each other and hung up finally after mutual declarations of affection.

C.C. jumped back in my lap once I put the phone down. I scooped up Slade Skinner's manuscript, laid it on top of C.C. and began to read again. *Cool Fallout* was a poor substitute for Wayne's warm body, but it would have to do.

A few chapters later, I had decided that Carrie was right. Slade Skinner was a good writer. After a brief, tantalizing glimpse of the nineties, he'd flashed back to the sixties and the people who lived at the Brightstar commune, selling illegal drugs to support an equally illegal underground railroad for Vietnam draft evaders. As I turned the pages I went back in time with them, back to a time when I had agonized over my boyfriend's draft status, learned of the death of my first friend in Vietnam and marched against the war the next week. I could almost smell the dope and patchouli oil. And hear the chants: "Hell no, we won't go!" And the songs: "Ain't gonna study war no more, ain't gonna study war no more . . ."

But Slade's characters did more than march. Jack Randolph was Brightstar's leader in the sixties, as handsome and as charismatic as a Kennedy. By the nineties he's a has-been actor dying of AIDS. Patty Novak was his lover and right-hand assistant at Brightstar, glimpsed briefly in the future as a real estate agent bearing a marked resemblance to Nan Millard. Jack's sergeant-at-arms was ex-Catholic Kathy Banks who loved Jack too, if only platonically. She also loved guns and justice in equal proportions. I already knew from the beginning of the story that she would return to the church more than twenty years later as a nun.

But I liked Peter Dahlgren the best of Slade's characters, a man destined to become a banker, who negotiated dope deals in the earlier years with a cerebral excitation that felt sexual in nature. And completely pleasurable. Then there was Warren Lee, who sat quietly in the background, intent on the passports he was forging, easily recognizable as Russell Wu even then.

By the time I put down the manuscript, I was convinced that Brightstar had been close to paradise. I wanted to be there working for a just cause alongside Slade's characters. And I felt a peculiar combination of dread and curiosity knowing that disaster was coming. I left my chair reluctantly and set the manuscript on a pinball machine. My eyes felt gritty. It was way past my bedtime.

I was glad for Slade's characters when I went to bed and pulled up the covers that night. I figured they would keep my mind off his murder. I figured wrong.

I closed my eyes and immediately thought of Mave Quentin and Phoebe Mitchell. Was Mave fit enough at her age to beat someone to death with a dumbbell?

I rolled over on my side. Then there was Donna Palmer and the Mafia connection. I wondered if Palmer was her married or maiden name. Not that Mafioso had to be Italian. Look at Bugsy Siegel.

Hours later, I fell uneasily asleep, only to wake the next morning from a dream in which a grinning Bugs Bunny wielded a machine gun. Then I saw what he was shooting at. It was a manuscript whose pages dripped blood as they floated to the floor.

I drowned my anxiety in Jest Gifts paperwork all of Friday morning and most of the afternoon. It was close to four o'clock when the doorbell rang, breaking my concentration as effectively as a joy buzzer detonating under a cushion. I even jumped in my chair. C.C. gave me one slow look of disgust and leapt from my lap.

I got up and opened the door cautiously, the dread from last night's visitation drying my mouth. But when I peered through the crack in the doorway, I didn't see a murderer. I saw Carrie looking back at me, a white-toothed grin on her round, freckled face.

"Carrie!" I greeted her, flinging open the door in my relief.

"I'm glad you're happy to see me," she said as she strode through the doorway. She gave me a quick hug, then stepped back to look into my eyes. "I wasn't sure I would be welcome."

"Of course you're welcome," I assured her as another part of my mind began to backtrack. Was she really welcome? It all depended on why she was here.

"I left work early," she told me. "I plan to visit each of the critique group members individually. I thought I might begin with Mave. Would you care to accompany me?"

I pursed my lips into the shape to say "No," and then the phone rang.

It was my ex-husband, Craig, on the line. I mouthed that information to Carrie as he spoke. I also crossed my eyes for emphasis, feeling guilty in the next instant.

"I've got some more ideas for computer-nerd gag gifts," Craig said, his voice low and seductive. "How about I come by and show them to you?"

"Sorry, Craig," I answered quickly. "I'm just leaving the house with a friend."

I looked across at Carrie after I hung up the phone. Her molasses-brown eyes were crinkled with repressed laughter.

"Well, get your purse, girl!" she ordered. "We *are* just leaving the house now, aren't we?"

Sitting next to Carrie as she drove up Highway 101 toward Hutton not much later, I realized that I should have asked Craig if he had been walking up my driveway the night before. But would he admit to it even if he was my nighttime intruder? I turned to Carrie, ready to ask her advice, but she spoke first as she took the Hutton turnoff.

"Did you know that Hutton has only seven non-white residents?" she asked.

I shook my head, still thinking about Craig as the town's tree-lined streets came into view.

"And of those seven people all but two are servants," she continued.

"Who are the other two?" I asked curiously. She had my interest now.

"An African-American couple," she told me. "He owns his own business. She's a stockbroker. They are either very brave or very foolhardy. Or perhaps both. But they are very, very rich in any case, so they'll probably do just fine."

We found Mave at home as expected.

"Howdy, women!" she greeted us at the door. She was wearing a lavender T-shirt and tight purple jeans today. They looked damned good on her too. "You two come all the way to Hutton just to grill this old woman?" she asked, tilting her head.

I swallowed guiltily, but Carrie just said, "Sure thing," and flashed a grin at Mave.

Mave slapped her thigh and let out a snort of laughter. "Well, come on in then!" she boomed, then turned to lead us down the hall.

I read the words inscribed on the back of her bobbing lavender T-shirt as we followed her: "If they can put one man on the moon, why can't they just send them *all* there?"

Carrie and I must have both finished the sentence at the same time, because we were laughing in unison as we stepped into Mave's living room.

"Never did have much tolerance for the male of the species," Mave commented as she turned around. Obviously, she had eyes in the back of her head. She squinted the eyes in the front of her head at Carrie as she continued. "Though Travis doesn't appear to be such a donkey's bottom as the rest of them, does he now, Carrie?"

I looked at Carrie, too, wondering what exactly Mave was getting at. Was she curious about Carrie's relationship with Travis? Or maybe she was warning Carrie off—

"I believe Russell Wu is a pretty acceptable human being as well," Carrie replied blandly.

And then I wondered if Mave had left Russell out of her question on purpose, because she suspected him. I gave my head a little shake, feeling like Alice in a Wonderland of innuendo and subtext.

"Well, sit yourselves down and we'll talk," Mave suggested, her bright eyes round behind her glasses.

I just hoped I hadn't missed any important implications as I took my seat next to Carrie on a comfortable purple couch. The whole room was comfortable, both physically and visually. I looked around as Mave sat across from us on a matching couch. The walls were a pale lavender, the windows trimmed in soft yellow and the carpet a darker lavender. The odd combination of colors was more soothing than I would have expected.

"Did you ever find your copy of Donna's manuscript?" Carrie asked, getting down to business.

"No, I didn't!" Mave exclaimed. She shook her head. "Now, isn't that the goofiest thing? Do you really think one of those mob critters got it?"

Carrie nodded solemnly.

"Well, I suppose it wouldn't have been all that hard to get in this place," Mave murmured, her eyes out of focus behind her glasses. "I don't lock up much. And I've been spending a lot of time in the back garden."

"Perhaps you might lock your doors from now on," Carrie suggested.

"You betcha," Mave agreed readily. "Though in this case the horse is already gone." She frowned. "You two think Donna's family situation's tangled up with Slade's death?"

"I don't know," Carrie answered carefully. "Though I'd certainly appreciate an answer to that very question."

"Me too," Mave muttered. "Not that I cared much for Slade Skinner. He was one of those males that you think might be of another species altogether, if you know what I mean. But still and all, murder isn't a good thing no matter how pesky the victim might be."

"How did you meet Slade, originally?" I asked.

"Good golly, I'd known Slade for donkey's years," Mave said. She stared up at the ceiling. "Met him through some neighbors, the Atchesons. Good folks, long gone. We started this here writing group maybe ten years ago. I was doing a series of articles for the *American Heritage*. Slade had just published his first thriller. And Amy Atcheson was writing gardening books, bless her poor little heart. She's dead now, of ovarian cancer. Her husband went not long after—" Mave shook her curly gray head as if to clear it. "I'll bet you two don't really want to hear all about Amy and the rest of the neighbors," she finished with a wink. "Ask your next question."

"How did you feel when Slade challenged you about meeting Phoebe Mitchell?" I obliged.

Mave's head jerked back as if slapped. "I felt a mite testy," she snapped, her eyes squinting in a fierce glare. But then her expression softened again. "Don't you worry, though. I don't kill folks when I'm feeling testy. And it wasn't as if I really believed I'd met Phoebe. It was just a little white lie I'd grown fond of. Made a good story to tell. George Jean Nathan said, 'Art is a beautiful, swollen lie.' And that about sums it up. Wouldn't be a whole lot of art without lies, now, would there?"

I didn't have an answer to that one. I turned to Carrie. But she seemed out of ideas too.

"Want to see a picture of Phoebe?" Mave offered.

Carrie and I nodded simultaneously. Somehow, we had become a team.

Mave stood up and led us to the wall behind our couch. It was covered in black and white photos of women. Mave pointed and identified each of them enthusiastically. Sojourner Truth, Susan B. Anthony, Alice B. Toklas, Gertrude Stein, "Red" Emma Goldman and Margaret Sanger were the only names I recognized. And, of course, Phoebe Mitchell. She was a handsome woman, with well-chiseled features and one impudently raised eyebrow above an eye that seemed ready to wink. I could see why Mave loved her so.

Carrie and I made polite noises over Mave's collection for a few more minutes and then she saw us out, pleading the need to write.

"Well?" I asked once Carrie and I were in the car again.

Carrie still hadn't answered me by the time we passed the lush lawn and beds of dahlias in front of the large redwood house next to Nan's.

"Look," Carrie said, extending a finger. But she wasn't pointing at the garden, she was pointing at the BMW parked in front of Nan's cottage.

"Nan's home. Real estate sales must be slow," Carrie drawled, sounding for a moment like Nan herself. She pulled to the curb, set the brake and turned to me, all in one motion. "Shall we?"

"After you," I replied.

Our visit with Nan wasn't much longer than our visit with Mave. Nan answered the door with an impatient, "Oh, you two," and ushered us into her living room, ten feet by six feet of spotless bare hardwood floors and cream-colored walls with two small, perfectly matched vanilla-colored sofas and one abstract painting in shades of cream, muted blue and pale yellow above a small, neat, unused fireplace. That was it. The room was perfect, tasteful, and utterly sterile. Nan didn't ask us to sit down.

I managed one phrase, "Hi, we were in the neighborhood," and she started talking real estate.

"Carrie says you're in Mill Valley," Nan told me, tossing a languid gold-bangled wrist in its general direction. "Not a good place to be right now." She shook her head, her shining blond pageboy swinging from side to side as gracefully as hair in a shampoo ad. "Prices are dropping in Mill Valley. You want to be in Hutton or San Ricardo. Ever thought about a condo? Larkspur has a great little . . ."

If she was trying to avoid our questions, she had a good technique. I looked over at Carrie. She shrugged and rolled her eyes. But ten minutes later, Nan paused for a breath.

"We were curious how you came to be in the critique group," Carrie put in quickly.

Nan blinked, her tan face blank for a moment.

"Oh," she said finally. "I took a class from Slade a few years ago. Well, he took one look at my writing and practically begged me to join his little group." She smiled smugly, animated once more. "Anyway, Kate. I can tell you right now that Mill Valley has had its day as a real estate hot spot. The areas that are—"

"Slade could give quite a rough critique," Carrie cut in again, not even waiting for Nan to breathe this time. I didn't blame her. It might have been ten more minutes.

"Slade, rough?" Nan said, eyebrows arcing. Then she chuckled. "Not really. You just had to understand Slade's sense of humor. Very sly, very subtle. He was really a darling man. But so misunderstood." She didn't have to add "by lesser mortals." The implication was enough.

"Have you found your copy of Donna's manuscript?" I asked.

"I haven't had a single little second to look yet," Nan told me. She shook a well-manicured finger in my direction, jangling her bracelets. "Been too busy showing hot properties. You ought to come by the office, Kate. . . ."

As we were leaving Nan's, I heard a car start up behind us. The sound seemed familiar. Was it the same sound as the car the night before? I turned my head and saw a beige Honda Civic alone on the wide Hutton street about a block behind us. I couldn't make out the features of the driver. The car was too far away. But still, I had a feeling. . . .

"What kind of car does Russell drive?" I asked, turning to Carrie.

"A Honda. A Civic, I believe," she answered. "Why?"

"Because, I think he's—" I began, swiveling my head to look behind me again. But the car had disappeared.

- Ten -

I STARED OVER my shoulder in disbelief. Where had the beige Honda gone? Had it turned onto a side street? Or had I imagined the whole thing? Goose bumps formed on my arms.

"Because what?" Carrie asked next to me.

I jumped in my seat, wrenching something in my swiveled neck. Something that hurt. I rubbed the sore spot as I turned my head back to look out the front window.

Hutton was still rolling by, tastefully as ever. But its well-groomed gardens and hedges had lost their appeal.

"Never mind," I whispered.

"Are you all right, Kate?" she asked, her voice a little louder.

"I'm fine," I lied. Then I shook my head. Lying was no good. Not that I was making a moral judgment. I just knew that Carrie would see through my lie. "Fine except that someone came and stood in my yard last night," I amended.

"And you think that someone is Russell Wu," Carrie told me.

I turned to her in astonishment, wrenching my sore neck once again. "How did you know?"

"Kate, you just asked me about Russell's car," she said impatiently. She threw up her hands for a moment, then grabbed the wheel again before I had time for a fresh anxiety attack. "Did you see his car last night?"

"I only *heard* it last night," I muttered. The whole thing sounded so ridiculous aloud. "At least, I think I heard it. And I think I might have seen it behind us a couple of seconds ago. A beige Honda Civic. But now it's gone."

Carrie frowned as she pulled onto the highway. Was she reconsidering her choice of an investigative partner?

"Look, I don't know if it really was Russell, but—" That was when I noticed that we were going north on the highway instead of south. "Hey, where are you going?"

"To Russell's," Carrie said. "Of course."

Of course.

Russell had an apartment in San Ricardo. Or maybe it was a condo. The complex looked upscale enough. We wound our way through the landscaped grounds until we found this building alongside a patch of lilies of the Nile and climbed a short flight of stairs to his upper-story unit. He appeared at the door within seconds of the doorbell's chime.

"Hello," he said without blinking. His tinted glasses looked even darker in the light of the doorway. I wondered if they were the kind that changed in the light.

"Hi, Russell," I said uncomfortably. "Carrie and I thought . . ."

I realized abruptly that I had no idea how to finish the sentence, especially with Russell just standing there, staring.

"We thought we might visit with you and discuss Slade Skinner's death," Carrie finished for me, her voice matter-of-fact. "After all, you do have a special expertise in these matters."

Something that might have been a smile tugged at Russell's lips briefly. Then he turned without a word and swept his hand in front of him, motioning us inside.

Inside turned out to be a Spartan living room with one blue-and white-checked sofa, a couple of bookcases, a stack of newspapers and a curling poster of Monet's "Water Lilies" on the wall. I had a feeling Russell didn't do a whole lot of entertaining.

Carrie and I sat on the checked sofa while Russell went to get a chair. The room felt cool for July, even cold. Or maybe it was me. A pretty tiger-striped cat approached and sniffed our feet curiously, then leapt up to sit between us. I felt relieved, even warmer, as if the presence of a cat proved that Russell wasn't a murderer. I hastily reminded myself that Hitler had liked dogs, as Russell came back with a wooden chair and sat down to face us.

He didn't even bother to make small talk. He just stared our way without speaking.

"May I ask how you happened to join the critique group?" Carrie said after a few moments of silence had passed. Her voice sounded easy, unstrained. But I glimpsed her hands out of the corner of my eye. She was wiggling her fingers again.

"I found out about the group through Vicky Andros," Russell answered, his voice as unruffled as Carrie's. But his body was still too, completely still as he spoke in a soothing hypnotic tone. "Vicky works as a computer programmer at a company called AB Networks. I'd done some freelance tech writing for them. Got to know Vicky. She invited me to join the group when she found out I was writing true crime."

There was another long minute of silence. But Russell didn't add anything to his statement.

"What was your opinion of Slade Skinner?" Carrie asked softly.

Russell's lips twitched, ever so gently. Yes, that was a smile. I was sure of it this time.

"He could be a real s.o.b., couldn't he?" Russell replied, just as softly. "On the other hand, I don't think he meant to be cruel. He was just completely self-absorbed."

"In that case, why did he stay with the critique group?" Carrie prodded.

"Good question." Russell lifted his eyes to the ceiling for a moment. That was a relief. He had moved almost naturally. "My theory is that Slade, like many self-absorbed men, was really lonely. And he was uptight about people wanting to be his friends. Afraid they only wanted a piece of his wealth and success." Russell brought his head back down and looked at us again with yet another twitch of a smile. "For some reason, he seemed to think writers were exempt from that kind of motivation. The group was like family to him, I think. A safe bunch of people to hang out with."

"Interesting," Carrie said thoughtfully. She paused, then bent forward to ask her next question. "How did you feel about his critiques?"

"I assume you mean his critiques of my own writing," Russell said.

Carrie nodded.

"They were nasty, but they were useful too. Slade was a good writer. People got so pissed off at his critiques that they never bothered to listen to what he was saying. And some of his tirades contained damn good advice. He had an eye for what worked in writing. And what didn't work. Especially in mine. A true-crime story should have all the elements of a good thriller. When he told me sections of my manuscript bored him out of his skull, I listened."

"You know, I believe you are right," Carrie said admiringly. She leaned back on the couch, her fingers no longer wiggling. "I never actually noticed the content of his critiques because they made me so angry. Not that he actually critiqued my own work. It was hearing the comments he made about the others."

"But he didn't piss you off enough to make you kill him," Russell stated.

Carrie leaned back and laughed. "No, he didn't," she agreed.

"Me neither," Russell said.

They smiled at each other. And I felt the interrogation slipping away. I took a deep breath.

"Didn't Slade make fun of you in his book?" I asked, my voice coming out too loud.

Russell shifted his eyes my way. "I don't think Slade really 'made fun' of me," he answered calmly. "He wrote a character who's a lot like me. And it's pretty weird to see yourself from someone else's perspective. But the fact is, he wrote about a stereotypical Asian kinda nerd. And I *am* a stereotypical Asian kinda nerd. I don't think there was anything derogatory in his portrayal. Of course, I think I have more aspects to my personality than he gave his character. But if that character was so obviously recognizable as me, then I guess Slade did a good job."

I was beginning to like Russell myself. He really was a good observer of people, just as Carrie had told me. And funny in his own way. I reminded myself that we were here to get some answers from him, funny and likable notwithstanding.

"Did you visit me last night?" I demanded. I couldn't think of any better way to ask.

"Visit you?" he asked back. He fixed an unblinking stare onto my face.

I felt the blood rise into my cheeks. If he wasn't my late-night visitor, he probably thought I was nuts. Most people know who their visitors are.

"Never mind," I said for the second time in an hour.

"So much for our mutual investigation," he commented, smiling gently. "Maybe we could continue over dinner."

I barely noticed the dinner part. Mutual investigation? Damn. What the hell did that mean? Carrie and I were the ones asking questions. At least I thought so.

"We were hoping to speak with Joyce while we were in the area," Carrie was saying as I began to listen again. "Though a meal does sound good."

"Maybe we can get Joyce to come to dinner, too," Russell suggested.

"Kate?" Carrie asked.

"Huh?" I said.

She frowned at me. My brain began to process again.

"Oh, sure," I said, belatedly trying to pump some enthusiasm into my voice. "Dinner would be great."

The next thing I knew, we were downstairs getting into Russell's car. It was a beige Honda Civic. Of course.

I climbed into the back of the Civic. Carrie sat up front with Russell. When he turned the key in the ignition, I realized he'd never really answered my question about the night before. I stared at the back of his perfectly still head. Was he my nighttime visitor?

Joyce's apartment was located above Operation Soup Pot's headquarters, up a long flight of steep stairs.

"I'm sorry there's no place to sit down," Joyce apologized as the three of us walked into her living room. She hadn't exactly invited us in, but she had stepped back from the door. And that was enough.

Carrie murmured something reassuring to Joyce behind me while I looked around the living room.

I had thought Russell's living room was Spartan, but Joyce had him beat hands down for simplicity. Russell owned a couch. Joyce had two cushions. One cushion sat in front of a framed photo of an aged, serene face that looked faintly Asian. I had to bend over to see it where it was hung on the wall a couple of feet above the floor. I couldn't tell if the face in the photo was male or female. I turned to ask Joyce who it was.

"This is my meditation area," she explained with a sudden blush that dyed her face all the way to the roots of her black hair.

"It's very nice," I told her, changing conversational course before I'd even started. "Very peaceful." Joyce's blush was enough to discourage me from asking any questions about the photo. Though now I had a new question. What was she so embarrassed about? But I probably wouldn't ask that one either.

I turned instead to look at the only other furniture in the room, a word processor laid out neatly on a low teak table with Joyce's other cushion in front of it. I wondered for a moment how she could sit on that cushion and type. Where the hell did she put her legs?

"We thought we'd take you out to dinner," Russell said.

"Oh dear," Joyce murmured, her eyes widening under her oversized glasses. At least the blush seemed to be receding. "I'm sorry. I was just soaking some beans for tomorrow."

"Have you eaten yet tonight?" Carrie asked.

"Well, no," Joyce admitted, shaking her head. "I haven't. But—"

"Then why don't you come with us?" Carrie cut in. "A night out would do you good."

"Well, I should—"

After a few more minutes of cajoling, Joyce finally agreed to go to dinner, her acceptance about as enthusiastic as a cat's considering a visit to the vet.

Once Carrie had twisted Joyce's arm sufficiently, we followed her into the kitchen to watch her soak her beans. At least the kitchen looked lived in. It was furnished with a stained and scarred teak table and four chairs. And a lot of cooking equipment. It smelled good too, of garlic and rosemary and yeast. An air-brushed painting of irises was on one wall, and a framed poem in black calligraphy on the other.

I read the poem as Joyce poured more than a quart of beans into a huge cast-iron pot and carried it to the sink.

"This existence of ours is as transient as the winter snow . . ."

Maybe I should jot it down, I thought, show some interest in other people's poetry. Joyce ran water over the beans and I read on.

". . . To watch the birth and death of beings is like watching the dance of a butterfly—"

"Can I help?" Russell offered as Joyce lifted the pot up onto the stove.

"No, I'm fine," she said, blushing again. "I can lift much heavier. You have to be strong to be a cook."

"A lifetime is like a burst of song . . ."

"I guess that's it," Joyce said with a wistful edge of sadness in her tone. She looked around her kitchen as if she were memorizing it. I read the last line of calligraphy quickly.

"Come and gone, like a flash of lightning in the sky."

And then the four of us left her apartment.

"So," I said as she and I climbed into the back seat of Russell's Civic. "Who wrote that poem in your kitchen?"

"What poem?" She tilted her head as she looked at me, her brows raised in inquiry.

"You know," I told her. "The one about life being transient—"

"Oh, that," she said with a little laugh. "The Buddha wrote it. Or at least he is said to have written it. Did you like it?"

"Oh sure," I replied. I wanted to say more, but I was afraid I'd betray my lack of spirituality if I did. I fished around in my mind for a way to change the subject. Russell saved me the trouble.

"How about that Chinese vegetarian place downtown?" he suggested from the front seat.

"That would be wonderful," Joyce breathed, a look of genuine pleasure appearing on her face for the first time. "I feel so decadent," she confided in a whisper. "I don't drive. I usually walk or take the bus. Sometimes I bicycle. And I almost never go out to dinner."

I shifted uncomfortably in my seat. It didn't take pictures of starving children to remind me of my own relative wealth. I not only owned a car, I owned a house. At least I owned the part of it I wasn't still paying for. And I took going out to dinner every once in a while for granted. Maybe I'd make a contribution to Operation Soup Pot when I got home.

"Joyce," Carrie said from the seat in front of me, "I never got a chance to ask you. Do you still have the manuscript?"

Joyce didn't blush this time. Her face went white instead. And she didn't answer Carrie. She looked too afraid to speak. What was wrong with the woman? Was she that afraid of the Mafia?

Carrie craned her head around until she was looking Joyce in the eye.

"Donna Palmer's manuscript," she articulated as if for a deaf person. She sketched an outline of a manuscript with her fingers. "Do you still have your copy of Donna's manuscript?"

- Eleven -

JOYCE'S BODY STIFFENED against the car seat as Carrie stared at her. Then she took a breath and her body seemed to melt into round-shouldered softness again.

"I still have my copy of Donna's manuscript," she said quietly, looking down at her lap now like a kid the teacher's yelled at. "I checked. It's still where I left it in my office at the Operation. Those men probably wouldn't think of looking there."

"Good work," I told her, keeping my tone light and teasing. "You too could have a career in espionage."

She glanced over at me, then looked back at her lap. I smiled like you do when you're trying to let an animal know you're not dangerous. I felt like holding out my hand for her to sniff.

"I didn't actually try to fool them," she said softly. "But thank you." Then she closed her eyes and took a series of deep breaths, in through the nose and out through the mouth.

I couldn't tell if she was meditating or suffering from hay fever or just having a private anxiety attack. But it was obvious to me that she wasn't in the mood for further conversation. Russell and Carrie respected her silence too, not that she was exactly silent. All that breathing was pretty loud, especially in the back seat. But no one in the car said another thing until we got to The Bodhi-Tree on Burlington Avenue.

The Bodhi-Tree is a little storefront restaurant in downtown San Ricardo that's easier to pass by than to notice, only identified by a small hand-painted sign in the front window. If you make it as far as the door, you'll find a yellowing article about the benefits of vegetarianism Scotch-taped to it. That article's been there for at least two years. The Bodhi-Tree seems to be doing all it can to discourage customers. Except for the food.

The food at The Bodhi-Tree is great. The sweet and sour walnuts, musee mock pork in pancakes with plum sauce, and almond press "duck" made from a vegetable product that never quacked in its life are all good enough to make the carnivores happy, at least the carnivores I've taken there. And the hot and spicy cabbage and gluten puff in black bean sauce are heaven on a platter as far as I'm concerned.

Russell pushed the door open and motioned us through, a gentleman of the old school suddenly. I didn't stop to question the gesture. I was hungry.

A reed-thin Asian woman in running shoes pointed to a table near the door.

"You sit," she ordered.

We sat, Carrie and I on one side and Joyce and Russell on the other. The thin woman tossed us four menus and then ran off to another table, literally. It looked like she was the only one waiting tables that night.

"This has gotta be the perfect place to satisfy everyone," Russell said as he looked over the menu. "I'm Chinese, and Kate and Joyce are vegetarians—"

"What about me?" Carrie demanded. She crossed her arms across her chest in feigned indignation, her brows raised over laughing brown eyes.

"Look," he said quietly, pointing at the menu. "Vegetarian

spareribs and Chinese greens. If they're collard greens, would that be close enough?"

I snorted back a laugh as Carrie stared at him for an instant, her brows pushed together in a frown. But when she exploded into a peal of laughter instead of anger, I let my own cackle out. Even Joyce smiled tentatively.

"Ye gods and goddesses, if you aren't the most deadpan joker I have ever met," Carrie said a moment later, wiping her eyes.

Russell's lips twitched in an acknowledging smile. Myself, I still wasn't sure that he'd been joking.

After that, we got down to the complicated business of negotiating our order. Carrie insisted she wanted those vegetarian spareribs. I wanted the hot and spicy cabbage, and/or the gluten puff. Russell wanted Szechuan eggplant. And Joyce wanted whatever the rest of us wanted. Of course. We added rice and two orders of pot stickers and we were ready.

After the harried waitress ran over and took our order, Carrie and I turned our smiles on Joyce, ready to pump her for information. Even Russell turned her way. I felt like I was one of a school of sharks.

"I always feel a little guilty eating out," Joyce whispered before we could start the interrogation. "With so many people out there going hungry."

I felt my shark's smile slipping. This woman could have made Mother Teresa feel guilty about her decadent lifestyle.

"But I do enjoy tasting other people's cooking," she followed up quickly. "Since I'm a cook, I suppose I can tell myself it's something I should do to perfect my art."

"Both my parents are cooks too," Russell offered.

"Really?" Joyce said, turning to him with a hint of animation on her pale face.

"Yeah," he confirmed. For a moment I thought that was all he was going to say. But then he went on, his low voice as soothing as a massage. "They own a Chinese restaurant in the city. Though I'm afraid it's not vegetarian." Russell was turning out to be downright conversational, and it made me suspicious.

"But that's wonderful," Joyce said. "You must have learned so much from them."

He shrugged. "Not really," he told her. "All that good food spoiled me. Oh, I can cook a hamburger." He blinked, seeming to remember he was in a vegetarian restaurant. "Or a tofu burger for that matter," he added. "But not much else." He bent closer, looking into her eyes. "Was it your parents who taught you how to cook?"

"Which set?" she asked, sticking out her lower lip like a rebellious teenager for a moment. "I had more than one set of foster parents," she explained before anyone had a chance to ask. "Now, Mother Johnson was a good cook. Though what I remember is her homemade doughnuts. Not the kind of food anybody should really eat, I know. But, boy, were they good." Her eyes went happily out of focus.

Great. Now I was hungry for doughnuts, something I hadn't eaten in years.

"Pot stickers," our waitress announced as she jogged up to the table. "Very hot."

They were too. Very hot. And very tasty, full of ginger, garlic and what tasted like chilies. I forgot all about the doughnuts as I chewed. Even Russell and Carrie gave up on questioning anyone as they gobbled up pot stickers. Joyce, though, was still nibbling her second one by the time the rest of us had finished, tasting carefully as if she were going to take notes. I should have known that she would eat as correctly as she did everything else.

Carrie turned her attention to Russell.

"What do your parents think of your writing career?" she asked.

He gave a minimalist shrug, his expression unchanging.

"Not much?" she persisted.

"They'd rather have a doctor or lawyer," he expanded. "But they don't bug me much anymore. My sister is a lawyer, anyway."

"Gluten puff, eggplant." The waitress named the dishes as she slapped them on the table. Then she turned around and was back in seconds with the cabbage, the spareribs and the rice. That was another plus for The Bodhi-Tree. They were fast. The cook probably wore jogging shoes too.

"You eat," the waitress advised with a sudden warm smile. And then she was gone again.

Carrie managed to talk and sample each of the dishes as they were passed around the table, as well as serving herself.

"Damnation, these are really good," she complimented the mock spareribs. Then she looked over at Joyce. "How did you come to be in the critique group?" she asked.

"Through Travis," Joyce answered readily enough. "He's such a kindhearted soul. He volunteers at the Operation, you know."

Carrie nodded, her dark eyes crinkling with affection. I was pretty sure that affection was for Travis and not for Joyce, however.

I took a forkful of hot and spicy cabbage. It was hot and sweet and sour all at the same time. My favorite combination. Joyce went on.

"Well, Travis was the one who came up with the idea for an Operation Soup Pot cookbook as a fund-raiser." Joyce stuck out her lower lip again briefly. "And you know how Travis is when he gets an idea. He took it right to the board of directors." She sighed. "I'm afraid I'm not much of a writer. It would have been better if he'd written the book. But the board wanted me to do it. Including the homey anecdotes." She looked down at her plate. "I shouldn't complain, though."

No, I thought. You should eat.

She picked up her chopsticks gingerly. "So Travis suggested the critique group. And that was a real blessing. I'm getting the help I need now to write the hard parts." She maneuvered her chopsticks around a tiny piece of eggplant and brought it to her lips.

"I only wish I could persuade Travis to return to college," Carrie said, giving Joyce a chance to eat. "He's taken most of the courses necessary to receive a computer programming degree. But he dropped out of school before he was completely finished."

Joyce chewed her eggplant thoughtfully and swallowed.

"You know," she said earnestly. "Even if Travis doesn't have a formal education, he studies all the time. He's more aware of ecological issues than anyone I know." She leaned forward. "And really, the only true goals in life are learning to love other beings and acquiring wisdom. I think he's very blessed."

"Oh, of course," Carrie said. Somehow, she managed to keep the sarcasm out of her voice. But I could see it in the shape of her brows.

I gave her a quick wink as Joyce bent over her plate to pick up another piece of eggplant. Carrie was right. Joyce was unbearably good.

Then I took a bite of gluten puff in black bean sauce, and the rest of the meal disappeared in a frenzy of good flavors.

"You come back," the waitress ordered as we left. I turned and nodded as she raced across the room with a steaming platter of vegetables. I wasn't sure about anyone else, but I'd come back. That was for sure.

Russell escorted Joyce up the stairs to her apartment while Carrie and I waited in the car. I wasn't sure if he was being protective, gentlemanly, or just trying to ask her some questions out of earshot. It appeared that Russell was doing a little investigating on his own. Did this mean he wasn't a suspect?

Not necessarily, I answered myself. He could be trying to find out how much anyone else knew. Or maybe he was trying to set someone else up for Slade Skinner's murder. Or maybe—

"Back to the ranch?" Russell asked, startling me as he opened the door to the Civic. I hadn't heard him walking up.

"Certainly," Carrie assented. Then she winked largely. "Perhaps we can rope some tofu steers when we get there."

Carnivore humor. I smiled. It always comes out after a good vegetarian meal.

But Russell didn't respond to her jest. In fact, he didn't say another word until he had parked his car back at his own place. Maybe he was thinking. I certainly was. Something was missing with this guy. One minute he's making conversation and the next he's Mr. Silent. Without the charm of Marcel Marceau. I still didn't know who he was.

"Can I use your bathroom?" I asked as we all climbed out of his car.

Carrie sent me a questioning look, but I ignored it. I wanted to see more than Russell's nondescript living room. I wanted to see where he really lived.

"Sure," Russell answered, no discernible surprise registering behind his tinted glasses.

We tromped back up the stairs and into his living room. Then he directed me down the hall. His bathroom looked like a typical single guy's bathroom, or maybe a typical *neat* single guy's bathroom. One bottle of shampoo in the clean shower, a clean toilet with the seat up and a small medicine cabinet. I opened the cabinet stealthily, under the cover of a running faucet. The first thing I noticed was a package of condoms. I slammed it shut again in embarrassment and saw my own red face reflected in the cabinet's mirror. Damn. What was I doing here?

I slunk back out of the bathroom, feeling ashamed of my nosiness, but I still couldn't resist a glance through the open door just a little further up the hall. I tiptoed a couple more steps and craned my neck through the doorway.

I saw a medium-sized room with only a straight-back chair and an exercise bench to sit on. A small TV sat on a low table on the other side of the room. And next to it, a barbell and some dumbbells were neatly arranged. Come to think of it, Russell did look pretty muscular under his flannel shirt. Then it hit me. Dumbbells! Slade Skinner was killed with a dumbbell. My ears began to buzz with adrenaline.

It was all I could do to keep from running back down the hall to tell Carrie. But I slowed my steps and joined her in a polite goodbye as we left Russell's apartment.

Once we were safely alone in her car again, I told Carrie all about the dumbbells. But she didn't seem impressed.

"A significant percentage of the population lifts weights, Kate," she said calmly as she turned the ignition.

"But Slade was killed with a dumbbell!" I insisted.

"I know that," she replied. Her voice was even, but I saw how tightly her hands gripped the steering wheel as she pulled onto the road. I had forgotten for a moment that I wasn't the only one who had seen the bloody dumbbell firsthand. "The murder weapon had to have been Slade's own personal dumbbell," she added. "You saw him play with it when he talked."

"But wouldn't it be more natural for someone who lifted weights to use one as a weapon?" I persisted, though I wasn't as enthusiastic as I had been. In fact, I felt a little sick. Too much of that good vegetarian food, I told myself. "Just knowing how to hold it. I mean—"

"Perhaps," Carrie interrupted. She was staring ahead now, but her attention didn't seem to be on the road in front of her. Her dark eyes were out of focus. Was she seeing the bloody dumbbell in her head? I was.

"Did you notice how talkative Russell was with Joyce

around?" I asked. It wasn't a complete change of subject, but it was the best I could do. "He was pumping her for information too, don't you think?"

"Yes, I do believe he was." Carrie gave me a smiling sidelong glance. My stomach felt better instantly. "Russell Wu is no fool. He knows that a wee bit of conversation is the right lever to open Joyce Larson up."

"Why'd Joyce get so uptight when you asked her about Donna's manuscript?" I demanded, forgetting Russell's dumbbells now in the memory of Joyce's stricken white face.

"I don't know," Carrie said slowly as she pulled onto the highway. She frowned again, thinking. "Although she certainly did look afraid."

"Afraid of what?"

"I don't know," Carrie repeated, sounding as tired of not knowing as I was. "Joyce is an odd woman. There is no doubt about that. But then again, everyone in the critique group is pretty strange."

"Including you?" I teased.

"Including me," she confirmed with a flash of white teeth. Then she got serious again. "The one thing I know about Joyce is that she's very concerned about violence. She can't even tolerate the mention of violence."

"Maybe she was worried that Donna's father's thugs would do something violent searching for the manuscript at Operation Soup Pot," I said, trying out the theory as I spoke. "Maybe she was deciding whether it was safe to tell us where it was."

"That's possible," Carrie admitted, but she didn't sound convinced. Not that she had a better theory about Joyce's behavior. Or about anything else for that matter. The car may have been moving, but our brains were stalled.

When we got to my house, Carrie and I sat in the car and talked a little more. But it was getting dark and we were getting nowhere. And I could tell she was tired. I could see it in the lines marring the round contours of her face.

"Let's call it a night," I suggested finally.

She nodded. "Thank you, Kate," she whispered. "For everything."

I gave her shoulder a quick squeeze and climbed out of her car. It felt like a hundred years since we'd left my house. I was tired too, I realized. Bone-tired.

I lifted my arm heavily to wave goodbye as Carrie backed out of the driveway. Then I climbed the stairs and opened my door.

I heard a frenzied rustling as I reached for the light switch. I turned toward the sound angrily. Were the neighborhood cats here again, stealing C.C.'s food?

And then something very large and human rushed at me through the darkness.

– Twelve –

I LEAPT OUT of the way of the shadowed form speeding toward me. A fraction of a heartbeat later, I saw that the form was indeed human and probably male. I couldn't make out anything else. My eyes still hadn't adjusted to the gray darkness of the entry hall. I caught a hint of a bulky profile, and then whoever it was bolted past me.

"What the—" I began, turning toward the door.

Then the second body pushed past me.

I stood frozen for a breathless moment. Then I inhaled sharply and ran out the door after them. It was lighter outside than it was in the entry hall. I saw the backs of two solidly built men running down my stairs. They wore tailored suits.

Probably Armani, I thought, remembering Carrie's description of the men she had seen. And with that thought, I stopped running. I was like a cat stalking deer. What would I do if I caught one?

So I stood on my deck, panting with anger and fear, and watched the two men run down my driveway. By the time I heard a car start and drive away, my whole body was shaking. Including my stomach. I just hoped none of its contents would shake on out.

I turned back to my front door, thanking the years of tai-chi practice—and the adrenaline—that had enabled me to jump out of the way as the two men hurtled past. What if I hadn't been fast enough? I thought of Slade, beaten to death with his own dumbbell. Had he gotten in these men's way, these thugs' way? I was sure by now that these were Donna's father's men.

I stepped back into the house on weak legs, turned on the light and trotted over to the pinball machine where I had last seen Donna's floppy disk. Sure enough, it was gone. Slade Skinner's manuscript was still there, though. How had they known in the dark that it wasn't Donna's?

And that wasn't my only question. Was one of these men the one who had stood in my yard the night before? No, I decided. Their shadowy shapes had been different than that of the previous night's intruder. Bulkier. And the sound of the car driving away wasn't the same as the previous night's either. Though maybe they were driving a different car. Then my mind came back to the main feature. Had one or both of these men killed Slade Skinner?

I jogged back to the front door and clicked both locks into place, something I almost never do.

Then I heard something behind me. Just the slightest sound, something, maybe a foot brushing the carpet ever so lightly. I would have never heard it at all without the leftover adrenaline running through my body.

I executed a 180-degree turn and looked around wildly for the source of the sound.

Then I heard a new sound, a meow. I lowered my gaze. C.C. looked up at me, blinking sleepy eyes. The adrenaline drained more quickly this time, leaving me shaking and sick at my stomach once more. And cold.

"Where the hell have you been?" I demanded.

C.C.'s eyes opened wide. She stared at me accusingly.

"Never mind," I said.

Then she began to meow in earnest.

I couldn't remember when I had fed C.C. last. Probably before I took off with Carrie. But I allowed the cat to shepherd me into the kitchen, where I fed her again, just in case, half a can of her favorite kitty entree. I even managed to replenish her water and dry food without spilling any. It wasn't easy, the way my hands were shaking. Not that C.C. thanked me for the service.

It wasn't until I was on my way out of the kitchen that I noticed the blinking light on my answering machine.

I set it for replay, flinching in advance. That always saves time.

The first message was the friendly, crisp voice of someone who wanted to interest me, Kate Jasper, in a wonderful refinancing opportunity. I fast forwarded till a new voice came on. It was just as friendly, but not nearly so crisp.

"Oh, let's see, my number is . . . um . . . oh dear." There was a pause and then whoever it was reeled off a phone number. The whoever was female by the sound of it, but that was the furthest I could go in identifying her.

"Anyway, I called because I was a little worried," she went on. "Things are incredibly complex over here and I'm afraid I may have, well, made a little mistake. My dad's men came by earlier and they asked your name—"

Donna. It had to be. My pulse began to pound again.

"They saw you with Carrie, I guess. Anyway, I told them your name. I hope that's okay with you. I know privacy can be very important to a person's integrity—"

It was Donna all right. If I hadn't been so frightened, I might have laughed.

"Anyway, the two of them aren't really dangerous or anything. At least I don't think so. But I thought I should let you know. Well, goodbye. Oh, by the way, I hope it's okay for me to call you. I don't want to infringe on your personal space or anything. Your number was in the phone book, so I guess it's okay."

That was it. She never did leave her name. I turned the machine off. Not only was my phone number in the phone book, so was my address. That's probably how the two goons had found me. Suddenly I wished I'd used an alias for the critique group.

I punched in the number Donna had left, not quite sure what I wanted to say to her. It was too late for her to undo the damage. But maybe I could get her to leave me out of any further communications with her family or their muscular friends.

"Hello," said a squeaky voice. A child, I realized. Great.

"This is Kate Jasper," I said slowly and clearly. Not having children myself, I tend to treat the little munchkins as if they're deaf. "May I speak to your mother?"

"What do you want?" the squeaky voice replied.

I was silent. How to explain to this child what I wanted? I thought of saying, I want to throttle your mommy, but that seemed excessive.

"I'd like to speak to your mother about her critique group," I explained instead.

"Oh," the voice responded.

"Can you call your mother to the phone?" I asked, keeping my own voice pleasant with an effort.

"Uh-huh," he said, if it was a he.

I waited for him to call her, but he didn't. He was still on the phone, though. I could hear him breathing.

And then I noticed something else, raised voices in the background. It sounded like two voices, one high and one even higher. Both of them were shouting.

"Is everything okay?" I asked, suddenly concerned. Would this kid just sit and talk to me on the phone if his mother was being murdered?

"Dacia fed another goldfish to the cat," the voice informed me. "Then the cat threw up. Mommy told Dacia last time that she would yell really loud if that happened again.

"And that's what she's doing now, yelling loud?"

"Uh-huh."

"Look, what's your name?" I demanded.

"Dustin," the voice said.

"Listen, Dustin," I said, back to my plan of speaking slowly and clearly, hoping he could hear me over the racket in the background. "Will you just call your mother to the phone?"

Dustin didn't answer me. I couldn't even hear him breathing anymore. Only the voices yelling, which sounded louder now.

"Hello," I tried.

No one answered. I read all the buttons on the phone console: "memo, pause, prog, redial . . ." Twice. Still no one answered. I said hello a few more times and then I hung up.

I punched out Carrie's number next. I was relieved to hear her hello. After not talking to Donna, I had been afraid I'd only get Carrie's machine. Or that one of Carrie's dogs would answer.

"The hoods have been here," I announced dramatically. "They broke into my house and took Donna's floppy."

"They have visited me again as well," Carrie replied, her rich voice as steady as ever. "While we were out visiting. I noticed the moment I stepped into my study. They had misplaced my box of floppy diskettes."

"Did they take Donna's floppy?" I asked.

"Yes," she answered simply. "They did."

"Well?" I demanded.

"Well, what, Kate?"

"Did they murder Slade?" I spelled it out impatiently.

There was a long silence. I hate long silences on the phone. They make me feel blind. I stuck the receiver under my chin and rubbed my cold arms, hungry for tactile sensation if I couldn't have visual.

"I think not," she said finally.

"Why do you think not?" I demanded. But even as I asked the question, I was calming down and thinking not myself.

The men hadn't been very interested in harming me. There had been two of them after all. They could have taken me on easily, tai chi or no tai chi. But instead they had run. And I had seen them. They had to know that. But they hadn't come back to kill me to cover up. Not yet, at least.

"I have no compelling evidence that these men are innocent of Slade Skinner's murder. But I have none that they are guilty either. And, ultimately, I just don't believe they were the ones. I think Slade was killed by a member of our group who was scheduled to meet him at five o'clock last Saturday." Carrie paused, then added, "I'm sorry to have mixed you up in this."

"That's all right," I assured her. Some day I would learn to knock off my knee-jerk sympathy. "Though I think we oughta—"

The doorbell rang, cutting me off as effectively as someone snipping the telephone cord. For an instant I thought my heart had stopped too, but then I heard it pounding again. Who the hell was out there?

"Ought to what, Kate?" Carrie asked.

"There's someone at the door," I told her in a whisper.

"Well, I'll let you go in that case," she said.

I said goodbye and hung up, wondering too late if I should have kept her on the line. I grabbed the phone console instead, poising my finger over the button programmed for 911, and carried it to the door, trailing the telephone cord behind me. I switched on the porch light.

"Who is it?" I shouted, wishing for the hundredth time that I had gotten around to installing a peephole in my solid wood door.

"Delivery!" The answer boomed clearly through the door.

Delivery? It was completely dark now, way past normal business hours. My skin tightened into goose bumps.

"What are you delivering?" I demanded.

"Flowers," the reply came back, softer now but still audible. And familiar somehow.

"I didn't order any flowers," I yelled.

"Oh, come on, Kate!"

Now I was sure I recognized the speaker. I put the phone down and yanked the door open, ready to scream.

My ex-husband, Craig, was standing there on my doorstep, looking more handsome than ever dressed in a tuxedo and a grin, a huge bouquet of flowers in his hand. Somehow the sight of all those flowers smothered my intended scream.

"Ta-da!" he sang out and bowed, one hand across his midriff, the other holding the flowers out in my direction.

"Damn it, Craig—" I began.

I watched the smile leave his face, and my heart twinged with guilt. His brown puppy-dog eyes widened. I had loved this man at one time in my life. And the hurt he had inflicted upon me hadn't been intentional. Not that it had hurt any less.

"You shouldn't have," I finished. And I meant it.

"Like 'em?" he asked, cocking his well-trimmed head, a tentative smile on his lips.

It was quite a bouquet. There were gladioli, poppies, chrysanthemums, daisies, snapdragons and five kinds of other flowers I couldn't identify, in a rainbow of colors. They must have cost a bundle and Craig was a notoriously cheap man. Now my stomach echoed my heart's twinge of guilt.

"They're very nice," I told him, keeping my tone as unenthusiastic as possible. That wasn't too hard. All I wanted at that moment was to figure out how I could get him to go away and never come back. Without hurting his feelings too much.

"You know what the orange said to the doctor?" he asked.

I shook my head. Maybe I should have screamed at him after all. Or bludgeoned him. Or—

"I haven't been peeling well," he answered himself. "Get it?"

"I get it," I said, adding ice to my tone.

Apparently I hadn't added enough ice. He stuck one foot through the doorway.

I stepped in front of him quickly, blocking his path.

"It's late," I told him. "And you'd better take those flowers home before they wilt."

"But they're for you," he insisted, his voice too high. His eyes were wide again.

"Craig, it won't work—"

"Just kidding," he assured me, smiling gamely. "I'm going to a fancy-dress dinner. These are the centerpiece."

I stared into his eyes for a moment, wondering if it were true. But all I saw was hurt.

"Then you'd better get going," I said briskly. "See you later."

"I've got some more computer gags—"

"Fine," I cut him off. "Goodbye."

He pulled his foot back through the doorway, still smiling. At least his mouth was smiling. His eyes were those of a dog unjustly accused of carpet molestation, wide with hurt and unceasing devotion.

I shut the door gently, then double locked it.

I should have given up and gone to bed then. But I knew I'd never sleep, so I went to my desk instead and worked on my computer-nerd earring designs in an attempt to drive hoods, murder, children on the telephone and ex-husbands from my mind.

I decided a keyboard hanging from one ear and a terminal hanging from the other might be interesting. I sketched the first draft in exquisite detail, my treat to myself. Then I got real on the second draft. I knew that any design had to be simple enough to be reproduced in inexpensive plastic. At least it had to be if I wanted to actually profit from my work, not to mention paying the salary of my two employees. And the design had to be uncomplicated enough to encourage the paint job to line up with the molded plastic. I had learned that hard lesson early on.

I let out a little sigh as I worked on my second draft. True, gag gifts weren't fine art. But occasionally, I still wished that designing didn't have to be an exercise in compromise as well as drafting.

A couple of hours later I was dead tired, but I still wasn't sleepy. I climbed under cool sheets and squirmed with reckless fatigue as I thought about Wayne. I missed him, damn it. I turned over on one side and then the other. After a few more turns, I had managed to short-sheet myself. I tucked the bottom of the sheet back in, then tried a new game, pretending that Wayne was right there by my side. I imagined his curly head lying on the pillow, then his muscular body—

That was a little too much imagination. My body was responding to his body and he wasn't even there. I jumped out of bed in frustration and padded into the living room for Slade's manuscript.

Cool Fallout kept me up another hour, and I barely made it out of the sixties. I read page after page as the main characters played their parts, selling illegal drugs and enabling draft resisters to escape to Canada. And as I did, Patty Novak and Nan Millard blended in my mind, Patty seeming more interested in Jack Randolph's family wealth than his leadership of the Brightstar commune and devotion to the cause. And Warren Lee, quiet and spooky as Russell Wu himself, seemed increasingly sinister with each appearance.

In fact, Brightstar felt less and less like Eden as I turned the pages, and more and more like a dysfunctional family ready to explode. And explode it finally did when Kathy Banks, the woman who would eventually become a Catholic nun, panicked and shot the sheriff who had discovered a few dozen bales of marijuana in the false back of the barn. Brightstar collapsed inward then. Jack Randolph's charisma couldn't save it. He didn't even bother to try. He abandoned ship, slipping out in the excitement, never to return. With his disappearance, the center was gone. And with no center, everyone else scattered.

In one final, sad scene, Peter Dahlgren drives away from Brightstar, weeping for all the deals he won't be there to negotiate. And with that final scene, the sixties are irrevocably dead.

Damn, I thought as I lay the manuscript down by the side of my bed. I'll never be able to sleep now.

But I was wrong. I closed my eyes and the next thing I knew it was Saturday morning.

Since it was officially the weekend, I dawdled an extra ten minutes over my soy yogurt and fat-free granola before starting in on my stack of Jest Gifts paperwork.

The phone rang while I was working on my payroll tax deposit schedule, C.C. perched on the back of my chair. I leapt up, grateful for the intrusion. C.C. dug her claws into the chair as I pushed it back, riding the chair like a rodeo cowboy.

"Yeehaw!" I encouraged her. I reached for the phone, hoping Wayne would be on the other end. But it was Carrie. "I hesitate to even ask," she said without any audible hesitation. "But are you coming to the critique group's regular meeting at my home this afternoon?"

I looked over at the stack of Jest Gifts paperwork. C.C. meowed sternly.

"It will be a potluck again," Carrie coaxed, tempting me further. "You are, of course, exempt from food preparation."

In the end, I agreed. I even thought about bringing a poem. For less than an instant. I made a potluck dish, though, a vegetable and rice salad with my own invention, a dressing made from lemon soy yogurt, miso, vinegar, garlic and ginger. It tastes a lot better than it sounds.

As I minced ginger, I thought about calling Felix for information. Felix was my friend Barbara's boyfriend and, more importantly, a newspaper reporter with police connections. If there was anything interesting to know about Slade Skinner's death, he would probably know it. Unfortunately, Felix was less a source of information than an information siphon. And an aggressive information siphon at that. I shook my head and returned my attention to the knife in my hand.

Once the salad was chilled through, I had no excuse to linger at home.

"I promise I won't get in any trouble," I said to C.C. on the way out the door.

She turned her back on me and stalked away.

I shrugged. If C.C. didn't believe me, she wasn't the only one. Then I walked slowly down the stairs to my Toyota, taking enough time to feel the heat of the July sun on my shoulders.

It was two o'clock sharp when I trotted up Carrie's apple-scented path and rang the bell.

An explosion of sound answered the ring.

– Thirteen –

BASTA HOWLED, SINBAD yowled and Yipper yipped as I stood at the front door. But I didn't have a chance to stick my fingers in my ears before I heard Carrie's "CEASE AND DESIST!" And then the explosion of sound ceased as abruptly as it had begun.

Carrie opened the door and peered out at me, blinking in the square of afternoon sunlight that shafted through the doorway. Yipper danced behind her, his claws making skittering noises on the floor while Basta pulled his old basset body up on her left blue-jeaned flank and Sinbad stalked up on her right. Then Carrie smiled, her white teeth a radiant contrast to her dark, freckled skin. No wonder Travis was in love with her. She might have been ten or fifteen years his senior, but the animation in her smile could have lit up the Golden Gate Bridge on a foggy winter's night.

"Thank you for coming, friend," she said solemnly.

"No problem," I told her. I put my rice salad down and opened up my arms for the traditional Marin greeting hug. I'm sure anthropologists will study it some day.

Carrie took a couple of steps forward and we embraced tightly. And this time she lingered, not pulling away immediately like she usually did. At first I assume she was lingering for my benefit, but then a revolutionary idea popped into my mind. Carrie was frightened. She who had saved me from Rosie some twenty years ago was seeking comfort for herself now, like a child seeking reassurance from an adult. I could even feel a tremor in her small, round body.

My own body stiffened with the realization. I didn't want Carrie to be frightened. I wanted her to be the rock she had always been.

She must have felt me stiffen. She dropped her arms and stepped back out of the embrace amid scurrying animals.

"Carrie, what are you so afraid of?" I asked.

Her eyes widened.

"I am—" she began.

"Hey, is everything cool out here?" came a deep voice from behind her.

She jumped and so did I. Even Yipper let out a startled bark. Then Carrie smiled again, a smile even brighter than before, and I wondered for an instant if I had imagined her fear.

"Everything is perfectly fine, Travis," she answered, turning her eyes away from me. "It's my friend Kate."

"Hey, Kate," Travis said and then turned back to Carrie, his face set in its usual handsome scowl. "Listen, Mave says there's going to be a rally for the homeless on Monday night. The cops have been rousting them in downtown San Ricardo again." He threw his arms out, looking crucified for an instant. "Like they have any other place to go, you know. And . . ."

Carrie shot me a look over her shoulder, rolling her eyes. Then she took Travis's arm and led him toward the living room as he went on speaking. I followed them and wondered what in hell was scaring Carrie so badly.

"Well, howdy there, Kate," Mave greeted me, her raspy voice loud enough to drown out Travis's for a moment. She was perched on one of Carrie's cornflower blue sofas in between Joyce Larson and Russell Wu.

"Hi, Mave," I replied with a wave in her direction.

". . . and it's a righteous cause, you know," Travis continued. He turned toward the occupants of the sofa for support. "Joyce says a lot of the folks they rousted can't get their meals at the Operation if they can't stay in the city overnight."

Joyce nodded emphatically, her face serious.

"So how are they supposed to eat?" Travis demanded. He flopped into the easy chair, his arms outstretched in question.

No one answered him. I wish I could have. I only wish our Government would. At least Joyce was doing good work, I thought with a warm rush of admiration. I studied her serious face, her solemn blue eyes. How many lives had she saved with her work?

Then I noticed the tilt of Russell's head on Mave's other side. He was staring up at me, studying my face as I was studying Joyce's.

I pulled my eyes away and looked around the living room. All the furniture, including the two sofas, the easy chair and a few kitchen chairs had been rearranged into a large circle with varying sizes of tables placed in front of most of the seats.

I might not have even noticed Vicky Andros if I hadn't been working so hard at not looking in Russell's direction. She sat waiflike in oversized khakis on one of the kitchen chairs, her bony arms wrapped around herself as if she were cold. Vicky looked a little like Audrey Hepburn in *My Fair Lady*, only she was too thin for the part. I nodded her way and she nodded back without unwrapping her arms.

"So how's our resident poet doing?" Mave asked cheerfully. I jerked my head back to look at her. Did she mean me? She was grinning in my direction. She *did* mean me.

"Oh, just fine," I assured her, smiling back inanely. "No muse today, though. But I guess no muse is good muse—"

The doorbell rang, detonating the animals again before I could make a complete fool of myself. I took a seat on the unoccupied sofa as gag-gift slogans for poets fluttered and crashed in my mind.

Carrie left and came back with Donna, who was dressed in a gauzy blouse and slacks today, but still wore the same floor-length sleeveless vest that she'd worn at the last meeting. I held my breath as she stepped forward. Sinbad added to the suspense, slithering in figure-eights around Donna's ankles.

But Donna did fine, making her way slowly and carefully into the room without mishap.

"Hi, everyone," she sang out gaily. Then she continued her painstaking progress across the room to my sofa. "Mind if I sit next to you?" she whispered, a beseeching look in her honey-colored eyes.

"Oh sure, have a seat," I said, then wondered if it might actually be dangerous to have Donna sit next to me.

Sinbad made one last pass around Donna's ankle as she was lowering herself onto the sofa. Then the doorbell rang and Sinbad jumped. Donna jumped too and fell the rest of the way onto the sofa with a *whumph*. I flattened myself against the back cushions.

"Are you okay?" I asked, sliding as far away from her as I could without actually getting up.

"Oh, I'm great," she said with a sweet smile. She moved closer to me. I tried not to cringe. "But I wanted to apologize to you for my dad's men. I know they can be, well, insensitive. Sometimes I think they don't understand personal space at all. I know I shouldn't have—"

"Kiss, kiss," Nan interrupted from behind us. I turned in time to see her blow one of those kisses over our heads to the group on the other sofa. Today's business suit was teal and miniskirted, accented by heaps of heavy silver jewelry. "While all you lazy bums have been enjoying your Saturday, I've been out showing hot properties. And selling them! The market is fast these days. Oodles and oodles of money to be made."

She sat down on the kitchen chair nearest to Vicky and crossed her long brown legs. Next to Vicky, Nan appeared to be the original California girl, a picture of tan/blond health and vitality. That contrast was probably one of the reasons she chose to sit there, I realized.

"Well, what's up?" she asked brightly.

Carrie sat down in the last available kitchen chair. "Obviously Slade cannot read today as planned," Carrie said, sweeping the small crowd with her eyes. "And many of us have been unable to review Donna's manuscript. Luckily, Vicky has agreed to read impromptu today." She waved her hand in Vicky's direction. "But I suggest that we talk about Donna's manuscript first. Apparently, her father's men visited here last night. The diskette—"

Travis leapt from his chair. "Here?!" he shouted, throwing his arms up. "They came here again! Carrie, you shoulda told me. I'll stay here with you. I—"

"It's okay, Travis," Carrie cut in, standing and waving a hand in front of his outraged face. "Everything is fine. I never even saw them."

He lowered his arms slowly, then shut his mouth. "Oh," he said and sat back down. He turned toward Donna. "They got my hard copy and floppy too," he admitted. "While I was out. Sorry."

Carrie took a deep breath and returned to her seat.

"Oh, no," said Donna, smiling graciously at Travis. "I'm the one who should be sorry. Well, maybe not sorry, but at least I should be able to learn from my mistakes. And to take responsibility. I shouldn't have put everyone through this trauma."

"No shit," Nan articulated clearly.

"But don't worry," Donna assured us with a big smile. "I still have my copies. They haven't found my little hidey-hole yet."

"I still have my floppy," Russell told us quietly. "In a place they won't be able to find."

I opened my mouth to ask him where, then closed it again. It was none of my business where he had hid it. And probably not something that should be mentioned in front of Donna, anyway.

"I've got the hard copy and the floppy hidden," Joyce added. She didn't say where, either. Maybe no one trusted Donna with her own secrets.

"Well, those pesky critters got my hard copy, sure as shootin'," said Mave. "I didn't check to see if I still had the floppy, though." She glared through her glasses fiercely. "We gotta do something about those dirt-bags. They're getting too big for their britches. Someone's gotta teach them a lesson."

"They stole my floppy," Vicky said quietly.

"Mine too," I chimed in, finally feeling like a member of the group.

Russell's head swiveled my way. "They didn't harm you, did they?" he demanded.

I shook my head, embarrassed by his intense stare.

"I saw them, though," I told him. "When they ran down the stairs."

"If you'd like me to stand guard, I'd be happy to," he offered diffidently. Damn. My favorite suspect for murder was offering to protect me.

"No, no," I answered, averting my gaze. "I'm fine by myself."

"The real question remains," Carrie reminded us, her tone somber, "did they kill Slade Skinner?"

"Um, I don't think so," Donna said. She looked around the room hesitantly. "See, Frank and Larry aren't like that. Some of the stuff they do is pretty inappropriate, but not like really violent. I've known them both since I was a baby. I talked to them this morning, and Larry said if they were going to kill anyone it would be me—"

"Oh, how very appropriate," Nan cut in. "What nice, intelligent men."

"They were just talking, just dealing with their angry feelings," Donna explained. Her eyes opened wide. "They wouldn't kill me or anyone else. Honestly. And I asked them to swear they hadn't killed Slade, and they swore."

"And we're supposed to believe them?" Nan demanded.

"Um, yeah—" Donna began.

Nan waved a hand in her direction, jingling silver bracelets. "Forget it," she said. "Good ole Frankie and Johnny didn't kill Slade—"

"Frank and Larry," Donna corrected her.

Nan whipped her head around to glare at the woman who dared to interrupt.

"Sorry," Donna whispered. She lowered her eyes and began to chew on her upper lip.

"If I may go on," Nan drawled, and then went on. "The two stooges didn't kill Slade. Remember, I live across the street from Slade's. I see a lot on that street and I didn't see them visit Saturday after the group." She paused and swept the room with her eyes. Then she smiled. "Which isn't to say I didn't see anything."

It took a while for her implication to sink into my mind. Russell was faster than I was.

"If you know anything at all about Slade's death, it's not wise to keep it secret," he cautioned her. His voice was low and hypnotic. "Tell us what you saw now, Nan."

But the hypnotic tone did nothing for Nan. She only giggled. "You just want the gory details so you can get a fat contract for your next true-crime book," she said, pointing her finger. "Well, you're not getting them from me. Anyway, I didn't say I knew anything about Slade's death. So forget it." Then she stretched, reaching her arms behind her and arching her back. "I'm starving," she announced. "When are we going to eat?"

"This is serious, Nan," Carrie declared. She stood slowly and stepped toward Nan, her small form looming suddenly, her voice prosecutorial. "Did you in fact see something last Saturday at Slade Skinner's house? Did you see someone?"

"I was just kidding," Nan snapped. "God, you guys are tiresome. You should all see your faces. You *all* look guilty."

I looked around. She was right. There was some combination of anger, fear and confusion on everyone's face, and nothing that would prove innocence on any of them.

"Are you just yanking our chains?" Travis demanded finally.

"Of course I am, gorgeous," Nan replied with a wink in his direction.

A blush crept up Travis's swarthy face, tinting it a deep shade of mauve. He jumped out of his chair, heading toward the kitchen.

"Fuck it," he said over his shoulder. "Let's eat."

So we ate. It was a great potluck. Carrie had brought out her good china. We feasted on pumpkin bread, green salad, tabbouleh salad, pineapple-bean salad, couscous, ratatouille and fresh sliced peaches. As well as my own offering of vegetable-rice salad, which was graciously applauded. Someone, probably Mave, began a conversation on the topic of why writers write, and the mouths were off and running.

Travis insisted at length that the message was everything. "Why write if you don't have something to say?" he summed up through a mouthful of food.

Nan argued money was what counted. But even I could tell she didn't mean it. And five minutes later she was insisting that it was the writing high, the exhilaration she wrote for. And I knew what she meant. Designing gave me that same high. Donna said writing was a gift, a chance to make something truly beautiful. Russell offered the quiet opinion that the process of writing was an addiction, if a benign one. And Carrie told us that the total absorption in the writing process brought a blessed relief from everyday self-consciousness.

"It's an obsession," Vicky whispered then. She lowered her eyes. "It's an obsession that blocks out all other obsessions."

I took a quick look at her pinched face and was glad that writing could help her, whatever her other obsessions were. She had eaten nothing but green salad again, only eyeing the rest of the food as it made its way into everyone else's mouths.

"'So I have loitered my life away,'" quoted Mave softly as she laid down her plate. "'Reading books, looking at pictures, going to plays, hearing, thinking, writing on what pleased me best. I have only wanted one thing to make me happy, but wanting that have wanted everything.'" She sighed. "William Hazlitt," she added dreamily.

Everyone seemed to be smiling now. Even Vicky. The group felt like a real family. And not a dysfunctional one. I took a last bite of pumpkin bread and pondered the miracle. Had their shared love of writing brought this state about? Or maybe there was no miracle. Maybe this was how they always functioned when writing was on the agenda instead of murder. Then I remembered the previous Saturday.

"What's for dessert?" Travis asked into the contented silence.

All eyes turned to Russell.

"Carob-dipped strawberries," he answered. "No animal products. Completely vegan."

Vicky cleared away dishes while the rest of us indulged ourselves in the rich, ripe carob-coated strawberries.

Once we were finished, Vicky took her place again on the kitchen chair to read aloud. Her voice was shrill as she began, her tempo fast, so fast in fact that I lost a lot of the words at first.

"'The room smelled of oranges,'" was the first full sentence

I could make out clearly. "'Of oranges and cinnamon. The mirror-lined walls reflected our bodies. Doug's skin was the rich color of chocolate, mine cream with a hint of raspberry. I wanted to see everything, to taste everything. I began with his mouth, the flesh of his lips so sweet and soft, his tongue tasting of . . .'"

I had forgotten that Vicky wrote soft porn. I hoped my face didn't reflect my belated recognition.

"'I was hungry for him now,' she read on. "'Hungry, so hungry, it was hard to believe anything would fill the void. I took his swollen manhood into my mouth, wanting to taste it. He sighed . . .'"

It was soft porn all right. And three gustatory orgasms later, I was completely sure. I just hoped I wasn't blushing. Hearing this stuff read aloud in a room with a handful of other people, two of whom were male, was far more personal than reading it alone would have been. I was relieved when her characters finally finished up and called room service for a feast of pastries and fresh fruit. Then I wondered if the fresh fruit would figure in the sexual adventures of the next chapter. Or even the pastries. And pretty soon I was thinking about Wayne. God, I missed him.

"Well, Kate," said Mave, interrupting my thoughts. "Why don't you take a stab at this critiquing business. Tell Vicky here what you think."

"Me?" I squeaked.

"Good golly." Mave laughed. "You gotta critique if you're in a critique group. Take a ride on the hay wagon. Give it a whirl."

"Well," I said. I could feel my skin pinkening. "It was very, well, sexy."

I looked over at Vicky. There was a tentative smile on her pinched face. I went on.

"I think all the food metaphors were great," I told her. Her smile disappeared. Panicked, I began to talk faster. "You know how we love to eat," I said. "The love affair your character has with taste and food is almost as good as the one she has with Doug."

I watched the color drain from Vicky's face. Her skin turned the color of cream, cream *without* a touch of raspberry.

Then she covered her pale face with her hands and ran from the room.

- Fourteen -

"WHAT THE HELL did I say?" I asked the silent room.

"Vicky has some unresolved issues involving food," Carrie answered when no one else did. She kept her voice down and looked over her shoulder before going on. "I would guess that she didn't realize they were reflected so obviously in her work."

"An obsession?" I asked in a whisper, remembering Vicky using that word earlier in talking about writing. My stomach felt queasy as I made the connection.

Carrie nodded.

I sat there feeling as guilty as if I had tormented a child. A helpless, disabled child. A poor, helpless —

"Don't you worry, Kate," Mave said softly. "You didn't do anything wrong. Vicky's a few sandwiches shy a picnic where food is involved. But she'll get over it. She'll have herself a good cry and be back."

"Uh, thank you," I said, trying to figure out if the sandwiches Mave had mentioned were actually part of Vicky's food problem or merely metaphorical.

"She's probably in the kitchen stuffing her face right now," Nan stage-whispered. "Vicky's true unrequited love affair is with food. At least she satisfies it occasionally." She winked largely in the direction of the other couch. "Some of us just deny our needs altogether."

I would never have known where that wink was directed if I hadn't seen Joyce's skin redden. She glared at Nan for a moment. Then she took a long breath in through the nose and out through the mouth, and her face softened again.

Now what was that all about? Probably Joyce's celibacy, I answered myself. Damn. This group wasn't one big happy family anymore.

" 'Oh, for a life of sensations rather than of thoughts,' " Mave said. I knew it was another quotation when she added, "John Keats."

"Food can be incredibly sensual," Donna added. She leaned forward suddenly, rocking the sofa with her motion. "But women are trained into all this weirdness around food and body type and all that stuff. I took this class on it. See, it's no wonder we're ambivalent. You have to eat. And food's like a metaphor for emotional nurturing on top of everything else, but it makes you fat. And no one in this culture wants to be fat—"

"Vicky isn't fat," said Nan dismissively. She shook her head. "I don't know why she's so hung up on food. It's no big deal."

"It is a very serious issue to Vicky," Carrie corrected Nan. "No matter how petty it may seem to others."

"Well, if she has to be so hung up on food, she could at least use it more effectively in her writing," Nan argued. "Henry Miller wouldn't have done a scene like that. If he used food, he used it." She giggled, but then her face grew solemn. "Of course, I met Henry Miller as a child. He was a truly amazing man—"

"Food's pretty damn important if you can't have it," Travis said. He glared at no one in particular. "There are plenty of hungry people in this country, plenty of folks who don't get enough to eat. Did you know that a bunch of activists who feed the homeless in the parks were arrested last week? The cops told them they had to stop feeding these folks and they refused and the cops arrested them. If Jesus Christ came, the cops would arrest him!"

He threw out his arms, looking crucified again. Now I wondered if he was trying to look that way on purpose. With his long black hair he was a dead ringer for Christ. Except for the scowl.

"Oh please," Nan drawled. "Do we have to hear all this gloomy-doomy stuff again? We're not here to talk about world hunger—"

"What would you do if you couldn't get food?" Travis persisted. He jumped to his feet and began to pace. "The U.S. will go bankrupt soon if they can't pay the interest on the national debt. And then the banks will fail. And then you'll need a wheelbarrow of cash to buy a loaf of bread. How will you get food then? Huh?" He gesticulated wildly. "Huh?"

"Pizza parlors are always open," Nan said.

I wondered if she was joking. Out of the corner of my eye I saw Vicky sidling back into the living room, with Sinbad trailing behind her.

"How will you keep warm when the heating goes off?" Travis demanded. When Vicky sat down, Sinbad switched his allegiance to Travis, pacing along with him as he spoke. "No more Pacific Gas and Electric!" Travis shouted. Sinbad arched his back. "No more Versateller! Rioting, looting! The inner cities will be war zones. And how many of us know how to protect ourselves?"

"I've taken self-defense classes," Mave answered as if the question hadn't been rhetorical. She crossed her arms and glared, looking anything but frail. "No bully-boys are going to bully me. Not this old lady."

"Who needs self-defense?" said Nan languidly. "You should buy a gun. I did."

"Now, that really is dangerous," Russell put in quietly.

"Not for me," Nan replied. "I know how to use it. Squeeze gently. Aim for the upper torso or the head—"

"How can you talk that way?" Joyce demanded. Her skin was flushed all the way to her permed black hair. Her low voice shook with emotion. "When you're talking about aiming a gun, you're talking about real injury. You're talking about taking human life."

"That's the idea," Nan agreed with a flash of white teeth.

Russell's voice was less passionate than Joyce's, but his words were at least as frightening. "One study of residential gunshot deaths showed that a gun in the home is at least forty times more likely to kill its owner, a spouse, a friend or a child than to kill an intruder," he said dryly.

"Oh, that's so terrible," Joyce whispered. She laced her fingers together as if in prayer. "I would never own a gun."

"Well, you can't just meditate yourself out of a riot," Travis said from where he stood. "If the U.S.—"

"But that's exactly what we must do," Joyce argued. "Violence breeds more violence. How can we hope to live peacefully if our lives are agitated by anger and hate? By attachment and fear?" She twisted her laced fingers. "We have to cultivate peace in our minds. As a way of life."

Travis put up his hands, palms outward. "Okay, maybe *you* can meditate your way out of a riot," he conceded. He sat back down in the easy chair, smiling for a moment at Joyce. "If anyone can, you'd be the one."

But Joyce didn't return his smile. She opened her mouth as if to say something more, then closed it again.

"Perhaps we could return to Vicky's work," Carrie said quietly. I turned to her, startled for an instant. I had almost forgotten Vicky's work. Carrie turned to Vicky. "I thought the piece you read aloud today was very well written. My only suggestion would be that you use more sensory detail."

"Like what?" Vicky asked. I was glad to hear her speak

normally. I snuck a glance. Her face didn't particularly show her recent upset. It just looked pinched as usual.

"I would like to have a better idea what Doug looks like," Carrie answered. "Except for the color of his skin, I'm unclear. I'd like to know what his voice sounds like. What his skin feels like."

"Okay," said Vicky, nodding eagerly. "I get it." She wrote something down on a pad of paper.

"How about what he smells like too?" suggested Mave. "Smell can be an evocative detail."

It sounded to me as if Carrie and Mave had covered every sense but taste between them, but I didn't comment.

"A few words seemed to be overused," Russell added, his low voice even lower now. "You might look through each chapter for repeated words and try to use different ones."

Vicky nodded and wrote something else on her pad. She looked back up.

"It was incredibly sexy," Donna offered, twirling a dark curl of her hair around her finger. "Um, I like Doug a whole lot, but I'd kinda like to know more about his life. Like what makes him tick, you know?" Donna yanked her finger, but it was stuck in the curl she'd been twirling. "Is he from an abused childhood, maybe?" She yanked again.

I couldn't stand it.

"Untwirl it," I whispered.

"What?" she asked, turning to me with wide open eyes.

"Twirl your finger the other way and your hair might untangle," I explained, uncomfortably conscious of the faces watching us.

"Oh, thanks," she said. She circled her finger the other way and pulled it away from her tangled hair. "But it was really incredibly good writing. Really sensual."

Vicky smiled wanly. Donna might be a klutz, but she seemed to have a kind heart.

"Any other comments?" Carrie asked.

"Read Henry Miller," Nan said.

Vicky frowned, but wrote something on her pad anyway.

"Joyce?" Carrie prompted.

Joyce shook her head, blushing. I wondered if she felt unqualified to comment on the explicitly sexual material.

"Travis?" Carrie asked.

Travis blushed too. I didn't even try to figure out why he was blushing.

"Well, this has been oodles and oodles of fun," Nan announced, rising from her chair. She clasped her hands behind her back and stretched. "But it's time to call it an afternoon."

Then everyone began getting up. Nan stopped as she was walking past Travis and stared intently at the side of his head. I was pretty sure she was looking at his earring. I'd noticed it before. It's hard not to notice a metal skull with a flapping jaw hanging from someone's ear lobe.

"Oh, your earring's just too, too precious," Nan cooed. Her raised eyebrows adding a mocking note to her words. But Travis didn't seem to notice.

"Hey, thanks," he said. "My dad bought a pair from this cool craftswoman in Maryland named Judy Danish. Then we split up the pair—"

"You mean, you both wear earrings?" Nan demanded, the mocking note gone now from her face and her words.

"Oh yeah," Travis assured her. "My dad's cool."

Nan shook her head slowly, but departed the room without further comment. I took a minute to wonder about Travis's dad. Was he some kind of Hell's Angel? Probably an old hippie, I decided. And here I'd thought all the old hippies had given birth to accountants and dentists.

Joyce was the next to say goodbye. Russell offered her a ride home and she accepted, telling him she'd gather up her things and wait for him outside.

I was about to say goodbye too, when Travis descended on Carrie with an offer of protection.

"Let me stay here with you," he said. "I've got my stuff out in the car. You'll be safe—"

"I will be perfectly safe here by myself," Carrie interrupted him. She stood up, her back as straight as the back of the chair she'd been sitting in. "I am not some helpless woman who—"

"But Carrie," he protested, flinging his arms wide. "These guys have broken in here twice. I'm not gonna—"

"Travis, it is not up to you—"

I tried to catch her eye as they discussed the issue, Travis's tones ringing and Carrie's tone even. Should I stay to protect her from Travis's protection? But Carrie didn't see me. Her eyes were on Travis as they circled each other with identically outflung hands.

"Ain't love grand?" Mave whispered in my ear. I swiveled my head around and saw a grin on her weathered face. "I'm going to mosey on out of here myself, but you be sure to tell Carrie goodbye for me," she added, and left.

Donna tiptoed out after Mave, tripping over the edge of the carpet on the way. And then a new voice whispered in my ear.

"If you're concerned about getting home safely, I'd be glad to accompany you."

It was Russell Wu. Of course. He stood less than a foot away from me, motionless, his eyes hidden by his tinted glasses.

"No thank you," I croaked. My mouth had gone too dry to speak normally.

He nodded and withdrew without a fuss. That was more than I could say for Travis, who was still trying to talk Carrie into his protective custody.

"Come on, Carrie," he was insisting. "It's not sexist to wanna take care of you. I just . . ."

"Carrie, can I speak to you for a moment?" I cut in. But Carrie didn't seem to hear me. And Travis just kept on talking.

". . . think I oughta stay. What's so bad about . . ."

I took a step in Carrie's direction. A hand tapped my shoulder. I turned, trying to remember who the hell was left. And came face to gaunt face with Vicky Andros.

- Fifteen -

"I THINK I owe you an explanation," Vicky whispered. Her deep-set eyes stared out of her skeletal face with all the urgent appeal of a starving child. Then she blinked. "You see, I've got this food problem." Her words were louder now, tumbling out faster than the whisper could handle. "I'm such a fat pig. I can't seem to stop eating. I just eat and eat and eat—"

"But you're not fat," I interrupted, knowing even as I did that it was probably useless. I couldn't be the only one who had tried to give Vicky a reality check. "You need to eat. Everyone does—"

"I gobble up food," she cut in, her words tumbling out faster and shriller still. "Gobble and gobble, cramming it in like an animal. Like a pig. A fat pig. Potato chips and cakes. Frozen cheesecakes and raw cookie dough. I can't stop. And then I'm so ashamed, I throw up. But I can't seem to stop eating, I'm so hungry—"

"Vicky, you're thin," I tried again. "Try letting yourself eat something good for you."

"No!" she yelped, shaking her head. She grabbed a handful of her slacks at stomach level. "Look at this, I'm fat. A fat pig. It's so disgusting. If I could only stop, but I just can't. . . ."

I looked into her face as she went on and saw insanity there.

The hair went up on the back of my neck. Could she die from her beliefs? Could she literally starve to death in between her binges on cakes and cookie dough? Probably. And then another question popped into my mind. Was she crazy enough to kill someone other than herself?

"Vicky, you must get professional help," a voice said from behind me. I turned and saw Carrie. Her freckled brow was wrinkled with concern. "I will be happy to help you find a therapist if necessary, but you can't go on—"

"No, no," Vicky interrupted, shaking her head roughly. "I just have to learn to control myself. I just need to stop eating." Then she closed her eyes for a moment. "I'll be fine," she told us when she opened them again. She tugged the strap of her purse over her shoulder. "Thank you for your hospitality."

"Damn," I whispered once Vicky was gone.

"Damn, indeed," Carrie agreed soberly. "And she's getting worse."

"Is there anything we can do?" I asked.

"Mave's been trying to contact Vicky's family, but . . ." Carrie shrugged a perfect mime of hopelessness.

"Hey, where's Travis?" I asked. Somehow, he'd managed to disappear while I was listening to Vicky.

"Travis is in the kitchen, washing the dishes," Carrie told me. She smiled. "I convinced him that housework was the most significant action he could undertake to protect me."

I chuckled. I told myself I shouldn't worry so much about Carrie. She could take care of herself. But I had seen fear on her face earlier. I was sure of it.

"Carrie—" I began. But she was faster.

"I'm concerned about Nan as well," she told me.

"Nan?"

"Don't you remember, Kate? All that innuendo about seeing something across the street at Slade's house after the group last Saturday."

"The murderer?"

"I don't know," she said. Then her eyes went out of focus as she thought.

What was she thinking? Whatever it was, it was frightening her. As I watched, her shoulders jerked in a sudden shiver.

"Carrie," I said softly. "Why are you so afraid?"

"I had a dream last night," she answered slowly. "Actually, I believe I should call it a nightmare—"

"Hey, Carrie!" Travis shouted from the doorway. "Where do the glasses go?"

"Ye gods and goddesses," she protested, winking largely in my direction. "It's so hard to find good servants these days."

"Carrie!" Travis shouted again. And Carrie turned to join him in the kitchen.

I would have asked her more about her nightmare if I could have pried her away from Travis. But I couldn't seem to get her alone. He even followed her to the door when she showed me out.

"Don't worry unduly, Kate," she advised before she shut the door behind me.

All the way home, I tried to apply the word "unduly" to my worries. Was it undue to wonder if Carrie's new sweetie was a murderer? Was it excessive to wonder if Nan had seen Slade Skinner's murderer? Or to wonder if Vicky was going to starve herself to death? I still wasn't sure by the time I rolled into my driveway. But before I could come to any conclusions, I heard the sound of another car rolling in behind me.

In the instant it took me to swivel my head around, my heartbeat accelerated to maximum cruising speed. But it slowed again when I saw the familiar Volkswagen bug parked in back of my own Toyota.

My friend Barbara Chu jumped out of the bug, looking cool and elegant in a sleeveless aquamarine jumpsuit. I always thought Barbara could have been a model if she'd have been a foot or so taller. At five feet, she had to settle for being a beautiful, well-dressed electrician. Not that she minded. She liked the electricity. She even swore working with it energized her.

"Hey, kiddo!" she shouted enthusiastically. Maybe she'd been playing with a live cable. "How the hell are you?"

"How did you know when I was coming home?" I demanded as I climbed out of my car and looked into her all-too-scrutable Asian eyes.

"I'm psychic," she answered with a laugh. I continued to stare at her. I never had figured out if she was really psychic, but her perfect timing could be spooky sometimes.

"I'm hungry too," she added as she pulled me into a hug. "Want to go for an early dinner?"

"I ate a late lunch," I said slowly, wondering if I wanted to go with her anyway, if only to tell her about Carrie's critique group. I was surprised she hadn't picked up any vibrations about the murder yet. I stepped back from her embrace and smiled. She wasn't that psychic.

"Yes, I am," she said. I hated it when she did that. "Anyway, there's this great new cafe in San Ricardo. Tamales and Cajun sausage sandwiches to die for." I opened my mouth automatically to ask about vegetarian dishes. "Grilled baby eggplant marinated in lemon-herb vinaigrette, pasta primavera and tofu burgers," she finished off.

I told myself it still didn't prove she was psychic as we climbed into my Toyota.

Cafe Cachucha was a small but sunny cafe with tables covered by fabric swatches in all the colors of the rainbow. The menu was colorful too. Worrying had to work off calories, I decided, and ordered a small cachucha vegetable salad and an herbal iced tea. Barbara asked for the Cajun sausage sandwich with fries and a caffe latte. At least her order made me feel better about my own gluttony. Not gluttony, I corrected myself, thinking of Vicky. I wasn't a fat pig, only a woman with a good appetite.

Then Barbara and I got down to talking. Barbara and her reporter boyfriend, Felix, were living in separate, adjoining apartments now. It was really cool, she told me. I smiled and nodded. I was happy for her in spite of the fact that I could never figure out how Barbara put up with the man. Though maybe Felix could be human when he wasn't trying to get a story. Maybe. My mind drifted to Slade's murder. Felix would kill to get a piece of that story, I realized. I just hoped he never found out that I had seen Slade's dead body firsthand.

Barbara's happy flow of chatter stopped abruptly. I brought my eyes back up to look across the table at her. She was bent forward, her hands on the bright tablecloth, her eyes focused on mine.

"Are you involved in another murder?" she demanded.

"Felix told you," I accused.

"Nope."

"You read about it in the paper."

She shook her head, a smile tugging at her lips. Then she got the smile under control and ordered me to tell her about it.

I knew I'd never get her to tell me how she figured out I'd been involved in another murder. So I settled down into my chair and told her about it as ordered. All about it. I described each meeting and everything I could remember about the individual group members. The only thing I left out was my attempt at poetry. She didn't need to know about that.

"So this Slade Skinner guy was a real weenie," she summed up once I was finished.

I opened my mouth to object.

"I know, I know," she said, putting up a hand. "You think just because he was a good writer, he couldn't have been a weenie. Jeez-Louise, lots of good writers have been weenies—"

"All right, he was a weenie," I conceded. "But who do you think killed him?"

Barbara closed her eyes and sat very still for a few moments, looking like a feminized Buddha. I held my breath, beginning to hope for an answer.

"I don't know who killed him," she said finally. I let out my breath in a long sigh. That wasn't the kind of answer I had hoped for. "But I've got some ideas," she added.

Uh-oh. I should have never gotten her started. Psychic or not, Barbara had an imagination that wouldn't quit. And it ran in all directions simultaneously. If you tried to graph her thought processes, you'd need graph paper the size of California.

"What if one of the women in the group was one of his ex-wives incognito?" she proposed eagerly.

In spite of myself, their faces flashed in front of me. Nan, Vicky. Joyce. Donna. Maybe. But Carrie? Or Mave? It was getting ridiculous.

"But why would they keep it secret?" I asked. "Slade had to know his own wife—"

"You said he was insensitive."

"Not that insensitive—"

"Okay, so what if he married this woman in the sixties and fathered a kid? And the kid's all grown up now." Barbara stopped mid-sentence and hit the table in front of her, her eyes lighting up like LED's. "No, not his wife. His own kid. What if he doesn't know what his own kid looks like grown up. But the kid inherits, so she—or maybe it's he—infiltrates the group to murder him. Then once the deed is done, he goes back home. I like Travis for this one."

My stomach tightened. For Carrie's sake, I didn't want it to be Travis. But no, Travis wouldn't work anyway, I decided. Travis had talked about his father. They'd shared a pair of earrings after all.

"Herbal iced tea and caffe latte," came a voice from above. I nodded gratefully at the waitress as she handed us our drinks. I took a sip of tea.

"Or Russell," Barbara added.

I choked on my tea. Damn. As I coughed, I thought about it. I'd put Russell at thirty years of age or so. A little older than Travis. And Slade was about fifty. I supposed it was possible. Just like it was possible to win the state lottery. Possible but not likely. Anyway, Russell had talked about his parents too—

"Slade put Russell in his story," Barbara went on, obliterating my train of thought. "And Nan. Maybe he was blackmailing one of them. Maybe one of them really is a fugitive from the law. So he says, I'll put you in my story if you don't pay up—"

"Slade didn't need money," I told her. "He was rich. If anyone was blackmailing anyone, it would have been the other way around."

"That's right," she agreed. Her eyes turned thoughtful.

"Forget I said it," I told her. "If someone was blackmailing Slade, why would they kill him?"

"They hated him?"

The hair went up on my arms. Someone must have hated Slade to beat him to death like that. At least temporarily. You don't do something like that calmly and rationally.

"But who?" Barbara asked.

"Maybe one of the women," I thought aloud. "Remember, Slade was a lecher."

Our food arrived as Barbara thought that motive over.

"Vicky's nuts," she said, biting into her Cajun sausage sandwich. "Maybe he did something to her that pushed her over the edge," she mumbled through her mouthful.

"But what?"

"Maybe he taunted her about her food problem. Or maybe he

tempted her with food. Or maybe"—Barbara stopped for
another bite—"maybe he told her she was fat."

That was an awful thought. I picked up my fork. The salad
looked good, glistening with bits of marinated vegetables. But
it was hard to eat while considering Vicky Andros. I could just
picture her hungry eyes on my food.

"And then there's the woman who's celibate, Joyce," Barbara went on. "Maybe Slade raped her."

I shook my head. "I don't think he was the rapist kind.
Insensitive, but not a rapist—"

"I've got it!" Barbara shouted. I looked around at the other
tables, but no one except me seemed startled by the shout. "It's
Donna's family. See, Slade seduces Donna. Donna tells her
family. They send out a hit man—"

"With a dumbbell?" I objected.

"Okay, how about Carrie?" Barbara asked. She stared across
the table at me.

"Well," I said uncomfortably. I shifted in my chair. "Slade
did tempt her with the possibility that he'd recommend her to
his agent, but I don't think Carrie's possible. She's just not like
that—"

"Of course she isn't," Barbara agreed suddenly. "I've met
Carrie, remember? She's not murderer material."

I ate a forkful of salad, relieved by Barbara's assessment of
Carrie, whatever its reason. The vegetables were tangy with
lemon. And there was a barbecue flavor to them too.

"Listen, Kate," Barbara said after I had taken another bite.
"If Slade was hitting on the women all the time, they must have
been used to it. So whoever killed him must have been
someone new to the group. Someone who hadn't had to deal
with him before—"

"I was the only new member that day," I interrupted.

"Oh," she said and went silent. But not for long.

"Maybe someone was protecting someone else's honor," she

started a moment later. "Like Mave. You said she was a lesbian. Maybe she decided to teach Slade a thing or two. Or Travis—he sounds hotheaded enough. Or Russell. Don't discount him because he's Asian. Asian-Americans can be just as violent as anyone else."

Just what I needed to hear. I pictured Russell's still face in my mind and shivered.

"Don't worry, Kate," Barbara assured me. She reached across the table to give my hand a squeeze. "I don't see any danger for you in the immediate future. And I've looked."

I never know what to think when she says those things. Was she really able to see into the future? There was no way I could tell. So I just said "thanks," and left it at that.

But Barbara had changed her tune anyway by the time we'd finished our meal—not to mention umpteen more murder theories—and returned to my house.

"Don't go looking for trouble," she warned me, her eyes glued to mine after we had hugged goodbye in the driveway. "This isn't a game. It might be dangerous."

I clenched my teeth. *I* knew it was dangerous. *She* was the one with all the goofy theories.

"I know that, Kate," she said, answering my thought seriously. "Just . . . just take care."

And exactly how was I supposed to do that? I wondered as she got into the Volkswagen. But before I had the chance to answer my own question, Barbara rolled down her window and stuck her head out.

"Don't be so shy about your poetry," she ordered with a grin. "I'll bet it's great."

All right, so maybe she really is psychic.

I stomped into my house and got back to work.

It was a good four hours later by the time I remembered that I'd never picked up my mail that day. I made my way out to the mailbox in the darkness, scuffing my shoes in the gravel as I went, enjoying the cool night air. And then I heard a car start up.

I took a step past the front fence as the car whooshed by, nearly unrecognizable in the dark.

Nearly, but not quite. I could still make out its shape, a shape very much like a Honda Civic. And even in the moonlight, I could guess at its color.

I guessed beige.

– Sixteen –

OF COURSE, I knew that Russell Wu drove a beige Honda Civic. I wondered for a couple of pounding heartbeats if that was why I'd guessed beige. Had I just conjured up the color in my mind? Or had I really seen it?

I walked back to the house, keeping my steps regular and centered on the gravel, refusing to panic. Even if it had been Russell in the car, I told myself, there could be a lot of good reasons for his presence. Like what? Murder, mayhem, abduction?

By the time I stepped through my front door, I was beginning to burn with anger. I could feel the heat as it climbed from my neck into my face. I had to confront Russell. I didn't care anymore if I looked foolish. I—

The phone rang, exploding my unfinished resolution.

"Saturday night and you're all alone," a smooth male voice purred when I picked up the receiver. "What a shame."

I stopped breathing. Then the voice registered. It was my ex-husband's voice.

"What the hell do you want?" I demanded angrily.

"Kate!" he objected, the hurt in his voice bringing an unwanted vision of his puppy-dog eyes to my mind.

"Listen, Craig, I'm tired," I explained, then wondered why I thought I had to explain. I hardened my heart and my voice. "State your business," I told him.

After a shocked silence, Craig stated his business. He'd thought up a new gag-gift design for me.

"A tie with sneakers on it—'cause computer nerds wear sneakers, but every once in a while they have to wear a tie to make a presentation—so their tie should match their shoes." He paused. "Get it?"

I told him I got it.

"How about a combination pocket protector and tie tack? See, computer nerds—"

"Craig, thank you, but I don't need any more computer-nerd gift ideas," I interrupted him. "Good night."

"Kate, I love you," he whispered before I could hang up.

Damn. He had finally said it. And I knew he wasn't kidding. My chest tightened. I took a long, painful breath before speaking.

"Craig, sometimes I like you. But I don't love you anymore," I told him as gently and clearly as I could. "I love Wayne. Wayne and I are going to be married."

There was a much longer silence than before.

"Oh boy, do I get to be a flower girl?" Craig asked finally, his voice a shrill falsetto.

I knew this was my cue to laugh, to pretend that our whole conversation was just kidding around. So I forced a laugh. It was hard because of the way my chest hurt, but I pushed it on out anyway.

And finally, we hung up. I thought about Wayne, then, counting the days until he'd be home again. And trying my best not to imagine how Craig felt. I tried all night long.

I climbed out of bed on Sunday morning tired and cranky but still determined to get some work done on the Jest Gifts backlog. I'd put in a couple of hours when the doorbell rang.

I snuck over to the window to peer out. Who would my visitor be this time? Russell Wu, the Mafia brothers, or my ex-husband? I wasn't sure who would be worse. But it wasn't any of them. It was Carrie.

I didn't even wait for her to tell me why she was there. I just got my purse from the pinball machine and walked to the front door.

"Who do you want to visit today?" I asked once I'd opened up.

"Donna," she answered instantly. Then she grinned.

Donna had a large house in the hills of San Ricardo with a big green yard that looked like a toy shop had blown up and landed there in pieces. There were swings and slides and brightly colored barrels to crawl through glittering in the sunlight, along with all modes of rolling things including a bunch of phosphorescent tricycles and an assortment of roller blades.

Inside, the house was filled with macrame, soft sculpture and more toys. Children's art work hung on the walls next to art posters. And then there were the animals. I counted at least four cats, two mice and probably twenty brightly colored fish in a large aquarium, plus a few more goldfish in a smaller aquarium. And two children: Dacia, age eight, who wore earrings and a silk headband to match her dress, and six-year-old Dustin, who wore a polo shirt with a lizard on it.

"I'm into cobras and anacondas," Dustin told us, "but Mom only lets us have fish and mice and stupid cats—"

"The cats are not stupid!" Dacia shouted. "They're a lot smarter than you are!" One of the cats took a moment to glance approvingly over its shoulder before returning its gaze to the contents of the smaller aquarium.

"Well, you're stupid too!" Dustin shot back. "Really, really stupid. And gorpy too."

"Mom!" Dacia yelled.

She didn't really have to yell. Donna was only a couple of feet away. So were Carrie and I, unfortunately.

"Remember what I told you two yesterday?" Donna asked, smiling as she knelt down in front of her children.

Neither child responded.

"Be like Mahatma Gandhi," she said, refreshing their little memories.

Dacia crossed her arms emphatically. Dustin stuck his fingers in his ears.

"Have you both been meditating on cooperation?" Donna persisted, still smiling.

The two children sighed identical sighs and marched out of the room. At least they were unified in their disgust, if not actively cooperating. Maybe Donna's method of dispute resolution wasn't so silly after all.

"So Donna," I said a little too loudly. My ears were still ringing from Dacia's shout. "Who introduced you to the critique group?"

"Um, Nan did," she replied, peering into my eyes, her own honey-colored eyes round with question. But she didn't ask why I was interested. Instead, she asked if Carrie and I would like to sit down.

"Certainly," Carrie answered and Donna began pulling plush toys and chunks of brightly colored plastic off the nearest couch. Finally we all sat down, Carrie and I on the couch, Donna across from us in an easy chair. All without mishap. Donna didn't seem so awkward in her own habitat. Maybe it was her clothes. She was wearing jeans and a tie-dyed T-shirt today. No floor-length skirts or vests conspired to impede her progress.

"Perhaps you could tell us more about meeting Nan," Carrie suggested once we were all seated.

"Nan and I took this creative writing class together, um, five or six years ago," she told us. "It was incredibly liberating, all that energy just flowing and flowing, trauma being transformed into beauty. And after that, Nan and I really bonded. We went to lunch, oh, maybe once or twice a year. And then I told her I was beginning my book and she invited me to come to the group. I was like, really, really honored that she would ask, you know?" Donna tilted her head.

I nodded encouragingly.

"Nan even dated my brother Freddy for a while—"

"Mom!" someone screamed nearby.

Donna jumped out of her seat and sprinted into the next room, grazing her shoulder on the edge of the doorway on the way. So much for grace in her own habitat. She was back within minutes, smiling and rubbing her shoulder with one hand, a long shiny plastic saber in her other hand.

"Aren't little kids just wonderful?" she breathed as she sat back down. She dropped the saber onto a pile of toys by her chair. "They're such extraordinarily complex little beings. So full of life, and well, intelligence. But a different kind of intelligence. And integrity."

"Yeah, intelligence and integrity," I agreed as enthusiastically as I could. I wasn't about to ask her about the saber. I just hoped it wasn't sharp enough to do any real harm. "So what happened between your brother and Nan?"

"Um, you mean Freddy?"

I nodded, assuming Donna only had one brother who had dated Nan.

"Oh, they stopped dating. The energies just weren't right for them, I guess. Freddy is really incredibly traumatized by his childhood." She lowered her voice a little before going on. "Wounded, you know? He's in business with my father. All that dirty money." She shook her head. "Sometimes I think Freddy's integrity is really, well, impaired."

"Donna," Carrie said. Her hands were folded but I could still see her thumb wiggling. "I want to ask you one more time if

you believe your father had anything to do with Slade
Skinner's death—"

"No," Donna interrupted calmly. "My dad said he didn't
have anything to do with it and I believe him. See, there's a
way my dad denies stuff for the record but you really know he
did it. He looks you in the eye, but there's like nothing there.
And then there's the way he says 'no' when he means it. Where
he waves his arms around and yells. And he told me 'no' that
way. In fact, he's agreed to let me do my book." She clapped
her hands together. "I'm so happy."

"He doesn't mind?" I asked in disbelief.

"Not anymore, he doesn't," she assured me. "We had an
incredibly good talk last night and we came to an agreement.
I'm going to use, well, a pen name."

"So how come Nan and Donna 'bonded'?" I asked Carrie in
her car fifteen minutes later. That relationship just didn't make
any sense to me.

"Donna and her family are wealthy," Carrie answered as she
snapped on her seat belt.

"Money or status," I murmured, remembering now that
Carrie had told me these were Nan's prerequisites for friendship.

Not that Donna's relationship to Nan really mattered. Her
relationship to Slade was what mattered. And she didn't seem
to have a more definite relationship to him than she had to
anyone else. I had even asked her if she and Slade had ever
been lovers. She just giggled at that one, and then started in on
a rambling explanation about the "incredible kind of integrity"
that would qualify a man to be her lover. In short, Slade hadn't
qualified.

"What the hell are we doing anyway?" I asked Carrie aloud.
"Are we really investigating Slade's murder by seeing all these
people? They're not telling us anything—"

"Not yet," Carrie interrupted. "Or perhaps they have told us significant facts and we haven't noticed yet."

"But Carrie, we've talked to everyone—"

"Not everyone," Carrie corrected me. "We haven't visited Travis or Vicky individually yet. We may learn something by speaking to each of them privately that we would be unable to elicit in the group setting."

Ugh. My stomach spasmed. I didn't really want to talk to Vicky privately. Or Travis, for that matter.

"Kate, we are accomplishing more than you think," Carrie went on. She turned her serious face in my direction. "We are learning more about the connections between the members of the critique group with every single person we interview. We are learning how they perceive each other, how they perceived Slade." She turned back to stare out the windshield as she turned the key in the ignition. "And perhaps more importantly, we are stirring the pot. Quite possibly, someone will react soon."

"Maybe someone is already reacting," I muttered, thinking of Russell Wu.

"I hope so," said Carrie as she turned the steering wheel. "I sincerely hope so."

Carrie was quiet on the drive to Travis's apartment. This visit had to be hard for her, with its implication that Travis was yet another murder suspect to be interviewed by both of us. Not just a man in love with her.

"Hey, Carrie!" Travis greeted her enthusiastically at his door, a smile lighting up his gypsy's face. Then he saw me and the smile disappeared. "Hey, Kate," he said with an inverse proportion of enthusiasm.

Travis's apartment was just as jumbled as Donna's house, though there were no toys or animals evident. Unless you counted the video games that were in pieces all over the living room waiting to be fixed. Or the animals that were on the posters, innocent bunnies being tortured to test cosmetics and innocent calves being tortured for the sake of veal. The rest of the jumble was made up of books, tools, magazines and clothing.

But it wasn't bad for a young man's apartment. I couldn't see anything actually rotting, and nothing smelled terrible. In fact, the room smelled rather pleasantly of incense, fried onions and male pheromones. Carrie was apparently temporarily immune to the allure of Travis's fragrance, though.

"We have some questions for you," she told Travis with a frown.

He frowned back at her. Their eyes locked. They might as well have been making love. I felt just as excluded, though maybe not as embarrassed.

"Could we sit down somewhere?" I broke in after a few more moments.

Travis looked at me as if I had just now landed on the planet.

"Hey, sure," he said after a beat. "How about the kitchen? Would that be cool?"

The kitchen was neater than I expected. And I could see where the onion smell was coming from. A massive wok filled with onions and vegetables sat on top of the stove with an industrial-sized rice cooker on the counter next to it, full and steaming. Travis was obviously ready for a snack. It was getting close to lunch time. My stomach churned hopefully. But Travis didn't offer to share as we all sat down at the wooden table.

"Kate would like to know how you first became a member of the critique group," Carrie said without further introduction.

Travis looked at me for confirmation. I moved my head up and down ponderously, resisting the urge to kick Carrie under the table. Why was she blaming the question on me?

"I rented a room at Mave's house a few years ago," he told us after a moment of thought that drew his dark brows together over his big brown eyes. "And we kept in touch. Mave is one cool old woman. A real activist. Man, she was part of the gay and lesbian rights movement before there was a movement! You should see her scrapbooks. Anyway, she was interested when I told her my idea for the survivalist manual. And she thought the group could help me get the word out better. So she asked me to come to a meeting."

"How about Joyce? You introduced her to the group, didn't you?" Carrie led him on. He didn't resist.

"Yeah, I know her from Operation Soup Pot. I volunteer there." He sat straighter in his chair, his features animated. "But Joyce is the one that made Operation Soup Pot really happen. She was a cook at this restaurant, see, and she noticed all the leftover soup going to waste. So she started taking it to a local homeless shelter. And then she got other restaurants involved. She saved all this food that would have gone into the garbage. And gave it to the homeless and the elderly and the dying." Then he frowned. "People think no one is hungry in the United States, but there are plenty of hungry people. All you have to do is look—"

"So you invited her to join the critique group?" Carrie said, shepherding him back on the path.

"Yeah, see the Operation always needs money. Most of us are volunteers, but there are a few paid, full-time folks. And then there's the rent and all. So I came up with this idea for a cookbook and the board of directors loved it. They wanted Joyce to do it, but she was afraid she couldn't write it, so I told her to come to the group."

Carrie nodded somberly.

"So, what's the deal, Carrie?" Travis demanded. "Do you really think someone from the group killed Slade?"

Carrie just frowned at him. And then their eyes locked again.

"Did you invite anyone else to the group?" I asked loudly. I could almost hear the pop when they broke eye contact.

"Oh, just Vicky," Travis mumbled. "I found out she was writing, uh . . ."

His face turned deep mauve.

"Pornography," I supplied helpfully.

"Right," he said, still blushing. I felt a nip of affection for Travis. There was a certain kind of innocence in his embarrassment that contrasted well with his handsome face. I just hoped that innocence stretched to acts of violence.

"Where did you meet Vicky?" Carrie asked.

"Oh," he mumbled. "At a meeting."

"What kind of meeting?"

Travis looked down at the floor in silence. Suddenly, he didn't look innocent to me anymore.

"Travis," Carrie said, her voice deep with command. "Tell us where you met Vicky. It may be important."

"I can't," he replied and crossed his arms.

When he raised his big brown eyes again, they were scowling.

– Seventeen –

"TRAVIS," CARRIE GROWLED. There was a real note of menace in her deep-throated growl. And in her frowning face too, her brows sharply angled together in a shape that might have been drawn by a cartoonist to represent anger.

But I could have told her that no amount of auditory or visible menace would do any good. Travis sat there scowling just as deeply, his arms crossed over his chest. He was going to be as stubborn as Carrie herself. Was it pure obstinacy that kept him from telling us where he'd met Vicky? Or did he have something to hide?

My mind explored the possibilities as the two glared at each other. Did the secret of where Travis and Vicky met have anything to do with Slade's murder? Try as I did, I couldn't come up with anything that made sense of that theory. Maybe a meeting of a revolutionary society dedicated to killing established writers? No. I shook my head to clear it. And found that I *could* imagine Travis and Vicky meeting in some kind of kinky sexual context, something that he was now unwilling to admit in his new role as suitor to Carrie. But I have a dirty mind. So did Travis apparently.

"Nothing sexual," he muttered, his skin coloring again. "Vicky's kinda strange, you know?"

Carrie's face relaxed a little.

"Listen," I said to Travis, feeling as if I were mediating a game of Twenty Questions. "Does where you met Vicky have anything to do with Slade's murder?"

Travis thought for a moment, then shook his head.

"Fine," Carrie said brusquely, rising from her chair. "If you find that you have anything you *can* share regarding Slade's murder, please call me."

Travis got up too. "Carrie?" he said. His voice had taken on a pleading tone. He wasn't scowling anymore. "None of this has anything to do with us, you know."

"I hope not," Carrie answered seriously.

"Well, it doesn't," he persisted, throwing his arms out in frustration.

She looked into his eyes. He returned her gaze and his arms drifted back down. Their eyes were locked together once more.

"Okay, Travis," she concluded after a few more heavy breaths. She jerked her head back, breaking eye contact. "I find you innocent of bad intent until proven guilty."

She smiled as she said it, but I had a feeling she wasn't joking.

When we got back to her car, I asked if she was serious.

"Yes," she said shortly as she pulled away from the curb.

"Carrie, talk to me," I ordered.

She sighed heavily.

"You're afraid Travis killed Slade," I said for her.

She whipped her head around to look at me. "Am I that obvious?"

"More than that obvious," I said with a smile, trying to lighten the tone. Trying not to worry about Carrie's eyes being on me instead of the road.

Despite the direction of her gaze, I don't think Carrie even noticed my smile before she turned her head back toward the windshield.

"Why do you think it's Travis?" I asked softly.

"I don't actually believe he murdered Slade," Carrie corrected me. But her voice didn't have much spirit. "I just don't know for certain that he didn't. And Kate, I have to know for certain. That's the only way our relationship will work, if it works at all."

"All right." I tried again. "Why don't you know for certain that Travis *didn't* kill Slade?"

She sighed again, but then spoke. "Travis was extremely hostile to Slade. You were present when the two men interacted. You saw how they were, like dogs sniffing and growling to protect their territories. And Slade was very patronizing in his critique of Travis's work. Very hurtful. And Travis is so young. He saw how Slade kept trying to date me. And he's so . . . so . . ."

"Hotheaded," I offered.

"Perhaps," Carrie agreed reluctantly. "Though I think 'excitable' might be a better description. In any case, I don't believe Travis is actually capable of violence."

"But . . ." I prompted. I seemed to hear the word in her tone.

"But . . . I had a dream Friday night," Carrie answered, her voice low and trembling.

I glanced at her face again and saw the fear there I had seen the day before, widening her eyes. A shiver prickled the hair on my neck. I didn't want to see that look on Carrie's face.

"It was actually a nightmare," she went on. "In the nightmare, Travis held a sword. It was dripping with blood. And then I looked down and saw Cyril's dead body. Travis had killed Cyril, Kate—"

"But he hadn't killed Slade?"

"No. He had killed my husband, though. It was frightening, to say the least."

"Carrie," I said slowly, thinking as I spoke. "Did you ever

wonder if the dream might be about your own feelings toward Cyril? He was your husband and you loved him. But he died, died of cancer." I talked a little faster, surer now of my interpretation. "And here you are, all this time later, almost in love with another man. I know you. You think if you love Travis you're killing Cyril, at least killing the part of him that lives in your memory—" I stopped short. "I'm sorry. It doesn't matter what I think the dream was about. I'm not a therapist—"

"I believe your interpretation might be correct, though," she said, interrupting my apology. But there was something wrong with her voice. It sounded too thick.

I turned my head just long enough to glimpse the tears running down her dark, freckled cheeks, then swiveled it back quickly. Sympathy squeezed my chest.

"It's all right to love Travis," I whispered, hoping I hadn't said too much already. "It's even all right to let go of Cyril—"

"As long as Travis isn't a murderer," Carrie finished for me, her voice husky but stronger.

And he might very well be a murderer, I answered her silently. All those country and western songs about looking for a heartbreak started playing in my mind.

"You see, Kate," Carrie continued, "that's why I feel so strongly that I need to identify Slade Skinner's murderer. If I am to have any kind of life at all with Travis, I must know who the murderer is."

Damn. What if we couldn't find out?

Carrie didn't say any more as we rolled along down the highway, but my mind was speeding, prodded by Carrie's need to know who had killed Slade. She deserved that much. At least that much. But what relevant facts had we uncovered about the group members? Donna's family was Family. That seemed relevant. Travis wasn't telling us where he met Vicky. Russell might or might not be following me. Joyce was a saint in the making. Nan was not. And Nan had been Slade's lover. Mave had known Travis a long time. Vicky was crazy or close to it. And Carrie had very badly wanted to be represented by Slade's agent.

I glanced over at her as she took the Shoreline turnoff. Her profile was stern. And distant. Had she fought with Slade before I arrived on the scene? Had she— No, I told myself, Carrie had not murdered Slade Skinner. I was sure of that even if I wasn't sure of much else.

There had to be something more we could do to find out who killed Slade. Maybe check into everyone's past. But how to do that? There was one thing I *could* do, I realized, finish reading Slade's manuscript. Maybe there was a clue there. Maybe—

It was then that I noticed we had passed the junction without turning. We weren't heading for my house, we were heading into downtown Mill Valley.

"Where are we going?" I asked Carrie.

"Vicky's," she said without turning her head.

Vicky's. Of course. My stomach churned in rebellion, but the rest of me kept quiet.

The apartment that Vicky lived in was neat to the point of sterility. There was very little to obscure the view of the spotless white walls and gray carpeting of the living room. One couch, one TV and one lone Georgia O'Keeffe print on the wall comprised its bare-bones furnishings.

"We were concerned about you," Carrie told Vicky once we were standing inside.

Vicky shrugged her thin shoulders, looking even more waiflike than usual in her oversized T-shirt and baggy pants. I wasn't sure what her shrug meant.

"You must learn to eat regularly," Carrie continued.

"I really know that," Vicky said. Those words should have been reassuring, but they were spoken in a voice too shrill to sound reasonable. "I just get wound up every once in a while and say crazy things. Just ignore me."

"Have you eaten today?" I asked, really concerned now.

"Yeah," she answered briefly, turning her head to look away from me as she wrapped her arms around herself and hugged. Was she lying?

I shot Carrie a glance. She gave me a tiny shrug. At least I knew what Carrie's shrug meant. It meant the eating issue was hopeless. It was time to move on.

"Travis tells us he introduced you to the critique group," Carrie said, her voice low and quiet. I recognized the tone as the one she had used on difficult patients over twenty years ago. Maybe she had practiced on difficult judges in the intervening years. She still did it well.

Vicky nodded, then shrugged again. But at least she had turned her head back in our direction now.

"Where did you and Travis meet?" Carrie asked gently.

"N.A.," Vicky answered.

"N.A.?"

"Narcotics Anonymous," Vicky expanded.

So that's why Travis wouldn't tell, I thought. Anonymity. He took the concept seriously. I found myself liking him a little better for his honorable intentions. But then another possibility came to mind. What if he hadn't told us about N.A. because he wanted to hide a narcotics problem from Carrie?

"I go to N.A. instead of O.A.," Vicky continued, her voice taking on speed. "I've really got an eating problem, so I should go to Overeaters Anonymous, but I hate those meetings. There're fat people there, awful fat people. It's so disgusting. They're such pigs . . ."

Vicky was off and running. It was at least ten more minutes before Carrie could ask her anything else. And all Vicky had to say when asked about other group members was that Travis was "kinda strange." That made two of them.

Carrie asked her how she felt about Slade Skinner, and got
another shrug of Vicky's skinny shoulders in reply. That was
the answer to the next three or four questions as well. Vicky's
attention seemed limited to subjects having to do with food and
disgusting fat people. Finally Carrie gave up and said goodbye.
I was just as glad when we left the apartment. Vicky's
obsession gave me the shivers. And I was tired of standing.
Vicky never had asked us to sit down.

"Did you know Travis had a narcotics problem?" I asked
Carrie once we were back in her Accord.

"I knew he went to N.A.," she answered. "He used to have
a drug problem. He goes to the meetings so he won't slip
back." I felt my tense muscles relax. Travis was an honorable
man. I just hoped he wasn't a murderer.

We drove back to the junction, but Carrie turned the wheel
in the direction of the highway instead of my house when we
got there.

"Wait a minute!" I protested, my muscles tensing all over
again. I was sick of interviewing group members. "Where are
we going now?"

"My house," Carrie answered with a flash of white teeth.
"I'll cook you lunch."

As it turned out, she had already cooked most of the lunch
ahead of time, a pasta salad with more of her garlicky
marinated capers, beans, onions, olives and mushrooms. Along
with onion-herb bread baked that day. And fresh fruit compote
for dessert.

"I thought a reward would be appropriate," Carrie explained
as she spooned out the last of the fruit compote. Basta was
sitting comfortably on my feet by then. Sinbad was curled up
on Carrie's lap. The black cat gave out little pneumatic hisses
each time Carrie shifted in her chair.

"And you knew I'd need a reward before we even got
started," I accused. Then I took another bite of the compote. It

was as good as the rest of the meal, flavored perfectly with maple, lemon and ginger. Carrie cooked as well as she practiced law, I thought contentedly. The only thing she did better was to manipulate her friends.

"Carrie," I said after I swallowed. "I still have no idea who killed Slade Skinner."

"I know you don't," she replied, her last word dissolving into a long sigh.

And with that sigh, Travis came to mind. Travis, young, passionate and apparently in love with Carrie. And Cyril as he lay dying, skeletal and distant. My full stomach twinged. Was that guilt or indigestion? Whatever it was, Carrie deserved a chance at a life with a man who wasn't guilty of murder. That much I was sure of.

"Tell me more about Slade," I ordered. Unless Slade really was the victim of random violence, the trigger for his death must have been something he did or said. Or something he was.

"Slade was an obnoxious man but not an evil one, I think," Carrie said, straightening in her chair. Sinbad hissed. "I imagine him as a child, one of the kids the other kids don't like. Observing the others, seeing their weaknesses and faults. I believe that was the source of his writing skill, this ability to observe. Unfortunately, this ability seemed to stop short with his personal involvement. Maybe his desires short-circuited it."

I ate another spoonful of compote as I listened.

"I would guess that he lived on inherited wealth for some years. This gave him the freedom to write. But I wonder if it didn't also damage him in some way. He never had to work, never had to depend on himself. He could buy whatever he wanted. And he couldn't trust people to like him for himself." She looked across the table at me. "Does that sound foolish? To believe that wealth somehow damaged him?"

"No," I said. Easy money often did do damage. "I'm just surprised he had the self-discipline to write."

"Ah, but his writing was what gave his life meaning." She raised her spoon and shook it as she made her point. "There wasn't anything else in his life. He hardly knew his family. He had no real friends. No religious beliefs. His writing was everything."

"Did he ever write anything but thrillers?" I asked.

Carrie smiled softly, her eyes going out of focus. "Oh, he wrote song lyrics too."

"What kind of lyrics?"

"Perhaps I was wrong when I stated that Slade had no religious beliefs," she prefaced. "He believed profoundly in self-actualization, to the extent of writing lyrics that paid tribute to the process."

"Like what?" I asked.

"I cannot tell you specifically, but I believe one of his songs went something like . . ." Her voice lifted. "'All of my love, all of my love for me.'" Then she put a hand over her face and chuckled into it.

"Oh, I get it," I said. "Stuff like, 'I will follow me . . . wherever I will go.'"

Carrie really laughed then. So did I. Then she started singing again. "Loving me was better than any love I've ever had before!" Sinbad jerked his head up and jumped off Carrie's lap with a great show of disgust.

"I never knew love like this until I looked in the mirror and saw my face," I chimed in.

After five or six more improvisations, we were pounding the table as we laughed. Even Basta stirred with that noise. Then suddenly, I remembered the man we were making fun of was dead. No more lyrics. No more self-actualization.

Carrie must have remembered at just the same time. She leaned back and the crinkles of laughter around her eyes flattened into a mask of sobriety.

We sat quietly for a few moments, Basta snuffling around to

get comfortable on my feet again. And then a new thought drifted into my head.

"You know what we haven't asked?" I said, breaking the silence.

"What?"

"Where was everybody when Slade was killed?" My pulse quickened. "Maybe Travis—"

"Had an alibi?" Carrie cut in. "I had hoped so. But Travis, like everyone else, went home after the meeting. None of the group members has anyone that can vouch for their whereabouts after the meeting and before we found Slade's . . . Slade's corpse. Except for Donna. She says she was with her children."

"You asked about alibis already."

She nodded. "When I called everyone about the emergency group meeting. It was the first thing I asked."

"Oh," I said, feeling my excitement ebb away into a pool of self-reproach. Why hadn't I thought of alibis before?

"Shall we discuss the suspects?" Carrie asked gently, forgiveness for any lapse on my part implicit in her tone.

"Russell Wu," I answered after a moment. I stuck out a finger. "One, I think he's still following me." I stuck out another. "Two, he lifts weights. Three, Slade wrote a character like him into his manuscript."

"Wait a minute," Carrie ordered, holding up her hand. She trotted out of the room and when she came back and sat down she had a yellow legal pad and a pencil. She shoved the dishes out of her way, set the pad on the table and wrote something down, then said, "Go."

I went.

"Nan Millard. She has the requisite temperament—"

"A consummate bitch," Carrie summarized as she wrote.

I thought about it, nodded and went on. "Nan was closer than the others to Slade. His lover in fact. Who knows what promises he made her? And which ones he broke? And he put a version of her in his manuscript too.

"Joyce," I said when Carrie had finished her notes on Nan. "She may be a saint, but she's a celibate saint. And Slade kept making passes at her."

Carrie lifted an eyebrow but kept on writing.

"And Donna," I went on. "Her family is organized crime. We know that now for sure, don't we?"

"I would feel safe in saying that we are ninety percent certain of that affiliation." Carrie shook her head. "Ye gods and goddesses, it's hard to believe that Donna is related to such thugs. She's a menses poet, for heaven's sake."

"A messy poet?" I asked.

- Eighteen -

"No, no," Carrie corrected me, shaking her pencil in counterpoint. "Not a messy poet. A menses poet, Kate, as in menstruation."

I must have still looked confused.

"Don't you remember Donna's recitation?" she asked. Then her voice went atonal. "'Red on white—my mother—my grandmother—blood ties—blood spilled,' et cetera, ad nauseam." She threw up her hands.

"But I thought that was Mafia poetry," I protested.

Carrie leaned back in her chair and exploded into laughter.

"Do you say these things to cheer me up?" she asked once she could speak again.

"Of course," I lied. What the hell. I felt like an idiot, but at least Carrie was having a good time.

"So what else do you imagine Donna is guilty of besides bad poetry?" she asked, still smiling.

"Well . . ." I hesitated to put forth Barbara's theory. I had already said my quota of foolish things for the afternoon.

"What is it, Kate?" Carrie asked, her smile gone abruptly.

"What if Donna slept with Slade?"

Carrie frowned. "I don't believe she ever did, but what would be the significance of such an act in any case?"

"What if she told her father and then her father thought she'd been dishonored?"

"And in response, he sent out a hit man?" Carrie's eyebrows went up. "You've been watching too many old movies. This is California. Nobody cares about honor. At least I don't think so . . ." Her words faltered and then stopped. She bent over her yellow legal pad and scribbled.

"Do you think the police are taking Donna's family seriously?" I asked.

"I would guess so. You heard what Russell said. The police are aware of the family's connections and considering them in regard to this crime." She shook her head abruptly. "But Donna's family doesn't fit the scenario in any case. Remember, Slade said he was meeting someone from the group at five o'clock. He did not say he was meeting the family of someone in the group."

"All right," I conceded. "How about Vicky?"

"Vicky seems to be suffering from a severe eating disorder. She's obsessed with food and out of touch with reality." Carrie sighed deeply. "But I can't for the life of me see how her obsession translates into murder."

"Me neither," I said glumly. "Though she acts like a bomb waiting to go off." I thought for a moment. "Maybe Slade triggered her rage somehow. What if he told her his agent was interested in her writing, just like he told you? And then, what if it turned out he was just stringing her along?"

"Vicky is obsessed with food to the exclusion of all other serious interests," Carrie pointed out. "I find it hard to believe that she would be concerned enough about her writing career to kill for it. I, on the other hand, am concerned to the point of desperation not only in having my writing published but in making enough money to finance my early retirement from the practice of law." I winced, wishing I hadn't brought the subject up. I didn't want to hear Carrie say any of this.

"But even if I were willing to kill to further my career," she went on, "there is still a gaping hole in the theory." She paused and stared at me across the table, her molasses-brown eyes as cool as her voice.

"Which is . . ." I prompted quietly. My pulse wasn't quiet though. It had climbed into my ears, pounding all the way.

"Which is . . . that killing Slade would *not* have furthered my career. Any possibility that he could engineer my representation by Hildegarde Tucker died when he did." She kept her eyes on mine as she finished. "The same is true for Vicky Andros."

"I don't think you killed Slade," I stated for the record. I knew we weren't just talking about Vicky.

Carrie let out a long breath. "Thank you, Kate," she whispered. "I wouldn't blame you if you did suspect me."

I let out my own breath and my pulse settled gently back into my veins.

"So who's left?" I asked briskly.

Carrie looked down at her legal pad.

"We've already discussed Travis," she answered just as briskly. I was glad to hear she considered him discussed. I didn't want to travel over that mine field again. "Which leaves Mave Quentin." She looked back up. "Any ideas?"

"He argued with her over her claim to have met what's-her-name, the sculptor."

"Phoebe Mitchell," Carrie filled in. "And she was a painter."

"Slade and Mave knew each other a long time. They might have had a private feud going that you never heard about."

Carrie opened her mouth as if she were going to argue with me, but then just closed it again and wrote a few more words on her pad.

"Well, that's motives," I said, just to pretend we had accomplished something. "If no one has an alibi, everyone has opportunity. How about means?"

"I would imagine anyone can swing a dumbbell given enough adrenaline," Carrie said quietly.

"So what do we have?"

Carrie looked back over her notes and then pronounced the verdict. "Zip."

"Zero?"

"Nothing."

"Nada."

"Shall I get a thesaurus for more synonyms?" she asked finally.

I shook my head miserably, thinking of her and Travis, then leaned back in my chair. My feet must have moved as I did. Basta snuffled and shifted his weight. I withdrew my right foot and rested it on top of him. The foot was asleep, and I was tired of the missionary position anyway.

"Is there some other approach we should be taking?" Carrie asked just as feeling began prickling back into my newly released foot. Her voice sounded uncharacteristically subdued.

I didn't say anything aloud as I thought about talking to Barbara's boyfriend, Felix the pit bull reporter. He did occasionally give out good information as well as take it. But I dreaded the pain of the process. My chest tightened just imagining him yelling and wheedling until he'd sucked me dry of information. Talking to Felix was like having a date with a vampire. Except that Felix wasn't as attractive as vampires are supposed to be.

"We don't know much about the backgrounds of the group members," I said finally. That was a safe statement.

"Do you think their backgrounds could be relevant?"

I shrugged, but even as I did, I was thinking. "Maybe someone has a police record for assault. Maybe someone went to college with Slade. Maybe someone . . . Jeez, I don't know."

"So how do we find out about people's backgrounds?" Carrie asked slowly.

"I could talk to a reporter I know," I offered without enthusiasm. I tried to breathe some air into my tight chest.

"But?" Carrie said.

"But he's . . . he's . . . obnoxious, hideous, grotesque—"

"Maybe I should get the thesaurus after all," Carrie said, chuckling. "Is he worse than old Mrs. Stuckey at the hospital?"

Old Mrs. Stuckey was a patient who had delighted in leaving open jars of Vaseline in the other patients' nightstands, the nightstands we stuck our hands into to clean out every morning. And sometimes it wasn't just Vaseline. But still.

"Felix is worse," I concluded, then looked across the table to share a laugh with Carrie. But Carrie wasn't laughing anymore. She wasn't even smiling.

"Perhaps I'm wrong," she murmured. She threw her arms out in a gesture that reminded me of Travis. "It is certainly possible that Slade's murder had nothing to do with the critique group. Maybe it was an interrupted burglary after all."

"Maybe," I agreed cautiously. I pulled my left foot out from under Basta and shoved my right foot back into the gap. Basta didn't object. He must have been as asleep as my left foot. "Slade knew other people too, people who weren't in the group. His ex-wives and kids just for starters. Maybe we could find out more about these guys."

"How?"

Ugh, we were back to Felix. Or we could talk to the police. Or hire a private detective. Or talk to Russell Wu. I would have bet he knew a lot more than he was saying.

"I believe I'm ready to give up," Carrie announced quietly.

It took a second for her words to sink in. When they did, my heart gave a little skip of relief. But then I saw the sadness in her eyes.

"Let's not give up completely," I offered. "Let's just think about it for a couple of days and then talk again."

And that's how we left it. Carrie drove me home, gave me a hug and another "Thank you, Kate," that made me feel even guiltier about abandoning our investigation. And finally, I was back at my desk doing Jest Gifts paperwork.

By the time I got to my sales tax form a few hours later, I realized that I didn't want to give up on our investigation. I wanted to know who had killed Slade Skinner. And not only for Carrie's sake.

By the time I had finished filling out the tax form, I was ready to resume reading *Cool Fallout*. It was getting late. And the manuscript might contain a clue. Even if it didn't, I wanted to know what happened next. I picked up the manuscript from the bedroom, where I'd left it, and carried it into the kitchen.

C.C. appeared magically the moment my foot touched the kitchen linoleum, yowling for food. I fed her as fast as I could and cut a couple of slices of jalapeño soy cheese to eat with my rice crackers. I wasn't all that hungry for dinner after lunch with Carrie. Then I spread Slade Skinner's manuscript out on the table as if it were the real feast.

I skimmed the last chapter I'd read, jumping back to the sixties, remembering Jack Randolph, the charismatic leader of Brightstar and his lover, Patty Novak. Was Patty really Nan in disguise? Absolutely, I decided, and not even that well disguised. And Warren Lee quietly forging passports in the background was unmistakably Russell Wu. I couldn't spot any living counterparts for the other characters, though: ex-Catholic Kathy Banks who panics and shoots the sheriff, or Peter Dahlgren, the wheeler-dealer who leaves Brightstar in tears. But after a while, I forgot I was even searching for clues as Slade took me through the collapse of Brightstar and back home into the nineties.

I was in Peter Dahlgren's office as he answered the phone.

He was a banker now, wheeling and dealing from his leather executive's chair. But someone's been calling him, someone who wants his services. Someone who wants the services of all the previous members of Brightstar.

Who is it? Peter Dahlgren doesn't know. And it isn't for the want of trying. He has two private investigators trying to track the caller. I watched as he answered the phone. The caller asks how long Peter thinks he could keep his job if his past with Brightstar were revealed. Peter's upper lip begins to sweat. But even as he listens in fear, he feels a reluctant surge of admiration for the skill with which his caller has researched and leveraged his former life. He has already decided that he will do what the caller asks if he can't find out who it is.

Jack Randolph doesn't feel any admiration, though. He doesn't feel much of anything anymore but sick. He is dying, dying of AIDS. He remembers the days at Brightstar as the best days of his life. He conveniently forgets how he abandoned ship at the end. Cash is his price. His family fortune was gone years ago. He needs cash to die in comfort.

Cash is Patty Novak's price too. She's a real estate agent in the Caribbean now. She's making money but she can always use more. A lot more.

Kathy Banks is the only one who won't give in. She's a Catholic nun now, devout in her faith. She'll go public if she has to. She's already confessed her sins to God. She's ready to confess to the world. And of all of them, she's the one who should be the most afraid. She was the one who shot the sheriff.

Peter Dahlgren knows how each of the former Brightstar members is reacting. Though his detectives haven't traced the caller, they have found Kathy Banks, Jack Randolph and Patty Novak for him. He has talked to them all by phone, for the first time in decades. It makes him feel strangely excited, stimulated in a way he hasn't felt in years.

The only one Peter's detectives haven't been able to track

down is Warren Lee. And that worries Peter, because Warren should have been the easiest. Peter had once seen Warren himself in the intervening years, almost five years ago. Warren had been a museum curator then, as quiet as ever. Was Warren Lee in hiding? Dead? Or maybe he was behind the whole scheme.

Peter couldn't decide. But if Warren was behind the scheme, whatever it was (so far, no one had filled him in on what the Brightstar alumni were supposed to do), Peter had to hand it to him. He'd done a good job. A quiet, meticulous job.

Was it Warren? I repeated the question as I turned the page. And if it was Warren, did that mean that it was Russell Wu? And if so, just what was it that Russell/Warren had been planning? Was there a current living counterpart to the scheme in *Cool Fallout*?

The phone rang. Damn. I still had two hundred of the six hundred manuscript pages to go. I stood up and approached the phone reluctantly, listening as the answering machine picked up the call.

"Just called to say I missed you, Kate," the low, rough voice said. Reluctance turned to excitement. "Hope you're out enjoying—"

I grabbed the phone and shouted, "I'm really here!" into the receiver. Wayne. I settled into my comfy chair as if I were settling into his muscular arms. "Damn, it's good to hear from you," I told him.

Two hours of conversation later, I had forgotten about *Cool Fallout*, forgotten about Brightstar. I'd even forgotten about murder. All I could think of was Wayne as I burrowed into my lonely side of the bed. Funny how just talking to him, hearing his rough-gentle voice, could leave me this aroused. Funny how just thinking of his unhandsome face and handsome body made it all the worse. And remembering the texture of his skin— Not funny at all, I told myself, and then thought again of Carrie and Travis. We'll find out, I promised Carrie sleepily and wrapped my arms around Wayne's pillow. It would have to do.

Carrie didn't call me Monday morning. If she had, things might have turned out differently. Judy called me from the Jest Gifts warehouse instead.

"Jean's geeky brother is here again," she whispered. "The mush-for-brains won't listen when I ask him to leave. Now he's going on about how Jean's parents wouldn't be getting a divorce if all their kids were good Christians. Hell's bells, Jean's just as good a Christian as him any day. And I told him so. But he just goes on and on. And Jean's just crying and crying. And I dunno—"

"I'll be there as fast as I can," I told her and hung up.

It was a long way from my house in Mill Valley to the Jest Gifts warehouse in Oakland. I tried to limit my trips there to once a week, but it would be at least two this week. As I pulled onto the Richmond Bridge, I began to wonder how far my role as business owner would take me. I'd played therapist to my employees, played mother, even played marriage counselor, but I'd never had to play bouncer before.

I glanced in my rearview mirror and pulled over a lane. A beige Honda a few car lengths behind me pulled over too. My heart thumped. I told myself it was just a coincidence, that I was getting paranoid about beige Hondas. Still I couldn't resist switching back to my original lane just to see what happened. I flicked on my blinker and turned the wheel. The Honda followed suit within seconds. Damn. My heart thumped even louder.

Was that Russell Wu? I wasn't close enough to see an actual face in the rearview mirror. But I could imagine him staring silently in my direction all too well. Russell Wu/Warren Lee, the fictional and real blended in my mind. I slowed down. The Honda slowed down. The thumping of my heart speeded up.

No more fear, I ordered myself. I signaled and steered all the way over to the emergency lane, then carefully slowed to a stop, remembering that I was at the very edge of the bridge. The water was a long way down.

But the Honda was a lot closer. It had pulled into the emergency lane only a few yards behind me.

- Nineteen -

I THREW MY door open and sprinted the distance between the two cars on a wave of adrenaline.

Russell Wu was climbing out of his Honda when I got there. As he straightened up, I saw a hint of concern in the curve of his eyebrows over the top of his tinted glasses.

"Are you okay?" he asked gently.

"What?" I demanded. Somehow I had expected something more sinister out of his mouth.

"I saw you stop," he explained in a low, classical music announcer's voice. "I was afraid something had happened to you."

"Oh." The adrenaline was wearing off. The sweat I had worked up during the sprint was cooling in the breeze from the water below. But I was still shaking. I tried to muster up some righteous indignation. He was making his presence sound reasonable, for God's sake!

"Were you following me?" I demanded hotly.

Russell nodded slowly, keeping his gaze steady in my direction. Not that I could actually see his eyeballs. His tinted lenses were more opaque than ever out here on the bridge. He might have been crossing his eyes at me for all I knew. But in spite of the tinted glasses, he didn't look even remotely guilty at that moment.

I tried again. "Why are you following me?"

"Just making sure you're all right," he answered quietly.

"Are you trying to tell me you're following me to protect me?"

Russell nodded again. This time he smiled ever so tentatively, his eyebrows curving over the top of his glasses again. He not only looked innocent then, he looked downright vulnerable. He certainly didn't look like a murderer to me anymore.

"I don't need any protection," I told him. I had meant my voice to be firm, but it softened a little at the end when I saw his smile disappearing.

I didn't know what else to say, so I said "goodbye" and got back in my car and drove. I checked for Russell in my rearview mirror a few times as I finished my drive over the bridge, but I didn't see his Honda Civic. Maybe he was waiting to start his car again until I was far enough ahead not to feel threatened by his presence.

But why the hell had he been following me in the first place? He had never really answered that question, at least not to my satisfaction. And my own answers weren't any more satisfying than his had been. If he'd really been following me in order to protect me, why single me out from the others? Did he know something that he thought put me in particular danger? That was a spooky idea. Almost as spooky as imagining Russell as the murderer himself. But if Russell was the murderer, what did he gain by following me?

My stream of consciousness continued to swirl and eddy as I drove south on Highways 580, 980 and 880 to the Jest Gifts warehouse in Oakland. Driving there had become more complicated after the 1989 earthquake wiped out the old 880 Cypress structure. At least the drive gave me time to think. And to worry. And to watch for Russell Wu in my rearview mirror. I still hadn't caught sight of him by the time I pulled into the parking lot in back of the familiar row of ancient warehouses on Joslin Street.

I walked up to the door of the JEST GIFTS warehouse, opened it cautiously and peeked in, hoping that Jean's brother had left by now. Everything looked pretty much the same as usual. Boxes of gag gifts were stacked in metal shelving up to the twelve-foot ceilings. Workbenches were covered in piles of mailing boxes, stacks of forms and scattered gift items ranging from toothbrush earrings for the dentists to uh-huh ties for the psychotherapists.

But there were three people standing around the back workbench where there should have been two. Judy and Jean both had their arms crossed over their chests, and a tall red-haired man who just had to be Jean's brother was jabbing his finger in their direction. Jean was tall and red-haired too. And muscular. That's one of the reasons I had hired her for the warehouse work. She was good-natured as well, a good fit to work with short and stocky Judy Mulligan who drove most people, including myself, a little crazy with her constant conversation. But Jean seemed to enjoy working with Judy. She was a good listener.

Today, however, Jean looked like she had done a little too much listening. Her eyes were swollen and glistening.

The red-haired man turned in my direction as I walked in. Anger was evident on his florid face. I shut the door behind me. I had already let enough air-conditioned air escape.

"So who are you?" he demanded.

"My name's Kate Jasper," I replied evenly as I sized him up. He had to be at least six foot three. And it looked like muscles ran in the family, big muscles. "I own Jest Gifts. Who are you?"

"I'm Peter O'Donnell," he snapped back. "I'm talking to my sister here, so why don't you just—"

"Jean," I broke in, keeping my tone even. "Do you want your brother to leave now?"

She nodded so violently that a matched pair of leftover tears jumped from her cheeks.

"Mr. O'Donnell, you're trespassing," I said. "Please leave."

"Are you going to make me?" he snarled, pulling back his muscular shoulders. Then he added, "Are you saved?"

It took a moment to figure out what the last sentence meant. It didn't seem to match the first one. And then I remembered Judy saying he was a born-again Christian. I tried to convince myself that Christians were supposed to be nonviolent as he strode toward me, his hands clenched into fists. When he was a couple of yards away, I took a deep breath and centered myself in a tai-chi stance, feet rooted to the floor, arms raised slightly. Ready.

"Mr. O'Donnell," I said, keeping my voice low with an effort. "Either I'll make you leave or the police will. And I'll be happy to press assault charges if you so much as touch me. As well as charges for trespassing. It's your choice."

I watched as his legs came to an instant stop. His face grew redder, outshining his red hair now. And then suddenly, he unclenched his fists.

"I'll leave," he told me sullenly. He turned his gaze away from my face. "But only because Jesus himself tells me to."

I nodded. If Jesus was telling him to leave, that was fine with me. As long as he got out. I stepped away from the doorway carefully, keeping my body centered and my arms raised.

Peter O'Donnell took his time walking past me. He opened the door, glared once more over his shoulder, and finally, he closed the door behind him. He was gone.

My legs melted into quivering rubber. And then I heard an explosion from behind me. I jumped and turned at the same time. But the explosion was only the sound of Judy and Jean clapping their hands.

"Thank you, Kate!" Jean shouted, a grin on her tear-streaked face. "You were incredible. Peter isn't usually so crazy, but ever since he lost his job he's been on this religious trip. Actually, it seemed to help him at first, to calm him down. But then when my parents decided to get a divorce, he really flipped. He keeps accusing everyone in the family of being bad Christians, and saying that we'll all go to hell—"

"And Jean goes to church and everything," Judy broke in indignantly. "Hell's bells, what a wacko he is!"

"Judy asked him to leave, but he wouldn't listen—"

"And then I called you—"

They kept talking and interrupting each other for a few minutes while I sucked in air and tried to calm my beating heart. To Judy and Jean I was a hero. Kate Rambo. If only they knew how Rambo's legs were shaking. The only reason I'd stood up to Peter O'Donnell was that I was tired of being afraid. Afraid of Russell Wu. Afraid of whoever had murdered Slade Skinner. Afraid of crazy Christians—

"Will your brother bother you at home?" I asked, suddenly afraid for Jean too.

"No, he's scared of my husband. He won't bug me there."

I thought of Jean's husband, a man who probably weighed all of a hundred and forty pounds, and I smiled. Peter O'Donnell was just a bully. And one who scared easily. I only wished I'd known that earlier.

I spent the next couple of hours on Jest Gifts business. Earrings were still selling like hotcakes, Judy told me, and the manufacturer hadn't delivered the new order on time. And there weren't as many shark earrings in the boxes as there were on paper. And . . .

Back home after a long hot drive, I treated myself to a late lunch of cold canned chili and rice crackers. Then I put in a call to Carrie. I wanted to talk to her about Russell. But all I got was her answering machine, which made sense since I'd called her at home during working hours. I'd forgotten the time in my anxiety.

"This is Kate," I recited for the machine. "Just wanted to talk. Nothing important." Then I went back to my paperwork.

Carrie didn't return my call until Tuesday evening. I should have been glad. I'd done a lot of Jest Gifts work in the meantime. The piles on my desk were even a little smaller than usual. But I hadn't been able to rid my mind of Slade Skinner. Or Russell Wu. Apparently, Carrie had been mulling too.

"I believe we should visit Nan Millard as soon as possible," she told me, her voice deep and serious.

"Why?"

"I am beginning to wonder if Nan really did see someone or something at Slade's house on the day of his murder. She insinuated as much at the last meeting, although she retracted it later." Carrie paused for a moment. "I told you I didn't think Nan was of the right character to murder, but I wonder if she might not be capable of blackmail—"

"And blackmail is dangerous," I finished for her, feeling a sudden pang. Even Nan wouldn't be foolish enough to try to blackmail a murderer, would she?

"Blackmail is dangerous indeed," Carrie agreed. "Though I certainly have no evidence that Nan has planned or executed such an act. But blackmail or not, I need to know if she truly saw something. I hoped the two of us might convince her to speak."

"I'll pick you up in ten minutes," I said. And then, feeling a pang of a different kind, I added hopefully, "Maybe we can have dinner at The Bodhi-Tree afterwards."

Carrie was still dressed in her business suit when I got to her house. The navy blue didn't do much for her caffe latte and cinnamon complexion, but it did seem to give her short body a certain authority. I wouldn't argue with her while she was wearing that suit. Maybe Nan wouldn't either.

"Don't you think we should tell the Hutton police what Nan said about seeing something?" I asked as Carrie climbed in my Toyota. Somehow her blue suit had reminded me of the Hutton authorities.

"Nan didn't really say she saw anything. She merely implied it." Carrie frowned for a moment, looking even more formidable. "Why don't we attempt to elicit the information first ourselves," she suggested. "If Nan doesn't respond, we can inform Police Chief Gilbert then."

"All right," I agreed as I backed out of her driveway. I didn't particularly want to see the Hutton police again myself.

"Kate, did you notice the resemblance between Chief Gilbert and his two detectives?" Carrie asked a little further down the road.

The memory of the chief and the murder scene at Slade Skinner's house blossomed in my mind's eye. I gripped the steering wheel a little tighter and tried to remember the faces of the three men instead of Slade's mangled head.

"That's right," I said once my brain obliged. "They all looked like British aristocracy."

"Including the African-American," Carrie added.

"Must be a job requirement."

She laughed. "Perhaps it is in Hutton. I wouldn't be surprised."

"Hey, what happens in the end of *Cool Fallout*?" I asked. I didn't want to think about the Hutton police any longer.

"What do you mean?"

"I've gotten to the section where the mysterious someone is calling all the old commune members. You know, the banker, the real estate agent, the nun and the guy dying of AIDS. But I still have two hundred pages to go. Is Warren Lee behind it all?"

"You'll have to keep reading," Carrie said with a low chuckle. "The suspense is part of the enjoyment. I told you Slade Skinner was a good writer."

"But I don't have time," I insisted. "I want to know who's behind the scheme. Is it Moslem Fundamentalists?" I glanced over at Carrie quickly, hoping to catch the answer in her eyes.

But all I saw was a twinkle. "Why would you guess Moslem Fundamentalists?" Carrie asked.

"Everyone else loves to blame them for conspiracies. Why not Slade?"

"I'll tell you this much," Carrie gave in. "You're on the wrong track with the Moslems."

"Is it environmentalists, then?" I tried.

Carrie just chuckled again. That chuckle was beginning to sound sinister to me.

"CIA? KGB?"

"I hear the KGB is officially out of business these days," Carrie offered.

As far as I knew, I still hadn't guessed who was behind the scheme in *Cool Fallout* by the time we got to Nan's house. I pulled my keys from the ignition and turned to Carrie. Her eyes were crinkled in a smug, feline smile.

"You'll have more fun finding out for yourself," she told me as she opened her door.

I shrugged as I opened mine. I still had all of dinner and the ride back to ask questions. She was right. I would have more fun finding out for myself. But I was going to find out by pumping her.

It was a great diversion. I was smiling as I got out of the car. But then I looked out across the street and saw Slade's house. Its redwood façade looked so peaceful behind the trees, the embodiment of gracious living. The hair on the back of my neck rose in memory of the last time I'd been in that house.

How could I have forgotten, even for a moment, that the author of *Cool Fallout* was dead?

"Kate," Carrie said sharply. I turned and saw a look of concern on her face.

"I'm fine," I told her.

She nodded, then pointed to the BMW in front of Nan's house. The real estate agent was in.

We walked past Nan's car to her front door. I looked at Carrie. She straightened her shoulders. I did the same. Between the two of us, we just might be able to convince Nan to speak.

I rapped my knuckles hard on Nan's front door. The door shifted open with a muted creak. That was weird. A still shot of Slade's front door swinging wide open glanced across my mind. And with it a burst of nausea.

That was then, this is now, I told myself. I took a deep breath and pushed the door open a little further. Far enough to peek into Nan's tiny but tasteful living room. And then I saw Nan. She was sprawled against one of her perfectly matched vanilla-colored sofas.

– Twenty –

"WHAT IS IT?" Carrie demanded impatiently.

She pushed Nan's door open even wider, wide enough so she could see into the living room. Then I heard the sharp rasp of her indrawn breath.

I didn't blame Carrie for the sound. I don't know why I hadn't made it myself. Maybe because I wasn't breathing. Somehow, I didn't have the energy. Because Nan Millard was dead.

I couldn't even find the strength to pull my eyes away. Nan lay splayed against her beautifully upholstered sofa as if she'd been thrown there. There was a bloody hole in her chest. It didn't go well with her teal suit, not well at all. And the hole actually looked burnt around the edges. But it couldn't be burnt, I told myself. There was a gun a few feet away from her on the floor. Guns didn't burn, did they? I couldn't seem to think straight.

Carrie pushed past me and stepped into the room.

"No," I said. At least I tried to. But my voice wouldn't work.

I laid a restraining hand on Carrie's arm and took a long, painful breath.

"Don't go in." My words came out in a wheeze. "Don't touch anything. We've got to call the police."

Carrie turned to look at me, her eyes wide.

"My Lord," she whispered. Then she shook her head hard. When she stopped shaking it, her eyes had contracted to normal size again. That was good, I supposed. Wasn't it?

"Are you okay, Kate?" Carrie asked, her low voice shaking.

Was I okay? The room was shimmering with light. And something was buzzing in my ears. I had the feeling that I could float away from the doorway if I wanted, just float and float—

No, I probably wasn't okay, I decided. But I had to be. I took another breath. Then I tried Carrie's method and shook my head hard. So hard, I almost fell over. Damn, I was dizzy.

"Fine," I answered a few moments later. "I'm fine. Let's find a phone."

But I wasn't really fine. I was chilled, outside and in. I looked over at Carrie once we were safe inside my Toyota again and I couldn't stop my mind from wondering. Had she arranged for me to be with her when she found Nan's body? Was it possible?

Then I noticed the grayish cast of her skin. And the way she kept breathing in and out in convulsive bursts. And the way her hands were shaking. She was as frightened as I was. I couldn't believe she'd known Nan's body was going to be there. Her present shock was too real.

"Do you know where the police station is?" I asked her finally.

She shook her head, twisting her hands together.

We sat a little longer. I had my voice back, but my brain still wasn't working very well.

"Perhaps a pay phone," Carrie suggested.

"With a phone book," I agreed and started the car.

But after fifteen minutes of speeding up and down the tree-lined streets of Hutton I was convinced the city didn't have any pay phones. I didn't even see any businesses. I was about to give up, when I turned another corner and Carrie pointed.

I followed her finger. We had found the business district. I drove by a market, a flower shop and a cafe. And then finally, I saw a pay phone. Right next to the Hutton Police Department.

The lobby of Hutton's police station reminded me of a doctor's office. White walls, institutional linoleum and a glassed-in counter. The only difference was that the man behind the counter was wearing a uniform and a gun.

"We need to talk to Chief Gilbert," I announced and then caught my breath. We had sprinted up the stairs and through the door.

"Yes, ma'am?" he replied, raising his brows with an inter-rogatory emphasis that could have belonged to a butler.

"We are here to report a crime," Carrie specified from my side.

The man shot her a glance and opened his mouth.

"A murder." I spelled it out for him. "We found the body." That shut his mouth for a second.

"Stay where you are," he ordered and slid the glass window shut. I wondered if it was bulletproof glass.

Maybe I shouldn't have asked for Chief Gilbert. As we sat waiting for him on an uncomfortable Naugahyde couch, I realized the man behind the counter had probably called him in from home. And no one had asked us for any details, not even our names, so I assumed that nothing would happen until Gilbert arrived. And meanwhile, Nan . . . I shuddered, not even wanting to think about it.

Twenty minutes later, Gilbert came bustling through the lobby to usher us politely into his well-furnished office. Even then, comfortably seated on real leather, it took us more frustrating minutes to make him understand that we weren't there about Slade Skinner's murder but about Nan Millard's.

"Nan Millard." He pronounced the name judiciously after

Carrie twice repeated our claim to have found Nan dead. "Who is Nan Millard?"

"She lives—lived—across the street from Slade Skinner," Carrie told him.

"And she was a member of his critique group—"

"And she is dead—"

"Dead?" asked Chief Gilbert, furrowing his aristocratic brow. Finally, we had gotten through. "In Hutton?"

"She was shot in her home, inside Hutton city limits," I said impatiently. "And the gun's still there."

Gilbert's brow unwrinkled. "Ah, suicide," he said. "How very sad."

Then he left the room, coming back before he'd even shut the door, to ask for Nan's address. Luckily, Carrie had it in her purse.

After that, we heard a lot of bustling and commanding, even a little muted shouting from somewhere outside Gilbert's office. Then we were asked to wait in the lobby by the uniformed man we had spoken to before. It was at least an hour later before we saw Gilbert again. Carrie and I didn't talk much in that hour. The only thing I wanted to talk about was Nan's death. Had Nan really committed suicide? Somehow I doubted it. But being in a police station was enough to discourage me from asking Carrie what she thought.

I had closed my eyes in an attempt to visualize a calming garden scene—actually any calming scene would have been nice—when I heard the sound of a man's voice coming in through the lobby door. An angry man's voice. I popped my eyes open and saw Chief Gilbert bearing down on our Naugahyde couch. The two other lean and aristocratically featured men who had accompanied him on the day of Slade's death were trailing behind him, identically cowed looks on their black and white faces. Uh-oh.

"Why in hell were you two there?" Gilbert demanded without preamble.

"We thought Nan might know something about Slade's murder—" I began.

"Certain statements that Ms. Millard had made in the setting of our critique group seemed to indicate that she might have seen someone or something on the day that Slade Skinner was killed," Carrie finished for me.

It was a good thing she was a lawyer. I might have said the same thing in far fewer words. Not that Gilbert was happy with her explanation.

"Why in hell didn't you tell us if you thought this Millard woman knew something?" he shouted.

"You were set in your belief that Slade Skinner's death was the result of an interrupted burglary," Carrie snapped back. "And Nan's insinuation seemed directed at someone in the critique group."

Gilbert's face flushed. "Separate 'em," he ordered. "I'll take this one in my office." He pointed to Carrie. "Zuleger, you watch the other one. Make sure she doesn't leave."

But for all his bluster, Chief Gilbert didn't have Carrie in his office for long. It couldn't have been more than thirty minutes before she was escorted out and I was escorted in. The chief asked me what time we'd arrived at Nan's, what we'd touched, whose idea it had been to visit Nan, if Nan and Slade had been lovers, and a few more fairly easy questions, about Carrie and the other critique group members. Then he asked what Nan had said to make me believe she knew something about Slade's murder.

That was a hard one. Because I couldn't remember exactly. And I had spent a lot of my time in the lobby trying to remember just that.

"It was something about being able to see Slade's house across the street that day," I told him uneasily. "But then when she was challenged, she said she hadn't really seen anything."

Surprisingly, Gilbert didn't delve any further. Carrie had probably been more specific. He only had one more question for me. Well, actually two. Did I kill Slade Skinner? And did I kill Nan Millard?

"No," I answered emphatically to both questions.

I just hoped I sounded believable. Even when I was a child, I'd always managed to sound guilty in the process of denying things that I really hadn't done.

But Gilbert didn't clap me in handcuffs. He just blinked and stood up from his desk to deliver me to yet another uniformed officer who took my fingerprints. And finally, I was free to go.

I was sure of one thing as Carrie and I left the police station into the darkening evening. If Nan had seen something, she would never tell us what it was now.

"Kate, I'm sorry," Carrie said to me when we got to the Toyota.

"Sorry for what?" I asked, my heart pumping a little faster. I couldn't make out her features in the waning light.

"For getting you into this . . . this mess."

Then she put her arms around me and hugged. It felt good. I hugged back, releasing fear and anxiety as I did. Releasing suspicion. I could feel it flow from my tense body as belated tears flowed from my eyes. My friend Carrie was comforting me. And for a time, that was all that mattered.

"Do you think Nan saw the murderer and blackmailed him?" I asked once we were back in the car rolling toward Carrie's house.

"Him or her," Carrie corrected. "And yes, it does seem probable. Though there are other possibilities."

"Like?"

"Perhaps she was killed for the same unknown reason that Slade was killed."

"Like?"

"I just don't know," she sighed. "Slade and Nan had so many connections. They were lovers. They lived on the same street. They belonged to the same critique group. They were both extremely insensitive to others' needs. They were both published authors."

"Well, I'm pretty sure of one thing," I told her. "Nan Millard didn't commit suicide. Even Chief Gilbert figured that out."

"Gilbert and his two clones," Carrie muttered.

"Hey," I said, trying for a cheery note. "Maybe it's not a job requirement for the officers in Hutton to look like Gilbert. Maybe they're Gilbert's illegitimate children."

Carrie laughed then and told me what a good friend I was. I was glad she couldn't see me blushing in the dark, the good friend who had suspected her.

We spent an hour or so at Carrie's house tossing around murder theories unenthusiastically. Neither of us had much real energy for the exercise. And when Carrie started calling the Hutton Police department "Gilbert and Sullivan" and singing operetta, I couldn't seem to stop laughing. I made a quick diagnosis of communicable hysteria and left to drive home, still giggling uncontrollably.

I'd finally stopped laughing when I pulled into my driveway some time after ten. What I saw in my driveway would have stopped my laughter anyway. It was a vintage '57 Chevy. And I knew it was turquoise even though I couldn't see the color clearly in the dark. Because a turquoise vintage '57 Chevy was what Felix Byrne drove. Felix, my friend Barbara's boyfriend, the pit bull of newspaper reporting. As I watched, he jumped out of his car, a short and skinny cauldron of steaming journalistic fervor running to meet me. I rolled down my window as he got to the Toyota.

"Found another one, huh?" he greeted me. I knew there was a hurt look in his soulful eyes just like I knew the color of his car. He always started in with a hurt look. "And didn't bother to tell your old friend Felix?"

I thought about backing out of the driveway as fast as I could and going back to Carrie's, but Felix had my car door open in the instant it took me to think of escape.

I stepped from my car cautiously.

In the dim light I saw Felix's mustache twitch in what might have been a smile. I flinched.

"Guess where I've been?" he ordered.

"The Hutton Police Department," I answered. I didn't even try to dissemble. Felix knew. Felix always knew.

"I shoulda gotten hip when the poop came in on the first Hutton stiff," he started in softly. Then his voice picked up volume and speed. "I shoulda thought about my *pal* Kate. My compadre. Always finds the body but never calls her friend, her friend who's a crime reporter for Christ's sake! But noooo." He drew the word out like a cow mooing. "I have to have strangers enlighten me when she finds the second stiff. Holy moly, were you going to hold out on that one too? Huh, Kate? Were you just gonna—"

"How come you didn't come by when you heard about Slade Skinner?" I asked, truly curious. Felix never passed up an opportunity.

"My contact didn't mention your name when she told me about the first one," he said, a sulk slowing down the speed of his harangue. But not for long. "I shoulda known something was up when Wu asked about you—"

"Russell Wu?"

"Yeah, Russell Wu. Russell Wu of your friggin' critique group! The critique group you never told me about. The critique group that both Nan Millard and Sherman Francis Skinner were in—"

"Sherman Francis?"

"What are you, a friggin' parrot?" Felix demanded. I could

feel his glare in the dark. "Sherman Francis Skinner was the poor friggin' shlunk who bought it. Slade was just his pen name."

I smiled in spite of myself. Slade's real name was Sherman Francis. I couldn't wait to tell Carrie. Of course, it would have been more fun if Slade were still alive, I realized, and my smile fizzled.

"So why was Russell asking about me?" I said, getting back to the first point.

"I don't know," Felix answered softly. "Wu was down at the Hutton cop shop taking notes after this Skinner weenie got roasted. So, just being friendly, I talk Wu up a little, trying to find out what he knows. He just gives me this real spacey, looney-tunes smile, like there's nothing there behind those weird-ass specs of his, and then he asks if I know Kate Jasper. Out of the blue. I told him we were friends, like real compadres, and Wu asks if you've been involved in other murders—"

"But why does he want to know?" I interrupted. I could only listen to Felix's stream of consciousness for so long.

"I don't know why, but he was real friggin' interested, if you know what I mean. Of course, he hacks out these true-crime books. Maybe . . ." Felix paused.

"Maybe what?"

"Kate, you didn't off Skinner and Millard yourself, did you?"

"No, I didn't, God damn it!"

"Hey, don't get your hemorrhoids in a lather," Felix protested. I could see his hands flash up in the dark, as if to ward off blows. "You were the one who asked. So you tell me, what's the real poop?"

I didn't fight it. I stood out there in the driveway and told Felix all I knew. Well, a lot of what I knew, anyway. I didn't tell him about Carrie's feelings for Travis. Or about any of my own theories. Or . . . Actually, I just gave him the bare bones. And I didn't invite him into the house. I'd have just had to get him out again if I'd done that.

After I finished, Felix was silent for a few moments. Then he said, "So, Kate. Do you think this Wu character whacked them?"

"I don't know, Felix!" I said impatiently. Then I remembered my dealing-with-Felix mantra, *Felix could give information as well as suck it.* "So what does Chief Gilbert think?"

"Gilbert's a real moron, you know, a real potato-brain. He doesn't think a whole lot. Holy moly, he's still going with the interrupted burglary routine."

"You're kidding," I said encouragingly. "For both of them?"

"Right. A burglar with the same potato-brain that Gilbert has, trying to rob the house across the street this time. And if he can't fit that theory onto some poor shlunk with a rap sheet, he's got the enraged lover theory. Someone who's hot to trot with Skinner or Millard, or maybe both of them, offs the first one out of jealousy and then whacks the second out of spite."

"How about suicide?"

"Gilbert would give his left nut to lay that one on Millard, but corpses don't wipe the prints off their own guns after they've offed themselves. Though the piece was registered to Millard . . ."

As Felix went on, I remembered Nan talking about owning a gun for protection. I shivered. That gun had killed her.

". . . now the potato-brain's starting to look at the critique group members. Especially since you and your friend found the stiffs. About your friend—"

"Carrie isn't the murderer, Felix."

"Hey, did I say anything?" he demanded in his most injured voice. "I did background checks on everyone. Wanna hear what I found out?"

"Yes, Felix," I said, keeping my voice calm. "I would like to hear what you found out."

"First off, your friend Carrie is a widow—"

"Her husband died of cancer!"

"Holy Toledo, Kate! You're touchier than a rhino with PMS."

My brain got wrapped around the image of a rhinoceros with PMS. Did rhinos even have periods? I almost missed it when Felix went on.

". . . Russell Wu's a goody-two-shoes. No criminal charges ever filed against him. But he's one trippy dude. Friggin' weird. All that true-crime stuff." I resisted a remark about the pot calling the kettle black. "Travis Utrelli's been arrested a few times. But it's for all this weenie political protest bullshit. Now, Joyce Larson's a real strange one. Outside of managing the kitchen at Operation Soup Pot, the woman's friggin' invisible. No driver's license. No credit cards. The woman could have just landed from Mars, if you know what I mean—"

"Not everyone drives, Felix."

"Donna Palmer's clean too. No criminal record. Divorced, two kids."

"Anything about her family being Mafia?" I asked.

"Mafia?" Felix said in a voice that was thick with lust. I was glad it was dark. I was just sure there was drool dripping down his chin. "Her family are Mafia?"

"I'm not sure if they're actually Mafia," I backpedaled, getting more cautious now that I'd spilled the beans. "Donna just mentioned the possibility of a crime connection a few times."

I could almost hear Felix's brain whirring.

"How about Mave Quentin and Vicky Andros?" I asked, hoping to derail him.

"They're clean," he answered absently. I should have never mentioned the Mafia.

"How about Slade's family?" I tried. "Who inherits?"

"His kids," Felix answered, his voice still abstracted. "Kids are grown now. Two different mothers. Got plenty of money from Skinner already. Though Gilbert's giving them the once-over." He paused. "Hey, about this Palmer woman, if she's connected, maybe she's some kind of hit woman—"

I laughed before I could help myself, remembering Donna tripping over her own clothes. A clumsy hit woman. The idea was deliciously funny. Until I thought of her wielding a gun and then thought of Nan Millard again.

"Good night, Felix," I said, suddenly very tired. "I'm going to bed."

"Holy socks, Kate! I've just started."

That was what I was afraid of. Then I heard a car driving up nearby.

"That must be Wayne," I told him, inspired by the sound. I just hoped Felix didn't know Wayne was on vacation. Wayne was the only pest repellent that had any effect on Felix.

"Okay, okay," Felix said nervously. He believed me! "Wouldn't want to get under the big guy's skin."

And then he backed his vintage '57 Chevy out of my driveway.

It was only after Felix had gone that I thought about the car I'd heard drive up. I was pretty sure its engine had stopped. But I'd never heard anyone get out of that car. I walked out to the mailbox in the dark, scanning the street with my eyes. I spotted an unfamiliar car across the street, behind my neighbors' Volkswagen.

Only it wasn't that unfamiliar after all. It was a Honda Civic.

- Twenty-one -

HONDA CIVICS ARE pretty common cars, I told myself. The one across the street probably belonged one of my neighbors' friends. But what if it didn't?

I shook my head angrily, pulling an overtight tendon in my neck. Damn it, I was too tired to put up with this stuff. I wasn't willing to be afraid anymore. If Russell Wu wanted to watch me get my mail in the dark, that was fine with me.

I turned to my mailbox and fished out a pile of bills, solicitations and catalogs. Then I trotted into the house and locked both locks on the front door. I wasn't willing to be afraid, but I wasn't going to be stupid either.

Once the locks were on, I sat down in my comfy chair and focused my mind on Russell, carefully avoiding all thought of Nan Millard. Russell hadn't just been following my car, he'd asked Felix about me. Would he draw attention to himself that way if he was the murderer? If he planned to do me harm? And just what had I done to earn Russell's interest anyway?

It took a while to come up with an answer to that last question. But piece by piece, a reasonable theory burbled up out of my mind. Russell Wu wanted to write a true-crime story about the man or woman who had killed the two critique group members. I had a reputation, at least in Marin, for finding dead bodies and murderers. Ergo, Russell believed that if he followed me I might lead him to the murderer. Did that make sense?

C.C. yowled from behind me.

"You don't like the theory?" I asked, craning my neck to see her.

She yowled again and jumped up onto the arm of the chair.

"Everyone's a critic," I complained and ran my hand down her velvety back.

Minutes later, my eyes were beginning to close. Unfortunately, Nan's dead body seemed to be painted on my inner eyelids. Was it going to be that kind of night?

It was. I went to bed and spent the night pouring off sweat and dreaming of corpses. "A stiff," Felix cackled in my dreams. "Shall I give it a friggin' stiff critique?"

The next morning my head was aching and my stomach was queasy. An adrenaline hangover. I lay in bed a few more moments, staring out the skylights and wondering if it would feel any fairer to me if I were suffering from a champagne hangover.

The phone rang as I was drinking my third cup of herbal blackberry tea. I took the cup with me to answer the phone. Carrie was on the line. Of course.

"I've called another emergency meeting to be held this evening at my home," she told me. Her voice sounded a lot better than I felt. "Six o'clock, potluck. Would you be willing to attend?"

"Is everybody coming?" I asked.

"Yes. I've reached each of the group members with the exception of Russell. I have left a message on his answering machine, however. I'm sure he'll come."

"All you have to do is ask me to go," I told her, an unwanted whine slipping into my voice. "Where I go, Russell follows."

"Is he still following you?"

"Uh-huh. And asking questions too. He asked Felix about me—"

"Is Felix the repulsive reporter?" Carrie interrupted, a touch of eagerness flavoring her low voice.

"Yeah." I took a sip of tea. "He caught up with me last night."

"Poor Kate," Carrie said in what I was pretty sure was mock sympathy. Then her voice grew more serious. "Did he say anything interesting?"

I took another sip of tea before going on. "Felix said Chief Gilbert thinks we've had two interrupted burglaries. Or maybe a lovers' quarrel. Felix also said Gilbert was a moron and a potato-brain."

"Perhaps Felix isn't so repulsive after all." Carrie chuckled.

"God, Carrie. That just proves you haven't met the man."

"Did he tell you anything else?"

"Oh, you'll love this," I told her. "Slade's real name was Sherman Francis Skinner—"

Her laughter came hooting over the line. She did love it. But then she stopped laughing abruptly. Was she frowning now? Had she just remembered that Slade was dead?

"Listen," I said. "Back to Russell. I think he might be following me to get a story. But it's still spooky—"

"Kate, has it ever occurred to you that he might be following you in an attempt to woo you?" Carrie asked.

"To woo me?" I repeated back, struck more by the archaic language than by what she was saying. Or was it a joke, Russell Wu *wooing* me?

"Perhaps he is courting you in the best way he knows how," Carrie expanded. "By protecting you."

I stopped noticing Carrie's language.. Because the awful sense of what she was saying was becoming clearer.

"You mean he has a crush on me?" I squeaked.

"Precisely."

I could feel my face flood with color. I was just glad Carrie couldn't see it through the telephone. I had to do something about Russell. I had to tell him about Wayne. Because the terrible truth was that Russell Wu was not an unattractive man. I thought of his deep, soothing voice and the vulnerability of his face on the bridge. And felt immediately guilty and disloyal to Wayne. Damn. I wished Wayne were home—

"Kate?" Carrie probed.

"What?" I said impatiently.

"Will you attend the meeting tonight?"

"Of course," I told her, coming back to the present. And as I came back, a question occurred to me. "How'd you get everyone together on such short notice?"

"There aren't that many members left to call," Carrie answered softly.

We said goodbye on that note.

I walked into Carrie's house at six o'clock sharp with a dish of vegetarian stuffed grape leaves in my hands. No one but me would have to know that I'd bought them at the health food store on the way and transferred them into my own dish.

Basta howled, Sinbad yowled and Yipper yipped when I walked in, but without their usual enthusiasm. Carrie didn't even have to raise her voice to get them to stop. She just put a hand up and led me first to the kitchen to drop off the grape leaves and then into the living room, with the quiet animals following. Where I saw why the animals were tired of their guard duties. Even at six, almost everyone was there.

Mave and Joyce were seated together on one of the blue sofas. Donna and Vicky were sitting on the other one. And Travis was on his feet, pacing as he spoke.

". . . gotta figure out why Nan died," he was saying. "She could be a real bitch, but still . . ." He waved his hands around, out of words apparently.

"I can't help but wonder if her tetchy personality didn't have something to do with her death," Mave said. She wrinkled her wrinkled brow a little more, her eyes thoughtful behind her violet-rimmed glasses. "Go around acting like a donkey's behind and sure as shootin' you're gonna run into someone who doesn't appreciate it."

"Oh, you mean like karma," Donna breathed. She bent forward eagerly with a sudden lurch that almost pulled her off the couch. Vicky flinched next to her. "People don't always understand how extraordinarily complex our karma is. If you abuse your environment, your environment may abuse you."

"I like that," Mave said, slapping her thigh. "Mother Nature playing tit for tat."

"But—" Travis began.

Then the dogs and the cat started up again, and whatever he was going to say was lost in the cacophony.

I took the opportunity to sit down between Mave and Joyce. I wasn't sitting next to Donna this time.

"Howdy, Kate," Mave yelled over the animal sounds and then magically the sound stopped.

Russell came walking in with Carrie a few moments later. He nodded quietly in the direction of each sofa and then sat down on a wooden chair. I tried to look at him without looking at him. He didn't seem to be looking back. Then Travis started in again.

"Much as I didn't like Slade's writing, he did a pretty cool job on Nan's personality with what's-her-name . . ."

"Patty Novak, the real estate agent," I filled in for him.

"Yeah," he said. "Her. I'll bet Nan was just like that, you know, someone who was out for herself even in the sixties when people were cool."

"So you assume that everyone was actually into peace and love in the sixties?" Russell asked. The smooth sound of his voice almost erased the essential sarcasm of the question.

"Yeah," Travis said excitedly. "See—"

"You weren't even old enough to understand," Carrie said with affection. "Just a baby."

"I was born in 1961," Travis said. "I was almost grown by the end of the sixties. I went on peace marches with my parents."

"I should have guessed," Carrie said and rolled her eyes.

"Carrie!" Travis protested, his beautiful dark eyes round with hurt.

"How about you, Russell?" Mave threw in quickly. "When were you hatched?"

"Nineteen sixty-three," he answered. So Russell was younger than Travis. Somehow I'd thought he was older.

"I'm 1963 too!" Donna squealed. "Isn't that amazing? We must share the same Chinese astrological sign and everything."

Russell nodded unenthusiastically.

"Babies," Carrie said. "All babies. Now, Kate and I certainly weren't babies then."

"Excuse me," Joyce murmured, standing up next to me. "I have to go heat up the chili." Maybe she hadn't liked the sixties as much as the rest of us. She had to be nearly the same age as Carrie and I.

"Good golly, you're all just babes in arms to this old lady," Mave said, grinning at Carrie. "And I suppose your generation reckons you're the only ones who discovered sex, drugs and rock 'n' roll too."

Carrie just laughed.

"Got to hand it to Slade," Mave went on, her smile dimming. "He caught the feeling of the era in *Cool Fallout*. All that goofy hope and optimism, everyone and their dog thinking they were going to change the world. And then the loss of innocence—"

"But *Cool Fallout* wasn't even original," Travis broke in, his voice shrill with excitement. "It was the same damn plot as that movie, you know, the one a couple of years ago with Robert Redford."

"*Sneakers*?" offered Russell.

"Yeah, yeah," said Travis, shaking his hands above his head like a referee. "That's the one. A bunch of former antiestablishment guys from the sixties get called together later—"

"But it was just one guy in *Sneakers* who—" Russell began.

"But blackmailing Redford with his past crimes, that whole shtick, you know. The same plot."

"I believe Robert Redford was only guilty of computer hacking in *Sneakers*," Carrie pointed out. "Killing a policeman is certainly a far more serious crime."

At the mention of killing, all the fight seemed to go out of Travis. "Yeah," he said, flopping down in the easy chair. "I guess so."

"Well, I have incredibly good news!" Donna's happy voice burst into the ensuing silence. "At least I think it's good news." She frowned for a moment.

"What exactly is your news?" Carrie asked.

"Oh!" Donna looked up and smiled again. "Well, I already told you and Kate. My dad says that it's okay if I write my book now, as long as I use a pen name. I mean, we're really repairing the structure of our relationship. It's really exciting." Her smile faded. She stuck a finger in her crystal necklace and began twirling the beads around it. "But I'm still not sure . . ."

"Sure of what?" Carrie prompted.

"Well, is it really ethical, like with real integrity, to use a pen name? I've talked to my woman's support group, and my personal best group, and my living with the planet group, and I just don't get an answer. What do you guys think?"

"Sure, it's ethical, honey," Mave answered. I was glad we had a qualified ethicist in the group. "Considering how riled up your kin have been getting, it's probably more than ethical."

Donna nodded violently. Then she gave her necklace one last twist and it broke, spraying crystal beads onto the floor.

Carrie and Donna cleared up the beads, clanking heads once in the process. Then Carrie said it was time to eat.

We all served ourselves from the kitchen and came back with plates stacked high. Joyce had brought a spicy chili studded with raisins, corn and cashews. Mave brought home-made garlic bread; Donna, sesame broccoli. And Travis had whipped up a carrot-nut loaf with lemon sauce that actually tasted good. I just hoped he wasn't the murderer. He'd make a great house husband for Carrie. And then I could always visit at dinner time.

Of course, some of the plates were stacked higher than others. Travis's was towering with food. Vicky's held a fistful of her own salad and nothing else.

"Sure you don't want some garlic bread?" Mave asked her once we were all seated again. "Skinny critter like you could use a little meat on her bones—"

"I know what I look like!" Vicky snapped. "So don't pretend I'm not fat. Slade and Nan were always teasing me too and look what—"

Then she stopped short and went back to watching everyone else eat.

Nobody said much of anything for the rest of the meal. A few muted compliments were made about the food here and there. Travis liked my grape leaves. He snagged the last of them on his fourth trip to the kitchen. Then Russell brought out dessert.

"Black Forest cake," he announced. His gaze turned slowly toward me. Then his lips curved into an ever so slight, tentative smile. My heart contracted. "It's totally vegan. I found a vegan bakery in Berkeley."

I remembered what Carrie had said about Russell courting me the best way he knew how. Was vegan Black Forest cake part of that strategy? I looked into Russell's face, trying to see beyond the tinted glasses. I reminded myself that it wouldn't be polite to run screaming from the room. Anyway, the cake looked good.

It tasted good too, of chocolate, honey, cherries and tofu cream. And something that might have been cherry preserves. I took another bite and told myself that later I would do my best to discourage Russell gently, without hurting his feelings. I just wished I knew exactly how to do that. Carrie's voice broke into my thoughts.

". . . are meeting here this evening to see if we can better understand the murders of Slade Skinner and Nan Millard. Has anyone any information that could help us?"

She looked around the room slowly. No one answered.

"Any theories?" she prodded.

"Anger," Russell suggested quietly. "They were both difficult people."

My skin prickled, hearing that quiet suggestion. What would make Russell Wu angry? Rejection?

"Slade was a real creep," Travis added helpfully.

"Well, my dad wasn't the one who did it," Donna piped up. "I asked him and he said he wasn't."

For a moment, I waited for Nan to take her to task. Then I remembered with a jolt that Nan wasn't here anymore. How could I keep forgetting? Suddenly the Black Forest cake didn't look so good anymore. Or feel very good on top of the other food in my stomach.

"Nan might have seen whoever murdered Slade," Mave offered. I was glad someone else had come up with the idea. "Remember all that hoo-hah about looking across the street?"

"Nan was always doing that, making a big deal about nothing," argued Travis. "She just wanted to be the center of attention."

He might just be right about that, I realized. Could someone have killed Nan because they *thought* she saw something? Even though she hadn't?

Surprisingly, no one else offered any other theories. In fact, no one else had anything at all to say about the murders. Nothing, no matter how many different ways Carrie posed her questions. Though maybe it wasn't so surprising. Who wanted to air theories that reflected on the other members of the group? Theories that might get the theorist killed?

Carrie gave up after a few more tries, and everyone began getting up and talking about how late it was and how they had to work the next day. Another emergency meeting over. And no murderer to show for it.

I was washing silverware in Carrie's kitchen when Russell came in. I didn't hear him until he was right behind me.

"Kate," he began. "Would you—"

I whirled around, spraying soap bubbles.

Russell's mouth dropped open for a moment, then closed again and settled into a half smile.

"Stop following me!" I shouted. So much for the gentle approach.

First his smile disappeared; then he tilted the direction of his tinted glasses downward. I looked down too. And realized I was holding a soapy spoon out in front of me like a sword.

I lowered the spoon. And lowered my eyes.

"Listen, Russell," I began again. "I'm sure you're very well-intentioned, but you have to stop following me. I'm not sure exactly why you're following me, but if you're interested in a . . . a . . ." Somehow I couldn't spit out the word "relationship." Maybe I'd just skip to the Wayne part. "Anyway, I'm very happy with—"

"I thought I'd say goodbye now," a soft voice interrupted.

I turned and saw Joyce standing in the kitchen doorway, carrying a casserole dish.

"Would you like a ride home?" Russell asked, turning to her.

"No, no," she answered, shaking her head. She looked down at the dish in her hands, cheeks pinkening. "The bus will be fine."

But Russell quietly insisted, and they walked out of the kitchen together. Russell turned at the doorway to say goodbye and flashed a little smile at me. I guess I hadn't been too rough in my approach. Too bad. I'd try harder the next time. But at least he couldn't follow me around if he had Joyce in the car. Unless they did it in tandem.

I shook my head and went back to washing silverware.

I was right about Russell not following me this time. I looked in my rearview mirror all the way home and never saw his car once. I just hoped Joyce was okay.

Early the next evening I was wearing out my pencil on the Jest Gifts ledgers, hoping I had heard the last of the critique group murders, when Carrie called again. Carrie wasn't a quitter. I had to give her that. But she sure could be annoying, as persistently annoying as my own conscience.

"We can't just allow these murders to go unsolved, Kate," she insisted. "If we keep on asking questions, I'm certain the answers will come."

"But who the hell's left to answer our questions?" I protested. "We've already talked to each and every group member—"

"That was before Nan died."

"All right, all right," I said, giving in ungraciously. "Your car or mine?"

We took her car. I'd worked myself up into a damned good snit by the time she picked me up. Why couldn't she just leave it alone? I slunk into her car, buckled my seat belt and crossed my arms across my chest. Then she announced that our first stop was Travis's.

Suddenly, I didn't feel so abused anymore. Poor Carrie. She

had to know who the murderer was. I looked over at her grim face and slowly uncrossed my arms. Then I tried to think of something to say that could make it all better. I never did, but at least we were speaking again by the time we got to Travis's.

"Hey, you guys!" Travis greeted us when he answered the door. For once his handsome face was smiling.

I had a feeling his smile was more for Carrie than myself, however.

Travis cleared some partially dismantled video games off a sofa that had to be older than he was and motioned us onto it with a flourish. Then he crossed his legs and sank to the floor in one fluid motion. I'd always wished I could do that. But I think the practice of yoga is a prerequisite. Or maybe it's youth.

"What's up?" he asked.

"Kate and I are investigating the possibility that someone in our critique group is responsible for both Nan's and Slade's deaths," Carrie explained. "We hoped to hear your ideas on the subject."

"Yeah," he said, standing back up. Maybe he could only talk on his feet. "I wondered about that too. Only I can't see who, you know?" He stood on one leg and then the other. "You're cool. Joyce and Mave are cool. Russell's—"

"Cool," Carrie finished for him. "Be that as it may, can you think of a reasonable motive that anyone in our group might have had to kill one or both of the victims?"

Travis sighed, walked to the other side of the room and turned.

"Well, Slade was a real asshole, you know," he said on the return trip. "And Nan. Jeez, she wasn't very cool either. Neither of them are great losses to the world. I mean, homeless people die every day and—"

"Travis," Carrie interrupted. She stood up now herself, somehow managing to appear taller than Travis as she straightened her back. "You have to stop saying those sorts of things."

"What things?"

She took a step closer to him. "That Nan and Slade weren't a big loss—"

"Well, they weren't!" he protested, throwing up his hands.

"That doesn't matter!" she shouted back, throwing up her own hands. "By making those statements you give the impression that you might have murdered them yourself."

"You think I murdered them?" he demanded, stepping toward Carrie. As the distance between them shrank, their relative heights became abruptly evident. He was towering over her now. He put his hands on her shoulders and looked down into her eyes. "Do you really think I'm a killer?"

- Twenty-two -

CARRIE STARED UP into Travis's dark gypsy eyes for one long moment.

"No, I don't believe you are a murderer," she said finally.

Travis took his hands from Carrie's shoulders. And Carrie began talking again as if a switch had been thrown.

"But I am concerned that you will be perceived as a murderer if you're not more careful about what comes out of your mouth." She lifted her hands and made chopping motions in the air. "You must learn—"

"I tell the truth," Travis interrupted, chopping back with his own hands. "I don't tell lies for anyone. . . ."

I stopped listening as I watched the two of them argue. Each of them had their head jutted forward, dark eyes flashing under puckered brows. Each punctuated their remarks with their hands. And each was absolutely sure that God was on their side. No wonder they were in love with each other. Despite differences in sex, race, age and height, they were identical in their gestures. And in their passion.

I smiled as I watched them.

Both of them turned to me at the same time.

"What are you laughing at?" Carrie and Travis demanded as one.

Then I really did laugh.

It was Carrie's turn for a snit on the ride home from Travis's. But hers didn't last any longer than mine had.

"Okay," she said finally, her voice far more friendly than it had been earlier. "What *were* you laughing about?"

"You and Travis," I answered. "Have you ever wondered if you were twins? Separated at birth, of course."

"No I have not," she shot back, turning a quick frown my way.

"The waving hands," I explained. "The burning eyes—"

"Ah," she broke in. The frown turned to a smile. "I begin to understand. I believe you may be right." She paused for a moment to guide her car into the next lane, then asked, "Do you think a little incest might be in order?"

"Go for it," I ordered, relieved that her sense of humor had returned. But the humorous phase didn't last long.

"I was telling the truth when I stated that I didn't believe Travis was a murderer," she followed up in a voice so serious she might have been giving evidence in a court of law. "But I was not stating the whole truth. Because I am still not entirely certain. I wonder if I ever will be."

"If the real murderer is caught—" I began.

"But that is exactly where we started!" She threw her hands into the air. I held my breath and hoped she was steering with her knees. "Believing we could discover the identity of the murderer."

"Maybe we still can," I argued as her hands grasped the wheel again. "You were right about visiting everyone individually. They may say things to us alone that they wouldn't say in front of the group."

I looked over at her. Her face was grim, but she seemed to be thinking about what I'd said.

"I have a hearing tomorrow morning," she told me finally. "However, I believe I might be able to leave the office for the afternoon. Would you be willing to join me then to visit more of the group members?"

I said yes. I couldn't really say no. After all, it had been my idea. At least, I was pretty sure it had been my idea.

Carrie left me off at my driveway. Once she drove away, I walked to the mailbox to get my mail and check for Russell. The mail was there. Russell wasn't. Maybe there was a God.

Barbara called while I was sharing a quiet meal with C.C., Friskies Senior turkey and giblets for her, rice crackers and soy cheese for me. And the terrible thing was that C.C.'s food was beginning to look better to me than my own. I told myself Wayne would be home soon. The man could cook. And not just in the kitchen. I sighed, my thoughts dancing into the bedroom without me. Luckily, the phone rang before I could get myself too worked up.

"Hey, kiddo," Barbara said. "I heard about the second murder—"

"You didn't pick it up psychically?" I asked, putting a full load of nasal sarcasm into my voice.

"Even psychics aren't on full time," she answered cheerfully. "Felix told me about it. But I knew you were distressed—"

"Right," I muttered.

"—especially about Russell Wu following you," she went on as if she hadn't heard the interruption. "I finally got a bead on him. I don't know if he's the murderer, but he does have a crush on you."

I kept my scream subvocal with an effort. For all the good that it did.

"Let it out, Kate," Barbara advised. "You need to scream a little."

"That's all right," I told her through clenched lips. "Do you happen to know who the murderer is?"

"Not yet. Sorry about that."

Barbara always seemed to know all kinds of nifty things

until you really needed an answer. She couldn't predict Lotto numbers either, much to Felix's loud annoyance. My thoughts returned to Russell. What in the world did he see in me?

"You're an attractive woman," Barbara answered the thought. "Look at Wayne. Look at Craig."

Damn. I had almost forgotten my ex-husband in all the excitement. Guilt washed over me.

"It's not your fault," Barbara told me. "Don't worry so much about Craig."

I said goodbye and hung up before she could catch me thinking that I damn well hadn't been worried about Craig. Not until she'd called.

I went to bed at nine o'clock, vowing to get up really early and get at least six hours of Jest Gifts work in before Carrie showed up the next afternoon.

I got in six and a half. Carrie knocked on the door a little after one, looking formidable in her gray pinstripe suit.

"Ready?" she demanded.

"Ready, Captain," I answered with a crisp salute. I picked up my purse and a bag of rice crackers as we went out the door into the bright sunlight. I had a feeling the bag of crackers was going to be all the lunch I was going to get.

We decided to visit Mave first. Not because she was the most suspicious member of the group, but because she seemed likely to be the most observant. Actually Russell might have been more observant, but he wasn't answering his telephone.

There was a Harley-Davidson motorcycle parked in front of the slatted gate to Mave's front yard. It looked strangely comfortable there, guarding the small Victorian estate. Carrie and I walked silently around the motorcycle and up the flagstone path to the house. Was the owner of the Harley-Davidson visiting Mave?

"Howdy, women!" Mave greeted us at the door. She winked

heavily from behind her thick glasses. "Want you to meet my special friend, Ellen Martin."

As Ellen and I dutifully shook hands across the doorstep, I decided she couldn't be the owner of the motorcycle. True, she was dressed in sturdy jeans, but Ellen still could have posed for Grandmother of the Year. She was comfortably plump, with rosy, round cheeks, twinkling blue eyes and gray hair pulled back into a neat bun at the nape of her neck.

"Nice meeting you both," she trilled before turning back to Mave. "See you soon, sweetie," she said in a much deeper voice and hugged Mave tightly.

My mind began to process the meaning of "special friend." But before my mind could even finish, Ellen grabbed a motorcycle helmet from a table near the door and walked past us. I turned in time to see her pump the Harley-Davidson into noisy life, and then she roared away.

Mave grinned at us, obviously pleased by the effect of Ellen's exit. I shut my gaping mouth.

"Some hog, ain't she?" Mave remarked and turned to lead us to the living room.

Carrie and I were seated side by side on a purple couch in Mave's lavender living room by the time I figured out that "hog" was probably a reference to the motorcycle and not Ellen Martin. Mave sat down on the matching couch across from us as Carrie began to speak.

"Kate and I thought you might be able to help us identify the man or woman who murdered Slade Skinner and Nan Millard," she said, bending forward and staring straight into Mave's eyes.

"So you think the same critter killed them both?" Mave asked, or maybe stated, as she stared back at Carrie.

Carrie nodded.

Mave tilted her head and pressed on. "And you think that very same critter is a member of our critique group."

"I'm not certain, but I believe it is possible," Carrie answered solemnly.

Mave leaned back against the cushions of the couch and laughed. "Ask a lawyer a simple question," she rasped, shaking her head merrily.

"I merely—" Carrie began, her eyes narrowed with annoyance. Then she took a deep breath. "Mave, are you testing me?"

"I guess I am at that," Mave replied. She sat up straight again, merriment gone from her wrinkled face. "I've got a feeling whoever killed those two had a tad more anger running through their veins than your average human. And I've seen you angry more than once. But how angry?" Mave shrugged her shoulders lazily, but kept her bright gaze fastened on Carrie's face. "Angry enough to kill?"

"No, I've never been angry enough to kill," Carrie answered tersely. "But you bring up an interesting point. I haven't really given the issue of anger due consideration. Even though I saw the result." Her eyes went out of focus as she stopped speaking.

Was she seeing a dead body in her mind? Or was she thinking of Travis? Travis who had enough anger to fuel Pacific Gas and Electric's operations for the next ten years. Maybe for the next century.

"The murderer might not be someone who's obviously angry," I offered. "It could be someone who's hiding their anger all too well. You know, someone who's repressed—"

"Well, that sure narrows down the field," Mave commented, turning my way. "Especially when we add newcomers to the herd of suspects, folks who we know next to nothing about. How's *your* temper, Kate?"

I didn't answer her right away. I was still taking in her transition from folksy old woman into hard-boiled interrogator. Both roles were probably an act, I realized with a little jolt. Of course everyone poses a little, I told myself. Mave had just been at it longer than most.

"I've got a temper, but not a murderer's temper," I answered finally. I congratulated myself on my calm, cool delivery.

"That's what Russell tells me," Mave confirmed with a knowing smile.

Russell? When had Mave talked to Russell about me? Maybe Carrie and I weren't the only two collaborating to solve a murder.

"He says you've been involved with murder before, but only as a witness," she went on. "But then Russell seems to be a mite prejudiced in your favor."

Damn. So much for being calm and cool. I could feel a hot blush crawling up my face. Was it my fault that this guy liked me? I had to tell him about Wayne—

"Who do you believe the angry one is?" Carrie asked Mave suddenly.

Mave opened her mouth, then shut it again. For the millionth time in my life, I wished I could read minds.

"I don't know," she said finally. "I've convinced myself it was each of us, one at a time. Travis, Joyce, Donna . . . I can make a case for anyone, including myself. But for all of that, I don't really know." She shook her head slowly, looking all of her seventy years.

"Well I, for one, cannot actually imagine any of the group members doing it." Carrie threw her hands wide. "If only we could ask Slade or Nan."

"'Tzu-lu asked how one should serve ghosts and spirits,'" Mave piped up. I could tell from her oratory tone and erect shoulders that she was quoting again. "'The Master said, Till you have learnt to serve men, how can you serve ghosts? Tzu-lu then ventured upon a question about the dead. The Master said, Till you know about the living, how are you to know about the dead?'"

Mave paused after the punch line, then smiled. "Confucius said that. Not that it gets us any further than a weasel can spit."

I was glad she had reverted to her old folksy self. She was harder to suspect that way. But harder to interrogate too.

"You've known Slade longer than anyone else in the group," I led in. "Did you ever meet any of his ex-wives? Or his children?"

"Nope, can't say that I've had the pleasure," Mave replied cheerily.

"Have you observed any connection between Nan and Slade that might explain their serial murders?" Carrie tried.

"Nope." She shook her head and got up from the couch. "Enough jaw-wagging. How'd you two women like some homemade zucchini bread?"

The zucchini bread was tasty. I told myself that it counted as a green vegetable for lunch, though after one bite I was pretty sure that it had more sugar in it than zucchini. And there seemed to be more fertilizer than information in Mave once she'd reverted to her folksy self. My head was reeling with quotations, country metaphors and aphorisms by the time we left.

"Do we know anything more than we did when we got here?" I asked Carrie on the way out to the car.

"Not to my knowledge," she answered.

It never hurts to check.

Our visit to Donna's house was even quicker than our visit to Mave's. Donna was at home. But so were her two children. And either Dacia or Dustin had taken one of the four cats and dumped it into the fish tank. Donna was trying to dry the dripping cat as she opened the door.

"Dustin did it!" Dacia shouted. The wet cat screeched and jumped out of Donna's grasp, leaving two bleeding stripes on her arms.

"Uh-uh," protested Dustin. "I don't even like the stupid cat—"

"The cats aren't stupid!" Dacia roared.

"Now, what are we learning about truth and cooperation?" Donna asked, kneeling in front of the two children.

"Yeah, Dustin," Dacia said, placing her chubby hands on her eight-year-old hips. "You lying little scumbag—"

"Am not! Am not!"

"Perhaps this isn't a good time," Carrie interjected.

"Oh no, it's fine," Donna said over her shoulder. Then she turned back to her children. "I want you both to go into the meditation room now and meditate on the karmic importance of telling the truth. And remember your affirmations. And then, when you're ready, you can come and tell me what actually happened."

The children glared at her for a moment, then marched into the meditation room and slammed the door shut. Donna stood up and motioned us through the front doorway.

"We wondered if you had any idea who murdered Nan and Slade," I blurted right out. I figured there was no time for subtlety if we were going to get any answers before Donna's kids came back in.

"Well, um, I—" Donna began.

Something crashed in the meditation room, something that sounded big and heavy. A body? Then we heard the screams. I listened carefully and was relieved to make out two separate voices. At least neither Dustin nor Dacia had been killed. Not yet anyway.

Donna sprinted to the door leading to the meditation room. She tripped over a pile of roller blades when she was almost there and hit the door with her head. The blow didn't slow her down any, though.

"Mahatma Gandhi!" she shouted as she wrenched the door

open. "Be like Mahatma Gandhi!" Then she disappeared into the room.

"Children are so incredibly spontaneous," she said when she joined us a few minutes later.

She was smiling, so I didn't bother to ask if her incredibly spontaneous children were all right. Or even which one of them had dumped the cat into the fish tank.

"Back to who killed Slade and Nan," I prompted instead.

Not that it did us any good. Donna told us she thought it must be "incredibly traumatic" to have committed two murders and not be able to talk about it. Then she assured us that some good would come out of the murders, at least karmically speaking. And finally she let us know once more that her father and she were communicating really well now and that he had nothing to do with the two deaths.

"Do you think Donna's trying to convince herself or us that her father's not a murderer?" I asked Carrie on the way out to the car.

"Both."

We went to my house after that and discussed murder theories while C.C. paced for us. If we didn't solve the murder, it wouldn't be for want of trying. Carrie had even brought a laptop computer for the exercise. She typed in four categories: suspect names, connections between suspects, notable facts and possible motives. The computer didn't cough up the identity of the murderer at the end of the exercise. Maybe it needed a special program to do that.

We did reach one unanimous conclusion, however. Dacia had been the one to throw the cat into the fish tank.

"I give up," I said finally. "Let's get something to eat and then go see Russell."

"Why Russell?" Carrie asked, her eyebrows going up. "Do you believe he's our murderer?"

"No, no," I said, squirming in my chair. "I don't know if he's our murderer or not. But he's gotta stop following me—"

"I thought he *had* stopped following you."

"Maybe." I squirmed a little more, embarrassed to share my fears. "But maybe he's just keeping out of my sight. Anyway, I have to tell him about Wayne, just in case he really does have a crush on me. And if he doesn't have a crush on me, then why the hell is he following me? If he can't explain himself, I'll . . . I'll . . ."

"You'll what, Kate?"

- Twenty-three -

"TELL THE POLICE?" I said. At least I tried to say it, but it came out more of a question than a statement.

Carrie nodded, though, as if satisfied, then asked, "And what will you do if Russell admits to having a crush on you?"

I worried about that question and worse all through dinner at Miranda's Restaurant. I should have been paying attention to their Indonesian tofu and vegetables. But even the spicy peanut sauce couldn't capture my full interest. It barely got a nod from my taste buds. Especially since Carrie had called from my house and made a date to interview Russell after we ate dinner.

"Hello again," Russell greeted us at his apartment door.

I stared at his tinted glasses, which had turned completely opaque in the light of the doorway, and searched for the hidden meaning of his words. Did he said "again" because he had been following me all this time? Or was he making fun of my coming to see him? What if he thought I was interested in him? What if—

"Thank you for agreeing to speak to us this evening," Carrie said as Russell motioned us through the doorway.

"Yeah, thanks," I mumbled, following her in.

The same tiger-striped cat that we had met before was on Russell's blue-and-white-checked sofa. I sat down on one side of her and Carrie sat down on the other. The cat sniffed me for a moment, then jumped into my lap and began purring. Great. Maybe she had a crush on me too.

Russell sat down across from us on a wooden chair, a hint of a smile tugging at his lips.

"What can I do for you, ladies?" he asked formally.

"We would like to discuss the murders with you," Carrie replied after a moment had passed. "But Kate had some specific issues she wanted to address first."

She turned to me, and I saw that she was wiggling her fingers, one by one. Maybe she was as nervous as I was. Though I doubted it.

"Listen, Russell," I said, my voice far too loud. I modulated it as I stumbled on. "I . . . I want to thank you for not following me anymore. It was making me really . . ." My mind searched for the right word. Upset? Frightened? Frantic? Nuts? ". . . uncomfortable," I finally finished.

He tilted his head gently downward. Was that a nod?

"Anyway," I pressed on, looking down at my own lap. I'd never be able to finish if I were looking him in the eye. Or in tinted glasses, for that matter. "I'm living with a really wonderful man right now. His name's Wayne. He's been on vacation, but he's coming back soon."

I stopped to take a breath and looked back up. Russell didn't look like he'd moved an inch, but his skin was pinker than it had been before. A lot pinker.

"So I won't need your protection anymore," I finished up as fast as I could. I was pretty sure I'd made my point. With a sledgehammer.

"I suppose I should explain," Russell put in quickly. "I knew you'd confronted a murderer before and I thought that by following you, I might learn something." He paused. "To use for my true-crime writing, that's all."

"Right, right," I agreed, bouncing my head up and down like a ping pong ball on an elastic string. "Of course."

Strangely enough, it was the plausibility of his alternative explanation that finally convinced me that he really had been infatuated with me. I was pretty sure he wasn't infatuated anymore, though. I was trying to think of what I could say to relieve his embarrassment, and my embarrassment, when Carrie spoke up.

"We spoke to Mave Quentin earlier today," she told Russell, her voice matter of fact. "Mave indicated that you and she had discussed the murders. We wondered if you had come to any conclusions."

I turned to Carrie gratefully and listened as Russell discussed all the conclusions he hadn't reached. He dismissed the idea of Donna's father being involved in the murders for a number of reasons that I had a hard time hearing over the sound of my pulse celebrating a successful mission. However awkwardly, I *had* finally managed to tell Russell about Wayne.

Russell went on to discuss and dismiss each of the group members as suspects. No one had the expected psychological profile of a serial murderer.

"But of course, anyone can kill given the right circumstances," he told us finally. He turned his head my way slowly. "Each and every one of us has that potential."

Uh-oh. The hair prickled on my arms. I had a feeling I had gone from object of desire to object of suspicion sometime in the last half hour. Probably around the time I'd used the sledgehammer on Russell.

"Perhaps something will be revealed to us at tomorrow's meeting," Carrie concluded briskly. She stood up. "Thank you for your help, Russell."

I jumped up after her, remembering the cat in my lap too late. The cat landed on her feet, though. I told myself Russell would do the same as we said our goodbyes.

Carrie didn't comment on the way I'd handled Russell as we drove to Joyce's place. She didn't even tease me. She was a better person than I would have been in her position. Much better.

"Thanks," I muttered once we got out of the car in front of Operation Soup Pot's headquarters.

"Thank *you*," she answered and gave me a one-armed hug before we climbed the long flight of stairs that took us past the headquarters to Joyce's apartment.

Not that we ever got inside Joyce's apartment. Joyce answered the door herself, but she didn't invite us in. She stood blocking her doorway instead.

"I'm meditating now," she whispered.

"Perhaps you could take a few minutes to talk," Carrie suggested as I peeked around Joyce. I couldn't see anyone or anything suspicious in her simply furnished living room.

As Joyce stared at Carrie, I noticed that her eyes were reddened behind her oversized glasses. I wondered if she had been crying. Or maybe she hadn't been sleeping well. Worrying about murder can do that to a person. Not to mention overwork and a few other things.

"Just for a minute," Joyce agreed finally, not moving from the doorway. She closed her reddened eyes and brushed the back of her hand across her forehead and over her permed black hair in a gesture that spoke of exhaustion. "I really do need to get back to my meditation."

"We wondered if you had any idea about the murders—" Carrie began.

But Joyce was already shaking her head. "I'm sorry. I don't have any answers for you now," she said softly. A faint blush stained her cheeks. "And I'm very tired."

"We will see you tomorrow, won't we?" Carrie asked.

Joyce nodded solemnly, then looked down at her feet.

We left her to her meditation.

"Do you think she was afraid of us?" I asked Carrie when we got back to the car.

"Probably. A visit from possible murderers could reasonably arouse fear in anyone."

"In anyone but the killer. The killer's the only one who knows we aren't killers ourselves."

"Yes," Carrie agreed thoughtfully. "It makes one wonder why the others aren't more afraid of us."

That topic kept us busy until Carrie dropped me back at my house. Not that we ever came to any conclusions.

"Shall we ride together to the regular group meeting at Donna's tomorrow?" Carrie asked me from her car window.

"Sure," I answered, swallowing a groan. "I'll drive."

I picked up *Cool Fallout* once I was safe inside my house. Maybe there was a clue buried in the manuscript. But if there was, did that mean there might be a clue in Nan's work too? Would I actually have to read Nan's work?

I shrugged away the questions and settled down in my comfy chair to read. Peter Dahlgren was calling his detectives again. He tells them they have to find Warren Lee. Then he stands up and looks out his window. His eyes fix on a figure twenty stories below on the street—

The phone shrilled. My phone, not Peter Dahlgren's. Though for a jarring instant, I wasn't certain whose phone it was. Sherman Francis Skinner could write, no matter what his name was, I decided, and picked up the receiver.

"Kate," a low, rough voice said.

"Wayne!" I whooped and jumped from my chair.

"Coming home Sunday night," he told me. "If that's okay with you—"

"Okay? Of course it's okay!" I danced in circles, pretending that the receiver was Wayne's shoulder, loving him long distance all the more for the misplaced humility that made him ask if it was okay to come home. We talked for two and a half hours. And I never mentioned the murders. In fact, I actually forgot about them.

Wayne was coming home.

And that was the only thing that mattered.

Unfortunately, I remembered the murders again as soon as I got up on Saturday morning. And I didn't stop thinking about them as I fed the cat, did paperwork and fixed an olive, garlic and caper pâté to take to the afternoon meeting of the critique group.

"Wayne's coming home tomorrow," I told Carrie when I picked her up at her house.

She wrapped her arms around me and squeezed in celebration. And as she squeezed, I couldn't help but think of her and Travis. Would Travis be able to come home to Carrie once he was cleared of suspicion of murder? And only if he was cleared?

Carrie didn't talk much as I drove to Donna's house. But her spine was straight and her brows were puckered in thought. The Toyota's gears weren't the only ones turning in the car.

"Hi, you guys!" Donna greeted us as we came in the door. She threw out her arms enthusiastically, almost knocking Carrie's Tupperware from her hands. "This meeting's going to be incredibly fun. . . ."

I checked behind her for children. I didn't see any. Or any toys. Only adults. I saw Mave and Russell on a sofa, and waved.

"Dustin and Dacia are at their father's," Donna went on. "We're divorced, but we still have this really complex relationship. . . ."

Across from Mave and Russell, I saw Joyce sitting next to Travis. And there were two men I didn't know, standing up. I took a closer look.

". . . but he had an incredibly painful childhood, so now he's trying to create a different one for our kids. . . ."

The two men were big and solidly built, dressed in suits. One of them started toward us. And as he did, my heart jumped in my chest. I recognized his stride.

". . . takes real integrity to, well, to overcome . . ."

It was one of the guys who had taken Donna's floppy from the top of my pinball machine. One of the guys who had broken into Carrie's. One of the guys who worked for Donna's father.

"Mafia," Carrie whispered from beside me.

I grabbed her elbow and took a quick step backwards toward the door. Too late.

"We'd appreciate it if you'd both sit down," the man walking toward us said in a surprisingly high voice.

He nodded toward a set of empty chairs grouped near the sofas. His hand was in his pocket. My own hands began to sweat. Did he have a gun in that pocket?

I looked at Donna, but she had turned already to walk to her own seat. All I could see was the back of her dark, tangled hair.

I turned to Carrie. She lifted her eyebrows ever so slightly, then made her way slowly over to a chair and sat down. I followed her example and wondered if her legs felt as weak as mine did. I scanned the faces around me once I was seated. Mave and Travis both looked angry. Joyce looked miserable. And Russell's expression was as unreadable as ever.

No one was smiling. Except for Donna. I could see the grin on her face now that we were both sitting down. Why the hell was she grinning? Was she happy to see these guys?

"What—" I began.

But then the doorbell rang again. Donna didn't bother to get up this time. The man with his hand in his pocket did host duty and ushered Vicky through the door. Silently. Vicky's eyes widened as he shut the door behind her, but she came and sat next to Carrie without further prompting. Then she wrapped her thin arms around herself and shut her eyes. Not a bad approach, all things considered.

Were these guys the murderers, after all? I still found it hard to believe. Slade had said he was meeting someone from the group, not someone from Donna's family—

"Oh goody, everyone's here now," Donna announced cheerfully from her chair.

The man with his hand in his pocket cleared his throat.

"Our boss asked us to apologize for any inconvenience we may have caused you in this group," he reeled off. Then he paused and looked down at the floor.

"Due to our overzealousness," whispered the other guy.

"Oh, yeah," said the first one. "Due to our overzealousness—"

"You mean stealing manuscripts and terrorizing people!" Travis burst out. He jumped to his feet and threw out his hands. My heart took another leap. What if this guy shot Travis?

"Listen, you two," Travis ranted on, unheeding. "You gotta stop this shit! You can't break into people's houses and take stuff. Don't you know you scared people?"

The man who had been speaking turned an ugly glare in Travis's direction. Then he took one deliberate step toward him. Travis stood his ground and glared right back. Damn. The man took another step. I held my breath. Then the other man caught hold of the first man's coat and gave it a good yank.

"We're apologizing," he whispered.

"Oh, yeah." The first man took a big breath and clenched his fists. I was glad to see that those fists were empty. No gun in either hand.

He screwed up his face and plodded on. "Although we have done no illegal acts, we realize our efforts to protect our boss may have been misconstrued. We are very sorry."

That said, the first man walked to the front door and opened it. The second man said "goodbye" politely and followed him out.

"Holy mother of jumping beans!" Mave shouted as the door slammed shut behind them.

And then suddenly everyone was on their feet babbling and cutting each other off.

"I thought we were goners—"

"I shoulda punched the guy—"

"Ye gods and goddesses—"

"Why didn't you tell us what they were here for?" I demanded, focusing on Donna.

"Can I use your phone?" Joyce asked her at the same time.

"Oh sure," Donna said over her shoulder and then turned back to me. "I wanted it to be a surprise, like a gift—"

"A gift!" Mave interrupted. "You almost ended this old woman's days with your gift."

We had all progressed to the stage of cheering and back-slapping when Joyce came back from the kitchen.

But Joyce didn't look any happier than she had ten minutes ago. Her face wore no smile and her eyes looked even redder than they had the night before.

"May I read today?" she asked in a near whisper. "I think today will be my last day here."

"Well, I was planning on reading," Russell said, the uncharacteristic grin leaving his face as quickly as it had appeared. "But if you need—"

"Hey," Travis cut in. "It's Russell's turn. We decided that a couple of meetings ago—"

"That's okay," Russell cut back in, his voice as subdued as Joyce's face. "It's fine if Joyce wants to take my place."

No one was cheering anymore when we all sat back down. Joyce's solemnity had infected us all.

What was so serious that she had to read now? That she wouldn't be coming back? Could she be ready to confess to murder? For a moment I was sure of it. I felt it in my bones, in the quivering of the blood in my veins. But why? Why would Joyce have killed Slade and Nan?

I took a better look at Joyce, saw the tears in her eyes, and my brain switched gears. Was Joyce sick? Terminally ill?

And finally, a third possibility occurred to me. What if she was going to name the murderer, and the murderer was a friend? I resisted looking in Travis's direction as Joyce walked over to her seat and picked up a tote bag with "Operation Soup Pot" printed across it.

She stuck her hand in the bag, then brought it back out empty.

"I'll just tell you, I think," she murmured.

Then she hugged the tote bag to her torso and began her speech.

"I have good reason to abhor violence," she declared, her voice louder than I'd heard it before. "I grew up in a series of foster homes. My foster parents were good enough people, it was me that was attached to anger and hatred. My sin—my karma—is violence."

She closed her eyes before going on. "They tell me I never 'bonded.' I had three or four temper tantrums a day, abused animals and my friends—those few that I had. I tore the wallpaper off the walls. And flailed. And hit. And hurt. My third set of foster parents put me in therapy. I was diagnosed with what they call an 'attachment disorder' today. Apparently, my mother couldn't take care of me as an infant and I was passed around to relatives and friends. It doesn't matter. I don't remember that part."

She took a series of deep breaths, in through the nose and out through the mouth.

Then she said, "What I do remember is trying to strangle my third foster parents' little girl."

– Twenty-four –

I STOPPED BREATHING. Joyce was confessing, all right. But what was she confessing to?

"What are you trying to say?" Travis demanded.

Joyce opened her eyes and looked at him, a half smile beatifying her plain face for a moment.

"I'm talking about violence," she explained, her voice just above a whisper. "How attachment to anger and hatred precludes real peace."

Travis frowned his confusion at her. I didn't blame him. Joyce hadn't really explained herself at all. Was she confessing to Slade's murder? To Nan's? Maybe the childhood Joyce had been violent, but the adult Joyce standing before us, clutching her "Operation Soup Pot" tote bag? No, she just couldn't be a murderer. I let out the breath I'd been holding. But if she wasn't confessing, what the hell was she struggling to tell us? I tried to see past her oversized glasses into her eyes. And then she closed them again.

"My third foster parents sent me away," she resumed, volume returning to her voice. "By then, I began to realize I had a problem. By my sixth foster home I really tried to improve. I did counting exercises when the rage came on me.

But it was no good. I beat up a boy at school. They say I almost killed him—"

"We know all about your feelings toward violence," Vicky interrupted, her voice harsh with impatience. "When are you going to do your reading?"

Joyce opened her eyes again, this time to look at Vicky.

"Just consider this my reading," she suggested mildly. "It is important to me. There is a point."

Vicky jerked her thin shoulders in what I guessed was a shrug. A very hostile shrug.

Joyce went on, keeping her eyes open now, focused somewhere in the space above our heads. "I spent the rest of my childhood in juvenile hall. A therapist there taught me to meditate, to find that place that is pure awareness. Pure stillness. Pure peace. She was good to me." Joyce took off her glasses and wiped a sparkle of tears from her eyes. "I really tried. I studied and meditated. And helped cook in the kitchen." Her voice broke as she said, "I was released on my eighteenth birthday."

Mave rose from her seat and put her arm around Joyce's shoulders. "You just say what you need to say, honey," she advised, her raspy voice low and gentle.

Joyce nodded and took a few wheezing breaths. It hurt just to hear her. Then she put her glasses back on.

"I went to college in the late sixties," she pressed on, her voice thick with emotion now. "And discovered politics. The United States was in a terrible war, the Vietnam War. Young men were dying in violence. I was against violence. I joined a radical group and dropped out of school, working in a restaurant to make a living. Then the group I'd joined became even more radical. We formed a commune and worked hard, smuggling and dealing dope to finance our own underground railroad for young men escaping the draft."

A jolt shot up my spine, jerking my back straight. Slade's manuscript. That was the connection.

"*Cool Fallout*," Carrie whispered next to me. Out of the corner of my eye, I saw Russell nod slowly.

But I still didn't want to believe this woman was a murderer. Buddhists didn't murder, did they?

Joyce kept one hand around her tote bag as she reached into it with the other. My pulse pounded even harder. What if she had a weapon in there? But the only thing she brought out was a Kleenex. She took off her glasses again and wiped her eyes, one-handed.

"It seemed worth it to help stop the violence," she told us, then dropped the glasses and the Kleenex into the bag. "One day a sheriff came driving out to the commune. We had over twenty kilos of marijuana in the back room. And a stack of forged documents in the front room. We tried to keep him out of the house. A guy from the commune grabbed his arm. But that just made things worse. The sheriff shook the guy off and forced his way inside. He looked around, smiled at us and went back out to make a call from his car."

She hugged her tote bag tighter. "Everyone started grabbing their stuff to leave. I took my purse and backpack; I didn't have time to pack anything else." Her voice took on speed. "The sheriff was walking up the middle of the driveway as I was driving the van out with two passengers. The sheriff waved his arms to stop us. But I was going too fast. I jerked the wheel and tried to miss him, but he jumped in the same direction. I hit him. And drove over him. And didn't look back."

Mave's arm came slowly away from Joyce's shoulders. But Joyce didn't seem to notice. She was too involved in her story.

"We heard that night on the radio that he was dead. Within an hour, I picked up a forged passport from one of our contacts and left the country for Canada. I never saw any of the people from the commune again. I dyed my hair black and permed it.

I put on thick glasses that I didn't need. And I cooked for a living. And meditated. And tried to atone. Once, I slapped a man in all those years, but only once. I thought the violence had left me.

"After fifteen years, I came back to the United States. An acquaintance smuggled me in for a price, no questions asked. And I lived without a legal identity. I was sure my fingerprints were on file. I couldn't undertake any profession where they took fingerprints. I was even afraid to get a driver's license. But I was a good cook. And I didn't allow myself relationships. Relationships mean questions."

Joyce clenched her hands into fists. Suddenly, I remembered her hands clenched like that before. Why hadn't I seen the violence in her? Of course Buddhists could kill. I thought of Jean's brother, the explosive Christian. The religious weren't exempt from rage.

"I cooked for a couple of the better restaurants in San Francisco. I was at Antoinette's up here in San Ricardo when I started taking the leftovers to the homeless. Pretty soon, I was making soups for the homeless, too. And after a while Operation Soup Pot was born. I kept out of the limelight. Then came the idea for the book."

"I didn't mean to . . ." Travis broke in, then faltered. I looked his way for an instant. His brown eyes were glistening with tears, his handsome face stricken.

"Don't worry," Joyce told him. She even managed to smile. "I always knew it was a matter of time. I've been blessed with good work for these twenty years."

"And . . ." Russell prompted.

The smile left Joyce's face.

"And Slade wrote a manuscript and handed it out at a meeting. When I read about a woman who'd been in a commune running drugs to support an underground railroad for draft evaders, who'd killed a sheriff and later become a

Catholic nun—I guess I could call myself a Buddhist nun—I thought for sure it was about me. I never even noticed the similarities to Nan, and to you, Russell. My ego was so great, I thought only of myself."

Joyce shifted her bag from one arm to the other. What was in that bag? Not a gun. I still couldn't believe Joyce would carry a gun. But what?

"I asked to speak to Slade after the group meeting at his house. And I asked him to keep our appointment a secret. After I left his house, I walked around Hutton for a while, then walked back at five o'clock for our meeting. I could tell he thought I'd finally decided to sleep with him." Joyce's pale skin flushed. "He was sitting at his desk, a dumbbell next to his word processor so he could exercise while he was thinking. I asked how he knew about me, how he'd found out about the sheriff and the commune.

"He looked up at me with this look of complete surprise on his face. I knew then that he hadn't known. It had just been my ego. Then he smiled. And he said, 'The media will love this.' I told him the media couldn't find out, that it would destroy Operation Soup Pot, but he wouldn't stop talking. He said, 'We'll do all the talk shows,' and started typing something. He kept talking and talking." Joyce clenched her fists again.

Yes, I could imagine her killing someone now. Nausea rose into my throat.

"I began to see red. I've always seen colors when I meditate. But this time the color was red, a red mist in front of my eyes. I picked up the dumbbell he had on his desk and hit him. Again and again. And then the red was everywhere." She took a breath. "I had to wear one of Slade's shirts over my clothes on the way home. I was covered. Covered in red blood."

As Joyce stuck her hand into her bag again, I heard the faint sound of a siren somewhere in the distance. The sound raised the hair on my arms. And woke me up. This woman had just

confessed to murder. And we were all just sitting here, listening
to her, watching her hold her tote bag. I pushed myself up from
my chair, but Carrie's hand touched my arm before I was ever
standing.

"Let her finish," she whispered.

"But—" I whispered back, watching as Joyce pulled another
Kleenex from her bag. Nothing else, just a Kleenex.

"We're safe, Kate," Carrie insisted. "I know this woman."

I sat back down. Carrie did know this woman. Better than
knew her. But how well was that?

Joyce blew her nose and then went on.

"I tried to meditate after I killed him, to embrace the stillness
inside myself. But all my mind could embrace was rage. The
stillness was gone."

She closed her eyes and shook her head slowly back and
forth.

"I need to atone," she whispered.

My pulse went into overdrive. She wasn't going to attack us.
But what if she was going to kill herself? I jumped from my
seat, ignoring Carrie's restraining hand. I wanted to be able to
grab the tote bag if Joyce stuck her hand in again. If she took
a gun or knife from that bag, I would be ready.

"There's still something to live for," I told her once I was on
my feet.

She smiled at me, this time a full smile that seemed to light
up her entire face.

"I'm not going to kill myself," she assured me, her voice low
and calm. "It's too soon for me to die. I want to die a peaceful
death, so I must once again learn to live a peaceful life.
Unagitated by anger and attachment and fear. No, I'll atone in
prison." She straightened her back. "I've tried to lose the
violence, the attachment to ego. I thought I had. No money, no
sex life, working with the poor. But I didn't know that all of

that was a different kind of ego, wanting so hard to be a saint. Not real surrender."

"What about Nan?" Russell prodded.

Her face tightened and all the light left it. I shivered. This was the face of a murderer.

"Nan saw me walking around Hutton and going back to Slade's house. She called me last Tuesday, said she'd pick me up for a little 'tête-à-tête' at her house. She wouldn't tell me why. She teased me all the way in the car, little hints, but no real accusations.

"When we got to her house, she left me in the living room for a minute. Then she came back, holding one arm behind her. She told me she knew I'd killed Slade. She said she didn't want to know why, she just wanted money. She figured I could siphon off the cash from Operation Soup Pot. Just a few thousand a month, she told me. I tried to reason with her. I stepped toward her . . . and she pulled the gun from behind her back.

"I panicked. Guns are dangerous. I tried to take the gun from her. But she resisted—and then we were struggling—and then it went off. And when I pushed her away, I saw she was dead." Joyce stopped speaking for a moment, her eyes wide and unfocused. "I even wiped the gun clean. I know no one will believe me, but I didn't mean to kill her—"

"I believe you," said Travis.

"So do I," I threw in, surprising myself.

"Listen, honey. We'll work it out," Mave said. "It'll be—"

The sound of a siren, closer to us, stopped her mid-sentence.

Joyce collapsed onto the couch and put her face in her hands. When she reached for her bag again, tears were streaming from her eyes. I tensed. I still didn't trust that tote bag.

But all she brought out this time was a stack of stapled sheets of paper.

"My confession," she explained, her voice hoarse. She

cleared her throat. "A copy for each of you. I decided last night that I had to tell. All the awful suspicion, it wasn't fair to the rest of you. I'm going with the police soon. Thank you all—"

"No, don't!" Travis shouted, on his feet, his arms waving. "We understand. We won't tell—"

"Yes," Mave cut in. "You don't have to—"

"I've already called the Hutton police," Joyce told us quietly.

In the silence, we heard the sound of pounding feet and then a knock on the door.

Donna opened the door and a man and woman in uniform came in.

"Is there a Joyce Larson here?" the woman asked.

"Yes, Officer, that's me," Joyce answered. Then she stood. "I want to confess—"

"Stop," the woman ordered, raising a hand. "You have the right to remain silent . . ."

Even after they had read Joyce her Miranda rights, they still wouldn't let her confess. Not completely. She kept trying, but they kept cutting her off. Even after she told them that she understood her rights completely. Even then. But she did manage to get out the word "murder." And the names Slade Skinner and Nan Millard.

The two officers finally agreed to take her to the Hutton Police Department, where she could make her full confession. And then they led her away, pausing at the door to put her in handcuffs.

A few minutes passed in silence once that door had slammed shut behind them.

"Did you know?" Carrie asked Russell finally.

"No," he said. "Not till she began to speak. And then I noticed everything I should have noticed before. She was the nun in *Cool Fallout*. She was the one who wouldn't talk about the story. She wouldn't talk about the sixties either. And she was the right age. She had no past. She had no legal identity."

"If only Nan—" began Donna.

"There are no 'if only's'," Carrie declared.

We stood and left not long after that.

– Twenty-five –

THE THREE OF us were positioned at the entrance of San Francisco Airport's Gate 54, waiting for Wayne's plane to come in. Carrie, Travis and I. I'm not even sure why I agreed when they offered to come to the airport with me. Maybe it was because I was still feeling the sting of my failure to spot Joyce as the murderer. Even though Carrie had insisted that having known Joyce much longer than I, *she* was the one who should have figured it out. As far as I was concerned, neither of us had really known Joyce Larson. Joyce Larson, whose real name turned out to be Louise Kimberly.

But the real reason I agreed to Travis and Carrie's company was that the two of them so obviously needed a chaperon.

Carrie and Travis were in the silly phase of their budding relationship. They sat in the bolted row of chairs across from me, casting burning glances at each other every two or three seconds and then looking away, all the time jabbering on about anything and everything. Except for Joyce's confession. Or their own relationship.

"So who's behind the plot in *Cool Fallout*?" I asked during a lull.

"Ms. Jasper, I'm afraid you'll just have to read the manuscript yourself to answer that particular question," Carrie replied with an exaggerated wink. Then she reached up with the fingers of both hands to twiddle the two white sharks that hung from her dainty ear lobes.

I figured I deserved something for the new earrings, hot off the Jest Gifts presses. I opened my mouth to tell her so. But Travis was quicker than I was.

"Oh baby, how long do I have to wait?" he droned in a Bob Dylan whine, scrunching up his big brown eyes and strumming an imaginary guitar. "Tell me, oh tell me, how the book comes out—"

I stuck my fingers in my ears. He may have been handsome, but he sure as hell couldn't sing.

At least Travis looked happy. Make that ecstatic. And certainly happier than he had been a few hours ago when the revised critique group had first met to talk about Joyce. Travis was still having guilt attacks about getting Joyce into the group. As much as I wished he'd give up the guilt, somehow I liked him for feeling it. Maybe Carrie and he wouldn't be such a bad couple despite their differences. Or their similarities.

I crossed my fingers for the two of them as I watched their continuing antics, all exuberant hand gestures and lavish wordplay. Was it true everlasting love? Or just hysterical relief at the way things had turned out?

Carrie had visited Joyce at the county jail where she was being held and reported back to the group. Joyce seemed to be doing fine, Carrie told us. In fact, Joyce seemed oddly content now that she had made her decision. I hoped Joyce would be all right. I especially hoped she'd find the place of peace inside herself once more. It looked like she was going to have plenty of time to atone in prison, despite the high-priced criminal attorney that Carrie had scared up for her. The attorney whose fees the Operation Soup Pot board of directors had unanimously voted to pay.

"Warren Lee," Carrie bent forward and stage-whispered my way, yanking me back to the present.

"What?"

"Warren Lee was behind the plot in *Cool Fallout*," she expanded.

Travis put an arm around her shoulders diffidently. She turned her head his way with a look of hope on her round, freckled face. Or maybe it was desire. Whatever it was, I hadn't seen a look like that on her face since the days of her marriage. The days before her husband had been diagnosed with cancer.

"But what did Warren Lee want?" I prompted.

Carrie pulled her gaze away from Travis with an obvious effort. A smile tugged at the corners of my mouth. Who cared if theirs was true everlasting love? Carrie was happy. That was enough for now.

"Lee wanted Dahlgren under his power, so he involved the entire membership of the defunct commune," she told me. "His real purpose was to gain computer access to all those plump accounts that Dahlgren controlled as a banker. The rest was a ruse to make it all seem more threatening."

"But why'd he want the access?"

"For the money, Kate." Carrie rolled her eyes. "Remember money?"

"That's all?" I said, disappointed.

She tilted her head and shook a playful finger at me. "I did warn you that it would be far more enjoyable to finish reading the manuscript than to listen to a secondhand account."

"But—"

I broke off as I saw a human tide flooding down the corridor from a plane. Wayne's plane. It had to be. My heart jumped up when I did, beating in my ears. Where was he?

And then I saw him, his head sticking out above the crowd, his low brows rising as he spotted me, his homely face breaking out in a smile.

"Wayne!" I shouted and began my run for him just as he ran for me.

"Hi, Wayne!" Carrie and Travis added their lesser shouts from behind me.

Once I got to him, I threw my arms around his sturdy chest and held on, inhaling the unique scent that was Wayne and only Wayne. He was home. I hadn't let myself realize how far away he'd really been until that moment.

When I turned my face up toward his, he bent down to kiss me. The airport disappeared in the heat of his soft lips.

But Carrie and Travis didn't.

"Ye gods and goddesses," Carrie teased from behind us. "Do you think they're stuck like that?"

I turned to her, ready to scream. I wanted to be alone with Wayne. As soon as possible. If not sooner. And then I saw the blush that Carrie and Travis shared. Were they embarrassed by our . . . our ardor? Of course, I answered myself. Their own kisses were much too near in the future to allow them to be unfazed by ours.

"Wayne Caruso, this is Travis Utrelli," Carrie said, making a formal introduction.

Wayne and Travis shook hands and then we each waited, in various states of inadequately suppressed lust, for someone else to say something.

"How are things?" Wayne asked finally, his low, rough voice an extra prod to my poor, over-stimulated libido. "Did you find any dead bodies while I was gone?"

I was sure it was a joke. Well, almost sure. But I still couldn't find the words to answer him. Not now. Apparently neither could Travis or Carrie.

The smile left Wayne's face slowly. Then his brows dropped over his eyes like curtains.

"You didn't, did you?" he demanded quietly.

"Hey, man," Travis said, a sudden grin on his face. "Kate told us you write short stories. We've got an opening in our critique group. Wanna join?"